BO
SHE E

BOOKS BY LISA REGAN

Hold Still
Cold Blooded
Kill for You
Finding Claire Fletcher
Losing Leah Holloway
Vanishing Girls
The Girl With No Name
Her Mother's Grave
Her Final Confession

THE
BONES
SHE BURIED

LISA REGAN

Bookouture

Published by Bookouture in 2019

An imprint of StoryFire Ltd.

Carmelite House
50 Victoria Embankment
London EC4Y 0DZ

www.bookouture.com

ISBN: 978-1-78681-640-5
eBook ISBN: 978-1-78681-639-9

For Monica Ebbenga and Bonita Klatt. Speaking your truth is a powerful thing.

PROLOGUE

The screams followed her, echoing all around her as she sprinted along the ridge and fled into the darkness, her feet scrabbling over the brush and loose stones. To her right was a sheer drop, hundreds of feet down. She didn't know just how far, but she knew the fall would be enough to kill her. To her left was a wall of dense forest.

When the first gunshot sounded, she veered left into the trees.

Branches slapped at her arms and face, slicing thin ribbons of blood into her fair skin. A tree root snagged her toes, sending her flying. Leaves and stones rose up to meet her and her elbow cracked against a large rock, sending an agonizing shot of pain through her arm and up into her skull. Still, she heard the screaming in the distance. Her breath came in gasps as she scrambled to her feet, holding her elbow close to her body. Tears leaked from her eyes, but panic and the will to survive drove her deeper into the forest.

Another gunshot shattered the night.

She had to get as far away from the encampment as she could, but the thickening springtime foliage overhead blocked out the light of the moon, plunging the forest into total darkness. Which way had she come?

Another gunshot cracked like a whip, but as the echo bounced around her, she couldn't tell which direction it had come from. Using her good arm, she began to move by feeling her way, praying she was going away from the shots, her fingers fumbling over tree trunks and branches, small sticks and stalks crunching beneath her feet. The muscles in her calves cramped. How long had she been running? It felt like hours but it couldn't have been.

The snap of a nearby branch pierced the roar of panic in her head. She whipped around, but she could see nothing in the blackness. Then came a voice, cold and calm, the sound slicing through her like a knife, paralyzing her.

"Did you really think you could get away?"

"Please," she whimpered. "Please don't."

She felt the hard circle of the gun's barrel against the base of her skull.

"You'll never leave me again."

CHAPTER ONE

Smoke billowed from Josie's oven, thick and black, spilling out around the edges of the door. Coughing, she hit the button to turn off the oven and waved a cloth to clear the smoke. From across the room, the smoke alarm shrieked.

"Shit," Josie said.

Abandoning the oven, she raced from window to window, flinging them open, trying to wave some of the smoke outside. Over the din of the alarm, she heard Noah's voice. "Josie? You okay—what the hell?"

She dragged one of her kitchen chairs across the room and stood on it, pulling the smoke alarm off the wall. Then, banging it against the table, she popped the batteries out to silence it. Tossing it aside, she managed a sheepish smile for Noah.

"What are you doing?" he asked, waving a hand to clear some of the smoke from his eyes.

"It's fine," she mumbled. "Nothing's on fire."

"Looks like something was," he pointed out.

Josie returned to the oven and, putting mitts on each hand, reached into the blackness in search of the edges of the cake pan. What she pulled out made them both grimace.

"What... was that?" Noah asked.

Josie threw the entire thing into the sink. "It was supposed to be a raspberry coffee cake. Your mom likes raspberries, right?"

Noah's face twisted into a look Josie recognized as part sympathy, part skepticism and just a little bit of him trying not to laugh. "Uh, yeah, but if you wanted to make something for dessert, brownies would have been fine. Or, like, a bundt cake or something."

Josie pointed to the kitchen counter where three other bake pans lay in a mangled, blackened heap. "Those are the brownies. That was a bundt cake, and that last one was a chocolate Devil's food cake from a goddamn Betty Crocker box, which I still managed to burn."

Noah leaned against the kitchen doorway and covered his mouth with his hand. Josie pointed an oven mitt at him. "Don't you *dare* laugh."

From between his fingers, he said, "Maybe something cold? Jell-O? Something simple."

"Are you out of your mind? I am not taking *Jell-O* to your mother's house for dinner."

"Something store-bought," he suggested. "That's simple."

There wasn't a chance in hell that Josie was bringing something *simple* to Colette Fraley's house. The woman was the consummate homemaker. Everything she cooked looked delicious and tasted even better. Her garden was lush, colorful and perfectly pruned and she even found time to sew beautiful quilts that she donated to foster children. Colette was the reason Pinterest was invented. People like Josie just couldn't compare to the Colette Fraleys of the world.

Colette barely tolerated Josie as it was, but for the first time ever, she had tasked Josie with bringing dessert to their monthly dinner. Josie saw the request for what it was—a challenge—and she was damn well going to rise to the occasion. Well, possibly. If she could pass something store-bought off as her own creation.

Josie sagged one hip against the counter. "She's never going to like me, is she? Even if I could whip up a chocolate soufflé with my eyes shut, it wouldn't change anything."

Noah moved across the room in two easy strides and took her by the shoulders. "You're overthinking this. Just be yourself. She'll come around."

No, she won't, Josie thought, but she didn't want to have the argument with Noah again. They'd been dating for a year, and in that time Josie had figured out that the most important person in Noah's life was his mother. He was the youngest of three but his brother lived in Arizona—all the way across the country—and his sister and her husband lived two hours away. Noah's parents had divorced when he was a teenager, and from what Josie could gather, none of the Fraley children kept in touch with their father.

Josie looked at the clock on her microwave. "I guess it has to be store-bought. We need to be there in a half hour."

"We'll tell her that you were busy with work," Noah offered. "And didn't have time to bake something."

Josie barked a laugh and pulled her mitts off. "Somehow, I don't think that will help." All talking about work with Colette did was remind her that a few years earlier, Josie had shot her darling son during a particularly tense and complex missing girls case. Both Josie and Noah were high-ranking members of Denton's police department and in the last few years they'd covered cases so shocking and high-profile, they'd made national news.

Noah started closing the windows. "Just get changed," he told her. "It will be fine."

Twenty minutes later, Josie sat in the passenger's seat of Noah's car, a box of store-bought brownies in her lap, feeling anything but fine as they weaved through the streets of Denton. The city was roughly twenty-five square miles, many of those miles spanning the untamed mountains of central Pennsylvania, with their one-lane winding roads, dense woods and rural residences spread out far and wide. The population was edging over thirty thousand, and it increased when the college was in session, providing plenty of conflict and crime to keep the Denton Police Department where they both worked pretty busy. Josie's gut clenched slightly as they pulled into Colette's driveway. Next time, she promised herself, she was going to make that damn raspberry coffee cake if she had to burn her damn house down.

"That's weird," Noah said as he put the car into park.

Josie's eyes followed his gaze to Colette's front door, which yawned open. She didn't have a storm door, just a thick wooden entry door which had been painted a cheery blue and decorated with a handmade spring wreath with sprigs of faux yellow flowers.

Josie left the brownies on the passenger seat and followed Noah up the front walk. Together they ascended the three steps to the concrete landing where potted flowers bracketed the door. "Mom?" Noah called.

Josie put a hand on his arm. "Wait," she said, her hand reaching for her shoulder holster only to find it wasn't there because today was her day off. "Should we call this in?"

He smiled uncertainly at her. "Call what in?"

Josie motioned toward the open door. "Something's wrong," she whispered.

Noah laughed. "What makes you assume something's wrong? Mom left the door open. She's been forgetting stuff lately, remember?"

Josie did remember. Noah and his sister had had several hushed conversations recently about having her tested for Alzheimer's or dementia even though she was only in her sixties. Still, she couldn't shake the sense of dread gathering in the pit of her stomach as she followed him through the door into Colette's living room, which was also decorated in blues. It was late afternoon and the waning sunlight cut across the room, making the hardwood floors gleam. The end table's small drawer was hanging open, items from inside scattered on the floor: a pair of Colette's reading glasses, a pack of tissues, a pen and notepad. Josie took a step toward it. There were still some things inside the drawer. Had Colette been looking for something?

"Mom?" Noah called again, moving deeper into the house.

The dining room was dark and undisturbed. Josie wondered if Colette had forgotten they were coming over. Normally, the table would be set by the time they arrived for dinner. In fact, on any other occasion, the entire house would be filled with the smell of Colette's superb cooking.

"Noah," she said. "I really think—"

But he was already in the kitchen, calling for his mother again. Josie moved quickly behind him. The overhead light glared down on the kitchen which was neat and clean, everything in its place except for two more drawers that hung open with their contents spread along the counter above them —dish towels, a wine opener, takeout menus, a flashlight, some candles and a lighter.

Josie clamped a hand onto Noah's shoulder, turning him toward the back door which was also open. Beneath her palm, she could feel him move with more urgency. As they passed through the back door, Noah called out again, "Mom?"

Their feet sank into the lush grass as they stopped to scan the large backyard. A tall white fence lined with blooming flower beds marked the perimeter, and a small wooden shed sat in one corner. Josie took a step in the direction of the patio in the center of the yard that was crowded with heavy metal furniture, her eyes tracing every inch of the garden. With a gasp, she pointed to something sticking out from one of the beds in the far corner. "Oh my God. Noah, is that—"

The words died in her throat as she sprinted across the yard, Noah behind her.

Colette was on her stomach, her upper body in the flower bed, her protruding feet the only thing visible at a distance. Up close, Josie immediately noticed the gardening gloves on her hands and a small handheld shovel in the dirt a few inches away.

"Mom!" Noah cried, panic ringing in his voice. He dropped to his knees, and Josie fell to hers beside him. Together, they rolled Colette onto her back. Her eyes were closed and dirt smudged her cheeks and clothes. Cold seeped from Colette's body into Josie's hands as her fingers searched Colette's neck for a pulse, but found nothing.

Noah was already leaning into her chest, one hand on top of the other, fingers laced, giving her compressions. As he counted out thirty presses, Josie angled Colette's chin so that her mouth was open, and pinched her nostrils closed.

"Now!" Noah urged her as he stopped pumping.

Josie's mouth closed over Colette's and she exhaled into her, trying to inflate Colette's lungs. Something fetid and granular stuck to Josie's lips, and the air wasn't moving through to Colette's chest like it should. Coughing, she sat back up and wiped her mouth.

"What are you doing? Jesus, Josie. Keep going. We have to save her," Noah cried.

He pushed her out of the way and sealed his lips over Colette's, but after one breath, he also pulled away, coughing and spitting onto the ground.

"It's soil," Josie said. "Jesus, Noah, it's soil."

She nudged him aside and hooked a finger inside Colette's mouth, scooping out a small clump of wet brown earth. She repeated the action three or four times but still, the airway wasn't cleared. Her heart seized in her chest. Beside her, Noah had gone perfectly still, his mouth stretched open in horror. "Help me," Josie cried. "Help me get her on her side!"

As if he was moving in slow motion, Noah reached forward, grasping his mother's shoulder and pushing as Josie turned her onto her side, her fingers still scrabbling inside Colette's mouth, trying to clear it of the hard-packed dirt. When she thought she had most of it out, she turned Colette onto her back again and tried to blow air into her chest. Colette's airway was completely blocked.

Somewhere in the back of her mind, Josie knew that Colette was gone but she couldn't bear the look of pure terror on Noah's face, so she kept working. "Call 911," she barked at him as she moved back to Colette's chest and restarted the compressions. He didn't move, his eyes locked on his mother's face.

Sweat poured from Josie's forehead as she pumped, dripping off the end of her nose and onto Colette's lifeless body. "Now, Noah. Go! Call 911!"

Josie worked until her shoulders and arms ached, until her face was streaked with the remains of dirt still packed into Colette's mouth, until her entire body was soaked with sweat, until the paramedics arrived and pulled her gently away. As if from very far away, she heard them shouting information to one another, taking over for her, and after several minutes she heard one of them call the time of death.

Then she heard a wail—low, guttural and heart-wrenching   tear from Noah's throat.

CHAPTER TWO

Josie sat beside Noah on his mother's couch, one hand on his back as he curled into himself, elbows on knees, face in his hands, intermittently sobbing and rocking back and forth. As her Evidence Response Team moved in and out of the house, Josie tried to wrap her mind around what had just happened. She had the sensation of watching herself from afar. It didn't seem real. This had to be happening to someone else, surely. Not them.

"Boss?" Officer Finn Mettner said. She looked up to find him staring down at them. How long had he been there?

"Yes," she said, voice shaky. Her fingers wiped at her mouth, brushing away the dirt that felt like it would never leave her skin.

Mettner gestured toward the door. "This is a crime scene. If you wouldn't mind—"

She stood abruptly. "Of course, of course. Noah?"

He didn't respond. Josie hooked a hand under one of his arms and gently guided him to standing, outside and into the passenger side of his vehicle. "I'll be right back," she told him.

Near the front door, one of the other ERT officers, Hummel, had cordoned the stoop off with yellow crime scene tape. He stood at the door with his clipboard, ready to log in each person who passed by him. In the driveway, the trunk of his cruiser stood open. Josie went to it and pulled out a Tyvek suit, slowly pulling it on, together with booties and a skull cap.

She heard footsteps behind her as Mettner appeared next to the trunk. "Hey, boss, we're all really sorry. This is… hard to believe." He glanced toward Noah's car. "How's Noah?"

Josie followed Mettner's gaze to where Noah sat staring straight ahead with blank, red-rimmed eyes. "I think he's in shock. Is Gretchen—I mean, Detective Palmer coming?"

Gretchen Palmer was another detective on Denton's police force. Her calm presence had a way of reassuring Josie and quieting her pounding heart during difficult times. A woman of pure integrity and one of the best investigators Josie had ever known, Gretchen had recently been placed on administrative leave following her involvement in a horrific murder that had happened on her own doorstep and brought secrets of her past into the harsh light of the present. Josie knew that after what had happened, it would take nothing short of a miracle for Gretchen to keep her job. But she also knew that Gretchen had done what she needed to do to protect the people she loved most, so Josie had used all the influence and good will she had in Denton to make sure Gretchen returned to the force in some capacity. Facing resistance from both the Chief and the Mayor of Denton on more than one occasion, Josie had used her press connections to garner support from the public, putting enough pressure on the Chief that he had agreed to bring Gretchen back for a probationary period which had started a week ago.

Mettner frowned. "She's still on the desk."

"Even now? Does the Chief know what's going on?"

Mettner nodded. "Yeah, he knows."

Josie threw her hands in the air. "Well, I need her here. She's the most experienced investigator we have, and this is clearly a homicide."

Mettner grimaced, and immediately Josie felt guilty. The Chief had been grooming him over the last six months to take the step up to detective, especially now, since Gretchen was out of action. He had been on the force for seven years, was meticulous, efficient and eager to learn. Although Josie and Chief Chitwood rarely agreed on anything, she knew Mettner deserved the chance at promotion. She sighed. "Mett, I'm sorry. I didn't mean—it's just that this is Noah's mom, you know? Gretchen worked homicide in Philadelphia for fifteen years."

Mettner waved a hand in the air. "I know," he said. "It's okay. I know she's the most qualified, boss, I get it. But the Chief isn't budging on this one, so you'll have to settle for me. I can handle this, you know?"

"I know you can," Josie replied. "Let's do a walk-through. I don't think Noah or I touched or moved anything. We sat on the couch in the living room, but everything else is as it was when we got here. Except the backyard, obviously. We tried to revive her, but she—" Josie broke off and her fingers swiped over her lips one last time. "Her mouth was packed with dirt."

"Hummel got here first. He said you found her face down in the garden," Mettner said as he suited himself up.

"Yes, but even if she had a heart attack or a stroke or something and fell, it wouldn't account for how much dirt was in her mouth. It was packed so deep that it blocked her airway. Mett, this was not an accident. Someone killed her."

Colette had been kind, gentle and decent. Josie's heart flipped in her chest at the thought of someone suffocating her. She must have been terrified.

Mettner gently touched Josie's shoulder, bringing her back to the scene. "We'll handle this, okay? Do a quick walk-through, then take Fraley home. The rest of us will work this with everything we've got."

Josie nodded, swallowing the lump in her throat. She went back to Noah's vehicle to let him know she would only be a few minutes, but he was still lost somewhere deep where no one could reach him.

Hummel signed the two of them in at the front door and they started in the living room. "We need to know what you touched or moved before you found Mrs. Fraley," Mettner said.

They moved slowly and carefully through the house as Josie retraced her and Noah's movements from the time they'd arrived, to them finding Colette dead in the backyard. Mercifully, the team had already photographed Colette's body, and someone had covered her with a sheet. They would wait until Noah had gone before transporting her to the morgue. Josie talked him through everything that had happened while Mettner used his thumbs to text furiously into a note-taking app on his cell phone. When she finished he gave her a sheepish smile. "I text faster than I write. Plus, I can email myself these notes and they're already typed."

Josie smiled. "Whatever works for you, Mett. Great idea."

Back to business, he asked, "When was the last time either of you spoke to Mrs. Fraley?"

"I haven't talked to her since last month. I think Noah spoke with her this morning. I can ask him," Josie replied.

"Mrs. Fraley lived alone?" Mettner asked.

Josie nodded. "I can get in touch with Noah's older brother and sister and find out when they last spoke with her. If you could, maybe someone should interview Colette's friends, neighbors…"

Mettner looked up from his phone. "Yes, I've already got someone canvassing."

"Great," Josie said.

Another member of their ERT knelt beside Colette's body. She was a new hire who had come to Denton with a few years of experience working on an Evidence Response Team in a city only slightly larger than Denton. "Officer Chan," Josie greeted her. "What've you got?"

Chan looked up and gave Josie and Mettner a nod, her gloved hands sifting through the dirt that Colette had turned up moments before her death. With her thumb and index finger she lifted a long, beaded object from the soil. Josie squatted down to peer at it. She pointed to the dirt-crusted crucifix that hung from the end. "Is that a rosary?"

Chan fingered a frayed end where the long chain of beads had broken. "Part of one, yes, I think so."

Mettner bent closer, squinting as Chan held up the rosary for him to inspect. "Looks old."

"It's pretty caked with dirt. Might have been here a long time," Chan agreed.

Mettner turned to Josie. "Maybe she was trying to dig it up? I know the timing isn't great, but could you ask Noah about this too?"

"Of course," Josie said, watching as Chan bagged it up for evidence.

Mettner cleared his throat, and Josie tore her eyes away from the upturned garden to meet his.

"We can take it from here," he said. "I'll be in touch when we know more. Why don't you get Noah home? Notify his siblings?"

"Right," Josie said, still feeling shell-shocked. "Of course."

CHAPTER THREE

Noah didn't speak on the ride back to his house, or when Josie settled him onto his couch. When she asked for his brother and sister's phone numbers, the best he could do was hand her his phone. His older brother, Theo, answered on the third ring. The conversation was painful, but Josie knew that Noah was in no position to tell them himself and she felt the other Fraley children should know right away. Noah would need their support sooner rather than later. Theo promised to catch the next available flight. Josie hung up and then immediately called Noah's sister, Laura. After more shock, more tears, and more questions, Laura agreed to be there within a few hours.

"Should I call your father?" she asked Noah.

Without looking at her, he said, "What for?"

"Oh, well, I know your parents are divorced, but maybe he'd want to be there for you and your brother and sister? Don't you think he'd want to know?"

"He doesn't deserve to know, and he hasn't been there for us since the day he walked out of my mother's house."

There was a bitterness in his tone that Josie had never heard from Noah before. She knew that his dad wasn't in the picture, but she didn't know much more than that. Noah never talked about it—never talked about his father at all, when she came to think of it. Besides, he was probably right. If Lance Fraley was not involved in his children's lives, then his presence would hardly be a comfort.

Josie set Noah's phone on the coffee table and sat beside him, taking his hand in hers. She knew there was nothing she could say.

She had lost both her husband and her beloved Chief suddenly and violently four years earlier. The pain was extraordinary and unavoidable, a great wave that would bowl you over and pull you under at any given moment. It wasn't pain that could be soothed or lessened, you just had to hold on to whatever shred of sanity you had as hard as you could until the current spat you back out into calmer waters. But, she remembered with a shiver, that sea of grief never truly left you, it was always below you, ready to pull you under when you least expected it. There was nothing she could do to shield him from it, and she knew from experience that there was little comfort she could offer. What she could do for him was to try to find out who killed his mother and put that person away forever.

After a pause, she asked, "Noah, is there any reason why rosary beads would be buried in your mother's garden?"

His head slowly turned in her direction. The redness rimming his eyes made her heart ache for him. "What?" he asked.

"I'm sorry. I know this is a terrible time to ask you questions, but the ERT found rosary beads buried in your mom's garden. It looked as though she might have been digging them up. Mettner wanted me to ask…"

"My mom's Catholic," Noah said as though that explained everything.

"Is it a Catholic custom to bury them?"

"When they're broken," he answered. "They were blessed. Mom always says they shouldn't be thrown away so she buries them with her flowers."

"Can you think of any reason why she would have been digging them back up?" Josie asked.

Noah dragged both hands over his face. "Is that what you think? She was out there digging up broken old rosary beads?"

"I don't know," Josie said. "I don't know what to think. Maybe she was just gardening and accidentally dug them up."

"That's possible, I guess."

"Noah, I know you've said that your mom has had some issues with her memory lately, but exactly how bad were things getting?"

"I don't—it wasn't—" he stammered.

She touched his arm. "I'm sorry. It's okay. We can talk about this later. When is the last time you spoke with her?"

"This morning," he said. "You know that. I told you I called her to confirm dinner."

"Do you think she was gardening because she'd forgotten?"

His eyes narrowed. "Why are you interviewing me?" he asked. "Why are you treating this like a case?"

"Because it is a case," Josie said, keeping her tone even and gentle. "Noah, someone killed your mother."

"We don't know that someone killed her. She could have had a heart attack or an aneurysm and fallen into the dirt. When we found her she was—she was—"

His voice broke and he looked away from her. Fresh tears streamed down his face.

"Noah," Josie said. "I know you're in shock right now. I know what that feels like. But your mom didn't get that much dirt in her airway from falling facedown into the flower bed. Someone—" she stopped. She couldn't bring herself to say the words. It was too cruel, especially in the state that he was in.

"No one would hurt my mother," he said. "You don't even have the autopsy results back. You don't know that this was murder."

"Someone was looking for something in her house, Noah," Josie replied. "You saw the drawers in the living room and kitchen."

"*She* was looking for something, probably."

"And she left the house in disarray and just decided to go out and start gardening?" Josie asked. "Noah, your mother's house has always been spotless."

He sighed. "Not recently. You want to know how bad she was getting?" he asked, wiping at a tear as it spilled down his cheek. "Last month I was over there and she forgot who I was. She started talking to me like I was my dad. They used to argue about how much money he spent on things we didn't need. She started chastising me about having bought a two-hundred-dollar VCR. A VCR!"

"I had no idea, Noah. I'm sorry. Every time I saw her, she seemed fine."

"Most of the time she was. These… episodes were just becoming more frequent. That's why Laura and I talked about taking her to a neurologist, but we never got around to it and now…"

He drifted off, leaning forward, elbows on knees and face in hands once more, but Josie heard the unspoken words. *Now, it's too late.*

Josie stroked his back. "I'm so sorry, Noah. So sorry."

CHAPTER FOUR

Laura Fraley-Hall arrived like a tornado a few hours later, bursting through Noah's door without knocking, tossing her purse and jacket onto the floor as she moved from the foyer to where Noah still sat on the couch. Laura was three years older than him and had the same thick brown hair hers flowing down her back in waves—and the same hazel eyes. She was a head shorter than Noah though, and her face was rounder and softer. She wore a tight navy sheath dress with a colorful scarf draped around her neck, just above her visible baby bump, which she covered with one hand as she fell onto the couch on the other side of Noah. Her arms encircled his shoulders, pulling him away from Josie and into her embrace.

"I can't believe it," she whispered.

Noah emerged from his stupor long enough to return the hug, his tears coming afresh and mingling with Laura's. Josie got up from the couch and went into the kitchen to give them a few moments alone. There, she busied herself making a pot of coffee. She checked his fridge to see if there was anything she could offer Laura to eat, but then figured Laura would have about as much appetite as she and Noah. Josie waited until the sobbing stopped and she could hear their voices before going back into the living room. She stood in the doorway, watching the two siblings for a moment.

"Where's Grady?" Noah asked Laura.

"He'll be here in another hour or two. He's packing us some bags. When Josie called me, I just got into my car and drove. I was at a work event."

Josie knew that in recent years Laura had been promoted to vice president at Sutton Stone Enterprises where Colette had worked as secretary and assistant to the owner and CEO for over forty years. It had started out as a small family operation at a nearby quarry, mining bluestone, limestone and boulders, and had since grown into a thriving multi-million-dollar enterprise. It now had its own construction arm, a trucking division and quarries all over the state devoted to providing asphalt aggregate for concrete, sand and gravel. Colette had bragged earlier that year that Laura had been placed in charge of getting their Bethlehem site up and running. She called Laura and Grady the family's 'power couple', with Laura rising through the ranks of Sutton Stone Enterprises and Grady running a thriving accounting business that allowed him to work from home most of the time.

Laura's hand flew to her forehead. "Oh dear. I'm sure Mr. Sutton will want to hear about this from me, not anyone else."

"Mr. Sutton—your boss?" Josie asked, but Laura ignored her.

"He will," Noah said. "He adored Mom. Can you—can you call him?"

Laura patted Noah's knee. "Of course."

Josie felt another sharp stab of sadness for Noah and his siblings; Colette's old boss was deemed more worthy of hearing about her untimely death than the father of her children. Inwardly, she chastised herself for not having gotten the full story about Noah's father before. Noah knew all her secrets and yet what did she really know about him? What could she really offer him in a crisis such as this? He'd always been her rock, supporting her and guiding her through the terrifying darkness life had plunged her into time and again. What could she offer him in return?

"Why don't you go upstairs and get cleaned up," Laura said softly to Noah. "Get out of these clothes. Take a shower. Maybe lie down."

Josie had suggested the same multiple times before Laura arrived, but this time Noah complied, getting to his feet and climbing the stairs slowly, his shoulders stooped. Josie and Laura listened for a few moments as he shuffled around upstairs. When they heard the shower go on, Josie caught Laura's eye. "Noah said that there was no need to notify your father."

Laura laughed bitterly. "No, I suppose there isn't, but I'll let him know anyway. He won't care enough to come to the funeral, but I'll text him. Mom would want us to tell him."

"We're probably going to need to speak to him at some point," Josie said. "At the very least to rule out any involvement."

"Involvement? Don't make me laugh," Laura told her. "Fine. I'll text you his number. Do what you must. Josie, do the police have any idea who did this to my mother? I want the truth."

Josie shook her head. "No, I'm sorry. Not yet. But our team is working on it as we speak. Laura, I need to know, is there anyone your mother had any issues with? A friend or neighbor? Even a boyfriend?"

Laura chuckled even as tears leaked from her eyes. "She didn't have a boyfriend. She dated a few times after my dad left, but she always said she didn't want to get married again. So no, there was no boyfriend. I'm sure my baby brother told you she was loved by many people. She was very involved in her church, and she kept up with her neighbors."

"Yes," Josie said. "I know she was very involved in helping local foster children, and Noah said she would often start meal drives if one of her neighbors was having issues. Laura, I know the kind of person your mother was, which makes it even more baffling that someone would want to hurt her."

"No one would want to hurt her," Laura said, her voice husky with tears, her words an echo of those Noah had used earlier.

"This could have been a random attack," Josie conceded. "It appeared from the state of her house that someone was looking for something. Do you know what valuables she kept? If you tell me what someone might have taken, I can get my team to confirm whether or not those items are still there."

Laura plucked a tissue from the box on one of Noah's end tables and blew her nose. "She didn't keep much cash in the house so it wouldn't have been that. She had some rings and necklaces that her own mother had passed down to her. When Grady and I got engaged, she gave him the ring that my father gave her, and Grady had the stones in it removed and a new ring made." Laura held up a hand and flashed a thick band of sparkling diamonds in Josie's direction. "Grady thought it was bad luck to propose with my mother's ring since my parents got divorced, but he understood the sentiment—that my mother was trying to pass down something valuable and sentimental to her."

"It's beautiful," Josie said. She waited a beat and pressed on. "Is there anything else you can think of that someone might have taken or even been looking for?"

Laura shook her head. "No, I don't think so. Nothing that would be worth killing over, certainly."

But Josie knew that for some criminals, it wasn't a matter of things being worth killing for—some people killed as easily as they breathed. On the other hand, if Colette had been out in the garden, someone could have potentially gone through her entire house without her even knowing they were in there. So why go outside and confront her? Why kill her in such a cruel and brutal way? Josie thought of the burglaries-turned-murders she had covered in her career. The perpetrators almost always carried guns. If guns weren't used in the crimes, there were almost always signs of a protracted struggle. Many times, the homeowners were restrained in some way. Colette Fraley looked like she had simply been digging in her garden and dropped dead from natural causes, except for the soil in her airway. Josie had seen plenty of crime scenes and this one was strikingly unusual. There had to be more to it. Josie told Laura about the rosary beads, and she said the same thing that Noah had said; their mother had been burying her broken rosaries in her garden since they were kids—both in the house they'd grown up in and in the smaller house she had bought after the divorce where she was living when she was murdered.

"Is that the only thing she buried in her garden?" Josie asked.

Laura's eyes narrowed. "What are you getting at?"

"I'm not 'getting at' anything," Josie said. "I'm just trying to piece together what happened to your mother. It helps narrow the suspect pool if we have an idea as to whether the crime was personal or random."

"Doesn't Denton PD have other detectives who can work on this?" Laura asked pointedly.

"Of course," Josie said. "But we're a little short right now. One of our best detectives is out of action for now, but we have another officer, Finn Mettner, who will be helping with the investigation. He'll likely be working through the night."

"Well," Laura said, her gaze penetrating. "A word to the wise. The best thing you can do right now is be there for Noah."

Josie's face flamed red with embarrassment at her implication. Wasn't she there for Noah right this second? Hadn't she been the only person besides Colette in his life for years now? Since they'd grown close, he'd only seen his siblings over Christmas. Josie had been the one to try to breathe life back into Colette's lungs even after she realized the task was damn near impossible. Still, Josie said nothing. The last thing she or Noah needed was a spat between her and Laura, not while the Fraley children were suffering from the loss of their beloved mother.

"I'll go check on him," Josie said, and walked up the stairs.

CHAPTER FIVE

Josie and Laura spent a good part of the evening making phone calls to notify friends and family members of Colette's death. Josie went up to bed to check on Noah before Grady arrived. She was grateful to find him asleep. She changed and climbed into bed beside him, drifting in and out of sleep as Noah slept fitfully beside her, waking her every few hours when he climbed out of bed to pace the room. Each time, bleary-eyed, she called him back to bed and held him until he fell back to sleep. Josie knew all too well the horror of waking in the night to realize anew that your entire world had been shattered.

A few times during the night, Josie heard Laura and her husband talking in the guest room down the hall, their voices muffled, their words indistinct. Then, as the light seeped around the blinds in the early hours of the morning, she heard the stairs creaking as Laura and Grady crept down to the kitchen, followed by the faint sound of dishes clinking. When the scent of breakfast foods wafted upstairs and under Noah's door, Josie's stomach growled.

"You're hungry," came Noah's muffled voice from under his pillow.

"Yeah, but I don't much feel like eating," Josie said. "We both need to, though."

They got dressed and went downstairs to the kitchen where Grady was cooking eggs and toast for what looked like a much larger number of people than just the four of them. Laura sat at the table, staring sightlessly straight ahead, a full glass of orange juice untouched in front of her.

Grady gave them a pained smile as they entered. Josie had only met him once and had found him nice enough; he had been very doting interacting with his wife. He was in his forties and tall with longish black hair and dark eyes, but he was thinner than she remembered. He turned off the burners when they walked in and came over to greet Noah, wrapping him up in a hard hug and clapping his back. "I'm so sorry," he said. "This is so… I just can't believe it. Neither of us can wrap our heads around this. We were going to give her her first grandchild—"

"Please don't," Laura croaked. "Please don't talk about it. I can't take it."

Looking at his wife, Grady said, "I'm sorry, Laura. I didn't mean to upset you more. We're all devastated." He turned to Josie. "Do you know who did this?"

"Our team is working on it," Josie told him. "I'll be in touch with Officer Mettner today to see if they've got any more information."

Noah sat at the table across from his sister, who said, "We'll have to start planning the funeral. I texted Theo. He'll be here in about an hour."

But Noah's gaze was on Josie. "Mett?" he said. "Shouldn't Gretchen be working Mom's case?"

"Chief won't let her off the desk," Josie said. "Not even for this."

Noah made a noise of disgust deep in his throat.

"Mettner's good," Josie tried.

"Not as good as Gretchen. Not as good as you. He doesn't have the experience—"

Laura cut him off. "Did you hear what I said, Noah? We need to plan Mom's funeral."

He looked at her but didn't respond.

Grady went back to the stove and cracked two more eggs into the frying pan. Confident she had Noah's full attention, Laura smiled and turned to Grady, "Darling, I think that's enough food."

Grady returned her smile, and Josie saw tears glistening in his eyes. "Sorry," he said. "I like to keep busy. Makes me feel useful."

"I feel exactly the same way," Josie shared as she moved over to the counter to make plates for her and Noah. "This is wonderful," she told Grady. "Thank you for cooking."

They ate in silence, the Fraley siblings moving in slow motion, their eyes vacant. It was almost a relief when Josie's cell phone buzzed in her pocket. "Who's that?" Noah asked.

"A text from Mettner. He said Dr. Feist fast-tracked the autopsy."

"What did it show?" Laura asked.

"He didn't say. I'll have to call him."

"Go," Noah said. "I know you want to."

Josie's mouth hung open. He hadn't said it with any malice, but he had said it. "I don't want to go," she replied. "I want to stay with you. I told you, Mettner is good. I think he can handle this."

Noah opened his mouth to speak, but Laura talked over him. "Actually, Josie, we would appreciate your finding out whatever you can. We'll all have to go to the funeral home to make arrangements today, after Theo arrives. Maybe you can talk to the other officer and the medical examiner and find out when our mother will be released to us. That would be very helpful."

Josie caught Noah's eye. "Only if it's okay with you," she said to him.

He rubbed a hand over his eyes and sighed. "It's fine. Really. Go see what Mettner has turned up. He'll probably want Theo, Laura and Grady to go in and submit fingerprints so they can eliminate their prints from any found in the house."

"Yes," Josie said. "He will." Or, if he didn't, she would make sure he did. This was his first homicide investigation.

"And one of us will need to do a walk-through to see if anything is missing. I can do it later, or even Laura."

"Are you sure that's a good idea?" Grady asked, addressing his wife. "I'm already worried about the stress this is putting on you with the baby. I don't know if visiting the scene where your mother was…"

Laura put a hand over his. "It's okay. I don't have to do it. Noah already said he can do it."

Noah offered Josie a wan smile. "Call me later, okay?"

CHAPTER SIX

Denton's city morgue was located in the basement of Denton Memorial Hospital, which was an old brick building that sat on top of a hill overlooking most of the city. The small suite of rooms that Medical Examiner, Dr. Anya Feist, presided over were windowless and drab with a lingering odor that was half chemical and half biological decay. Josie had grown used to it over the years, but she could tell the moment she stepped into the large exam room that Mettner had a long way to go. He looked green as he stood beside Dr. Feist at one of the tables, a file spread out between them.

On the far side of the room, Colette's body lay covered, her brown-gray hair showing from the top of the sheet. A shiver ran through Josie. It was still so difficult to believe this was happening. Her heart ached for Noah. She had always envied him his normal upbringing and had felt grateful and a little jealous that he had had such a kind, loving mother.

"Didn't expect to see you today," Dr. Feist said when she saw Josie. Offering a sympathetic smile, she added, "Please give Noah my condolences."

"You didn't have to come," Mettner added. "I just wanted to keep you up to date with what was happening."

Josie jammed her hands into her jeans pockets. "Noah wanted me to come. The family wants to know what happened."

Dr. Feist frowned, then reluctantly she held up a page from the file in front of her. "I don't really know how to tell you this, but Mrs. Fraley was definitely murdered. Asphyxiated. She aspirated on the dirt when she breathed it in."

Josie swallowed over the lump that had formed in her throat. "You mean she choked on it?"

Dr. Feist put the page onto the table and stepped toward Josie, regarding her with sympathy. "Josie, are you sure you want to hear this?"

"I have to," Josie croaked.

Dr. Feist motioned toward Officer Mettner. "I'm sure Mett can handle it. He told me this is his first homicide, but everyone has to start somewhere. Maybe he can catch you up on the details later? After you've taken some time. We can release the body to the family tomorrow. Then perhaps after the funeral, if you still want to know the details, Officer Mettner can fill you in?"

Josie felt tears stinging the backs of her eyes as her gaze drifted back to Colette's small, shrouded body. Josie didn't want to know the intimate and gruesome details of her murder, but she owed it to Noah to continue. Mettner was a fine officer, and Josie had no doubt that one day, he'd be one of the best detectives Denton PD had ever had, but she couldn't trust an investigation this personal to him alone. When Noah had taken enough time himself to process some of his shock and grief, he would need justice and closure. Josie knew this from her own experience of losing loved ones to violent crimes. She also knew how crucial the early stages of a homicide investigation were. She had to make sure that everything was done according to procedure; that no detail was left unexamined; and that Mettner explored absolutely every avenue of inquiry.

Josie blinked back the moisture in her eyes. "I'm fine. Please. Just tell me what you found."

With a sigh, Dr. Feist continued, "I say 'aspirate' because there was particulate matter—small amounts of soil—in her lungs. She inhaled it. But to answer your question, yes, she choked on it. Her airway was completely blocked. There are small petechiae in the conjunctiva of her eyes."

Mettner pulled out his phone, swiping until he pulled up his note-taking app. "Petechiae?" he echoed.

Josie said, "Petechial hemorrhages. They look like tiny, pinpoint red marks in the eyes and sometimes on the skin—sometimes only visible with a microscope and sometimes as large as a couple of millimeters. They occur when the body is deprived of oxygen. The tiny capillaries in the eyes leak or rupture from the pressure on the veins in the head."

Dr. Feist nodded approvingly as Josie spoke. "Exactly. They are indicators of death by asphyxia. Sometimes by hanging or strangulation, but in this case it's quite clear how she was asphyxiated."

Mettner used one finger to tap the page that Dr. Feist had discarded. "There were some marks on her arms—bruising and lacerations—that we believe were defensive. No sign of sexual assault."

Dr. Feist added, "Her brain showed—" she broke off, looking back toward Colette's body and shifting from one foot to the other. Josie had never seen Dr. Feist look so uncomfortable. Josie guessed she wasn't used to discussing the clinical aspects of her examinations with people so intimately connected to the victims.

"It's okay. Noah and his sister suspected she had some form of dementia. Is that what you found?" Josie asked, urging her onwards.

Dr. Feist nodded. She waved Josie over to a corner of the room where a long, stainless steel counter jutted out from the wall. A microscope rested in the center with several glass slides beside it. Dr. Feist leaned over and studied the slides—all of which bore Colette's name—before sliding one into the viewer. She took a quick look and then motioned for Josie to do the same.

To Josie, the small square in her vision looked like a child had scrawled on it with a fuchsia colored crayon. Uneven purple dots scattered across the slide, and in the center was a large, dark splotch, almost brown, with another, purple dot inside of it—this one much larger than the others. "What am I looking at?" she asked.

Dr. Feist said, "I took several samples from Mrs. Fraley's brain. That one was taken from her hippocampus. It's a pyramidal cell from the CA1 area of the hippocampus."

Josie looked up. Behind them, Mettner said, "The hippocampus is responsible for memory."

Dr. Feist said, "Basically, yes."

Josie pointed to the microscope. "So this specimen is from Colette's hippocampus."

"Correct. The large, spherical mass you see in the center—"

"With the purple dot inside of it?" Josie asked.

Dr. Feist smiled.

Josie said, "Simplistic is better."

"Very well," Dr. Feist said. "Yes, the purple dot. That's evidence of a Lewy body."

Mettner's thumbs froze. He looked up from his phone. "A what?"

Dr. Feist waved him over. He placed his phone on the counter and gazed into the microscope while Dr. Feist explained. "The simplistic explanation is that a Lewy body is an abnormal mass of protein that develops inside nerve cells. These deposits of protein affect chemicals in the brain and that leads to problems with cognition, movement, perception, behavior…"

She drifted off. Josie thought of what Noah had told her about Colette mistaking him for his father—not just mistaking him but going back in her mind to a time when she was married to his father. Sadness engulfed her. A woman as kind as Colette deserved better. She hadn't deserved to lose her faculties just as her first grandchild was about to be born. Still, had she lived, there might have been treatments or medications that could have improved her quality of life or perhaps extended her periods of lucidity. Now they would never know.

Dr. Feist said, "Josie?"

Mettner had abandoned the microscope and picked up his phone again. He looked back and forth between the two women, waiting for more information to add to his notes.

Josie shook off her grief. "I'm fine. So, she had dementia? Alzheimer's?"

"Well, Lewy body dementia is a common form of dementia. With Alzheimer's, I would also expect to see amyloid plaques and neurofibrillary tangles in the brain so this may have been Lewy body dementia."

"May?"

"Well, the other diagnosis associated with findings of Lewy bodies is Parkinson's. Did Mrs. Fraley have any noticeable physical symptoms? Poor balance or coordination? Trembling of her extremities? Stiffness of limbs or trunk?"

Josie shook her head. "No. I don't think so. Noah never mentioned that, and I never saw her struggle physically."

"But you said her children were concerned about dementia," Dr. Feist said.

Again, Josie mentally put aside the emotion that was in danger of taking over. Without meaning to, her eyes drifted once more to Colette's covered body. She tried to speak but her voice came out as a rasp. Clearing her throat, she tried again, "Uh, yes, she was, um, having cognitive issues. Memory problems."

Dr. Feist nodded. She stepped directly in front of Josie, blocking her view of Colette. Elegant fingers reached out and brushed Josie's arm. "Well, I'd have to do an in-depth interview with her family to be absolutely sure, but my initial diagnosis would be Lewy body dementia. Although I'm not sure it's really relevant now."

Mettner's thumbs stopped moving. "Not relevant?"

"Well, yes," Dr. Feist said. "The finding of dementia is really incidental. It has nothing to do with her death and didn't contribute to it at all, unless, of course, she wasn't lucid when the she came into contact with the killer."

Josie said, "Meaning she may have thought the killer was someone she knew, someone she trusted? Maybe if she had been lucid, she wouldn't have let him into her house?"

Dr. Feist shrugged. "Perhaps. It really doesn't matter though. As I told you, the cause of death is asphyxiation; manner of death is homicide. You've definitely got a murder on your hands. I'm so sorry, Josie."

CHAPTER SEVEN

Mettner and Josie took separate cars to Colette's house. The crime scene tape had already been taken down. Someone on the team must have removed it for Noah's sake, knowing he would have to come back. Parking their cars, they walked up the front drive together. "Did you get anything from the neighbors?" Josie asked.

"Nothing," Mettner said, pulling a key from his pocket as they reached the front door. Unlocking it, he let them in. There was a strange stillness inside that made Josie's skin crawl. "Nothing unusual at all. Colette's car was in the driveway all day yesterday. No one noticed any visitors or strangers in the area. The only call Colette made or took was one to Noah in the morning. It lasted about five minutes. From her cell phone. There's no landline."

"Did you check her call log going back a few weeks?" Josie asked.

"Of course. Gretchen handled that. We went back a month. There were calls to and from her children; a call to her family physician's office; calls to three church friends and one call to a Thai takeout place."

"No red flags."

"Not one," Mettner agreed.

The house had been left as Josie had found it. She knew her team had photographed and printed the place, but they had not cleaned up. That wasn't their job. That would be up to the Fraley children when they were strong enough to face it. Josie followed Mettner out to the backyard where he pointed out an impression in a patch of dirt. It looked like something round had been pressed hard into the soil. Colette's skull, Josie realized. "Someone held her down," she said to Mettner.

He nodded. "I think so. And here, the grass makes it harder to see, but there are two indents in the ground." Both he and Josie squatted down, and Josie saw where two smaller, rounded indentations tamped down the grass. If Josie were to lay down on her back, she'd be able to fit her skull into the larger indentation and the other two would fall roughly on either side of her hips.

"Someone *straddled* her," Josie remarked.

"Right. Whoever the killer was, he straddled her, pressed her head into the dirt and stuffed her mouth with soil. I'm thinking it was a man because of the strength that would have taken. Mrs. Fraley was in her sixties, but I understand she was physically healthy. Against a smaller opponent, I would expect to see more evidence of a struggle. More bruising and lacerations on her body, more of the dirt and grass disturbed out here. I'm thinking this guy was big enough to overpower her completely and hold her here until he was finished."

"Then he turned her over onto her face," Josie said.

"Boss," Mettner said.

"Just Josie, now, remember?"

Mettner corrected himself shyly. "Josie. I think this was personal."

Josie nodded. "It doesn't get much more intimate, does it? Looking down into someone's eyes while you suffocate them? Then turning them over so you don't have to see what you've done? You should alibi the family."

"I thought the family lived far away from here," Mettner said.

"Well Noah's oldest brother has a pretty airtight alibi since he lives in Arizona, but you should still make some calls—find out where he was at the time of Colette's death and who can corroborate his whereabouts. It's just good practice. Laura and her husband, Grady, live only a couple of hours away, and I think Colette's ex-husband lives in the state. They're closer. Even more reason to alibi them. Rule out those closest to Colette right off the bat."

"You think any of them are capable of this?" Mettner asked.

Josie shrugged. The grief she had seen at Noah's house was genuine. "Probably not, but the first thing we'd do if this was a case that didn't involve one of our own would be to make sure everyone close to the victim had an alibi."

"Right," Mettner conceded. "I thought Mrs. Fraley divorced Noah's dad years ago."

"She did," Josie said. "But we really have no idea what kind of relationship they had then, or if they maintained one afterward. It's worth looking into."

"You got it. By the way, come upstairs with me. There are some drawers disturbed up there as well."

The upstairs rooms were in a similar state of disarray to the downstairs. Just like the living room and kitchen, the upstairs rooms looked as though Colette had simply been looking for something. The drawers in her night stands and the top dresser drawers stood half-open, some of their contents scattered onto the floor. The closet doors had been pushed open and the lids from various shoeboxes sat crooked, as though hastily replaced. A large, standing jewelry box in the corner of the room had also been disturbed. A quick glance told Josie that whoever had raided the room had left behind several—if not all—valuable pieces of jewelry. They would be better able to tell what might be missing after Noah did a walk-through.

"Someone was looking for something, like I said," Josie told Mettner.

"Yes," Mettner agreed. "Looks that way. Come, see the rest."

In the bathroom, the medicine cabinet stood open, a bottle of Advil and a tube of toothpaste discarded in the sink beneath it. Cleaning supplies spilled from the cabinet beneath the sink. The heavy top of the toilet tank was askew.

"What the hell?" Josie said. "What did this guy think she had?"

"That's what we've got to find out," Mettner said. "Did Noah or his sister tell you anything at all?"

"There's nothing for them to tell," Josie said. "They say she wasn't having problems with anyone, didn't have many valuables in the home and that no one would hurt her."

"Then what secrets was she keeping?" Mettner asked. "Even from her children?"

Josie said, "That's what we have to figure out."

Colette's spare bedroom, which Josie knew her other children slept in when they visited, was undisturbed except for the closet where several of Colette's old handbags had been pulled out and left on the floor. The other bedroom had long ago been converted to a sewing room. Its dozens of plastic drawers against the far wall had all been pulled open. The large sewing machine that sat in the middle of the long, narrow sewing table in the center of the room had been knocked onto its side. Other than that, the room appeared to be in order. The shelves of fabric and spools of thread lining the opposite wall were undisturbed as were the baskets of yarn. In the corner of the room stood a waist-high wooden quilt rack draped with Colette's latest masterpiece.

"If she could sew like that, she definitely didn't have Parkinson's," Josie remarked as she stepped into the room.

"We've already photographed it and printed what we could," Mettner said. "So you can take a look around."

Josie walked reverently around the room, thinking of the hours Colette must have spent at her beloved sewing table. Had she made the newest quilt for her forthcoming grandchild, Josie wondered? The thought caused a small ache in her chest, and she tried to turn her mind back to the facts of the case, the clues. Surely the killer had been the one searching the house, not Colette in a state of dementia? She wondered if he had found what he was searching for and made off with it. Was that why the place was not more thoroughly ransacked? Or had he been trying to make it *look* like it was just Colette searching for something? She ran her fingers over the quilt hanging on the rack, the beautiful, perfect work causing the ache in her chest to bloom once more; Colette would never sew again.

Mettner watched from the doorway, arms crossed. "Do you want to try to clean things up before Noah does the walk-through? We could start in here where there's not too much of a mess."

Josie knew that restoring Colette's home to its usual neatness might make Noah feel better so she turned to the wall and started pushing all the small drawers back into place. Then she moved to the table and righted the sewing machine. Back up the right way, it still wobbled unevenly on the table. "This is heavy," she muttered.

Mettner came over and grabbed each side of it, shifting it to try to make it sit level.

"Careful," Josie admonished, although she wasn't sure why. Colette would never use the machine again, and Josie was fairly certain that none of her children were going to take up sewing.

Mettner tilted the sewing machine and turned his head to get a look at the bottom of it. "The base is loose," he said.

Josie moved around to his side of the table, bending to see. "Oh no," she said. "I see a crack on one side. That's why the bottom is loose. Still, it should sit upright. Try again."

Mettner spent several seconds trying to make it stand straight before they heard another crack.

"Oh no," he said. "Damn. I'm sorry."

"Shit," Josie said. "Just lay it back on its side. I don't want to do any more damage. We'll leave it like that. I can try to fix it later, before her children do a walk-through. It's just plastic, a spot of glue should do the trick."

Mettner's large hands cupped either side of the machine, but he hesitated to move it again and cause more damage. "Mett," Josie said. "Seriously. We'll get some crazy glue and fill those cracks right in."

He didn't look convinced, but he slowly lowered the machine onto its side. "It didn't just crack," he said. "Dammit. Look at this."

The plastic panel at the bottom was hanging almost completely loose.

"Oh geez," Josie said. "Okay, just leave it like that."

Gently, she tried to fit the base back on, but it wouldn't click into place. Mettner stood by silently, arms crossed tightly over his chest, as though he was watching an operation. Josie shook her head, and was about to turn and usher them both out of the room when something caught her eye. She drew closer, peering at the machine. Poking out from amongst the inner workings of the sewing machine was the edge of a clear sandwich bag with a sliding clasp.

"What's this?" Josie asked.

Mettner stepped forward and peered over Josie's shoulder while she gently tugged on the corner of the plastic bag. The baggie fell out, making a small clunk on the wooden table. Josie and Mettner stared at it. Josie said, "Do you have gloves?"

"You think it's important?" Mettner asked.

"Well, I don't know, but if it is, I'd like to be wearing gloves."

Mettner reached inside his jacket and pulled out a pair of protective gloves which he handed to Josie. She snapped them on and picked up the bag, holding it up to the light so they could get a better look at what was inside.

Josie shifted the bag in her hands, inspecting what appeared to be three items inside of it.

"Should I call the ERT?" Mettner asked. "Establish a chain of custody?"

Josie nodded. "I don't know what these things are, but it sure is strange that Colette would hide them in the base of her sewing machine."

Mettner took out his phone. "I know when my grandmother got older and started getting confused, she was always putting things in strange places. Once I found her car keys in the freezer."

Josie shook her head. "No. I think she hid this on purpose. This wasn't an easily accessible hiding spot. And look how wrinkled and rumpled the bag is—it's been in there for some time. Call the ERT."

CHAPTER EIGHT

Mettner called Hummel, who was the head of the Evidence Response Team. Hummel arrived ten minutes later, photographed the bag and the sewing machine and then, with gloved hands, he shook out the three items onto the sewing table. Mettner also donned a pair of gloves as he watched Josie pick up the items one by one. The first item was a flash drive with some writing on it.

"What does it say?" Mettner asked as Josie squinted at small, handwritten letters squeezed onto its surface.

"Pratt," Josie answered. She looked up at Mettner and Hummel. "Does that mean anything to you?"

Both shook their heads. Josie put the flash drive aside and picked up the second object. It was a flat stone that fit easily in her palm, narrowing to a point at one end. The other end was wide and straight-edged but notched in on both sides.

"What is it?" Mettner asked.

Josie turned it over in her gloved hands. "I think it's an arrowhead." It was light brown, its uneven rocky surface dulled and smoothed. "Jasper," Josie added.

"What's that?" Mettner asked.

"This is a jasper point. The Native Americans who were here in Pennsylvania before this country was established used stone to fashion their tools, jewelry, and all kinds of things. They made arrows out of a few different types of stone found here—flint, quartz, and jasper. Ray and I used to look for them in the woods when we were kids."

"I think my grandfather had one of these," Mettner said, taking the arrowhead from Josie and feeling its weight in his palm. "But it was a different color."

"Probably flint or quartz then," Hummel said. "What else do we have here?"

Josie picked up the third item—a belt buckle which was heavy and large, easily the size of her palm, and gold plated with two rifles on the front, their barrels crossed over the top of an etching of several pine trees. Below that, it was embossed with the date 1973. She handed it to Mettner.

He asked, "How old was Colette Fraley in 1973?"

"Her early twenties, I think," Josie replied. "But I don't think that belonged to her."

"What about Mr. Fraley?" Mettner asked. "Could this be his?"

"I suppose. All I know is that Colette and Noah's dad divorced when Noah was eighteen. He moved away. None of the kids keep in touch with him, but we could track him down and ask him about it. Laura, his sister, is supposed to text me his phone number."

"We'll do that but if it's not her ex-husband's, whose is it? What's a woman like Colette Fraley doing with a forty-five-year-old belt buckle, a Native American arrowhead, and a flash drive marked 'Pratt' on it hidden in the bottom of her sewing machine?" Mettner said.

Hummel held up the flash drive. "This seems like the most sensible place to start. You should take it back to the station house and check it out before we dust it for prints. The fumigation from the printing process might compromise the contents."

Mettner held out a paper evidence bag and Hummel dropped it inside. "Will do," he said.

"Get a warrant," Josie told him. "For the contents. If we don't get one, and it turns out to be of critical importance, it could be inadmissible."

"Okay," Mettner said. "I'll write one up. Then we'll see if this is what our killer was looking for."

CHAPTER NINE

Josie knew it would be a couple of hours before they had a warrant to access the flash drive, but when she drove back to Noah's house she found no one home. A quick text to him directed her to the nearest funeral home—the same funeral home where her late husband, Ray Quinn's funeral service had been held four years earlier. Her heart did a double tap as she passed through its heavy wooden doors. It was just as she remembered, with thick carpets and walls that muffled any sound, decorated in somber tones probably meant to soothe but which only made Josie's stomach turn. She had been to more than her fair share of funerals since the missing girls case that killed Ray and had no desire to attend anymore, certainly not one for Colette Fraley.

But there Colette's children sat in the director's office, ringed around a large desk, faces tear-stained and stricken as the funeral director showed them a selection of caskets from a large binder. After quietly nodding at Laura and Grady and giving Theo a quick hug, she sat down beside Noah and took his hand. Josie tried to focus on the discussion, but her mind kept drifting back to the items in Colette's sewing machine. Who, or what was Pratt?

"Josie?" Noah asked.

She shook herself back into the room and offered him a smile. "I'm sorry, what did you say?"

Laura spoke up. "Did you speak to the medical examiner? When will our mother be released to us?"

"Oh, sorry. Yes, I did. She'll be released tomorrow."

All heads turned back toward the director as a discussion about dates ensued. Then came the issue of money; even if they went for the more inexpensive route of cremation, they were still looking at thousands of dollars. There was a small discussion amongst the siblings which was eventually resolved by the agreement that they would each pay one third of the costs, and they would be reimbursed when the payout from Collette's small life insurance policy came through.

Once the meeting was over, they decided to go to lunch, although none of them looked as though they had an appetite. Theo drove off toward the restaurant in his rental car, and after Noah assured them he would get a ride with Josie, Laura and Grady followed in her SUV. Josie and Noah hung back, standing at the entrance to the funeral home. At least it was a nice day, Josie thought as the sun warmed them and a cool breeze caressed their faces.

"My car is right over there," Josie said when Noah made no move toward the parking lot.

He stood staring into the distance, face blank.

Josie touched his arm. "Noah?"

"I'm fine," he mumbled.

"You know, you don't have to go to lunch. I'm sure your brother and sister would understand."

He said nothing.

She didn't want to do it, but she also had no idea when the next time they'd be alone would be, so she cleared her throat and said, "Noah, does the name 'Pratt' mean anything to you?"

He turned his head to look at her, brows knit together. "What?"

"Pratt," Josie repeated. "Is it familiar to you? Do you know anyone by that name?"

"Why are you asking?"

"I was with Mettner at your mother's house earlier. A few things upstairs were disturbed. We were trying to straighten up in your mother's sewing room and found some... things hidden in the base of her sewing machine. One was a flash drive with the name 'Pratt' written on it."

Noah shook his head. "I don't know anyone named Pratt, and neither did my mom."

"You're sure?"

"It must not be hers."

"But it was hidden in the bottom of her sewing machine. She used that machine almost daily, didn't she? Where did she get it? Did she buy it new?"

"No, I gave it to her as a Christmas gift a few years ago," he answered.

Josie took out her phone and pulled up photos of the belt buckle and arrowhead to show him. "Do you recognize these?"

Noah shook his head. "No, I've never seen them before. I mean, that just looks like an arrowhead, like you used to find in the woods."

Josie pocketed her phone with a sigh. "What about the belt buckle? Could it have belonged to your dad? Or someone else your mom knew?"

He shook his head. "No. My dad never wore stuff like that, and my mom didn't have any men in her life after he left. I have no idea where that came from or whose it is. Why are you asking me all this now?"

"I'm trying to get to the bottom of what happened," Josie said quietly.

"My mother is dead, that's what happened," he said flatly, walking off toward her car.

"Noah?" Josie called.

She jogged after him, moving around to block his path. "I know you're hurting right now, but someone killed your mother and it's my job to find out who. As far as we know, he's still out there. I don't want anyone else to be hurt or killed. You know I have to ask these questions."

He stared at the asphalt for a beat then a gravelly laugh sounded from deep in his throat. "You can't just be… *Josie*, can you?"

She took a step back. "What?"

His hazel eyes zeroed in on her face. "It isn't your job to find the person who killed my mom. It's not your job to ask these questions. You don't need to be out on some crusade. We have other people for this. Gretchen, Hummel, Mettner."

"You know that Gretchen is on the desk. Hummel's the head of the Evidence Response Team, he's not a detective, and Mettner is good, but he's inexperienced. Do you really want your mother's case handled by the most inexperienced member of the team without any oversight?"

"Oversight from you, you mean."

"Unless I can get Gretchen off the desk, yes."

He said nothing but looked past her, his face awash with grief and frustration.

"Noah," Josie said. "You can't see it now because you're hurting too much, but I promise you that one day it's going to matter very much that your mother's killer is behind bars."

He pushed a hand through his hair. "It won't bring her back," he said. "Nothing that you do is going to bring her back."

"You think I don't know that?"

He met her eyes. "Then just be my girlfriend right now."

She felt the hot sting of tears in her eyes. She pressed a hand to her chest. "I am your girlfriend, Noah, and I'm here with you right now. Listen, I know you're upset, but—but why aren't you more—"

"More what?"

Josie shook her head. "I don't know. I just know that if someone I loved was murdered, I wouldn't be able to sleep or eat or concentrate on anything else until I found the killer and put them away. Chitwood would have to lock me up to keep me away from the investigation."

"You think I don't care that someone murdered my mom?"

"That's not what I said. I just—"

He cut her off. "That's just what you meant."

"No, I didn't mean that. You know damn well I didn't mean that. Noah, I just want to see that this is made right."

"But it can't be 'made right'," he said. "Don't you get that? Find the killer. Put him in prison. It won't bring my mom back. It won't get the image of her face out of my mind—you know, when we were doing the CPR." He hung his head, but not before Josie saw fresh tears glistening in his eyes.

She touched his arm gently. "I know," she said. "I'm so sorry."

He took a moment to compose himself and then waved a hand in dismissal. "Let's just go to lunch, okay?"

Tentatively, Josie reached down and took his hand in hers. She led him to her car and drove to the Denton diner with Noah staring out the window, not saying a word. It had been less than a day since they'd found Colette. He was still in shock. She could feel pain radiating off him in waves—raw and edgy. She wished more than anything that she could take it away from him; that she could somehow restore what was lost to him. But she knew that she could not. The best she could do was stand by him and try to find his mother's killer.

CHAPTER TEN

Lunch was painfully awkward with no one speaking or eating much. Grady tried desperately to engage each of them in conversation—asking Laura if the baby was moving much; asking Theo about the weather in Arizona; and asking Josie and Noah what was new at work. Each time, Laura shut him down in an exasperated tone. "Grady, no one cares about the weather and you know damn well what's new with Noah and Josie at work—our mother was just killed."

Grady's face colored, and he looked down at his uneaten turkey sandwich. Josie said, "Well, I don't think it's true that no one cares about the weather." She turned to Theo. "Is it true that you have massive dust storms in Arizona? What are they called?"

"Really?" Laura snapped. "We're going to talk about the weather right now?"

Grady said, "Laura, please."

Josie opened her mouth to reply but Noah spoke instead. "It was your idea to come to lunch. We're in public. We can make an effort to be civil to one another. Mom would want it that way."

Theo cleared his throat and gave Josie a pained smile, but she could see the lines around his hazel eyes loosen with relief. "They're called haboobs," he said.

Ignoring Laura's icy glare Josie engaged him, "I've only seen videos of them on the news. They look terrifying. Do you get many where you live?"

She was aware in her periphery of the clink of silverware against plates and of Noah picking up his coffee to sip it.

Theo said, "The first time I saw one, I thought I was in real trouble." He laughed. "Not something a Pennsylvania boy is prepared for."

They made small talk during the rest of lunch with only Grady joining in. Still, when the check came, most of the food they'd ordered remained on their plates. When the waitress asked if they would like takeout boxes, they all refused. Grady paid for the meal and they left in silence.

Back at Noah's house after lunch, Josie was tasked with going back to Colette's to bring over any photo albums she could find there. The job of putting together family photographs for a slide show for the funeral services was the only small thing that seemed to lift the Fraley children out of their grief—if only temporarily—particularly after Theo found a bottle of wine in Noah's pantry. Josie was heartened to see Noah smile at many of the memories from their shared childhood. Josie ordered pizza for dinner and afterward, Noah even kissed her when she left to return to her own home for a change of clothes. Josie's overnight bag was packed by the time Gretchen called her.

"I'm really sorry about Mrs. Fraley," Gretchen said. "Please give Noah my condolences."

"Thanks, I will," Josie said. "Any chance you're calling me because Chitwood let you off the desk?"

Gretchen gave a short dry laugh. "No chance. But I've been helping Mettner out with everything I can. As long as my ass doesn't leave this chair, Chitwood's fine with it. I know Noah needs you right now, and I wouldn't normally ask, but at the moment you're our unofficial family liaison."

"What've you got?" Josie asked, relieved that Mettner was delegating what he could to Gretchen.

"Some things I'd like you to have a look at, see if you can make sense of them and then maybe ask the family about. You have time to come by the station?" Gretchen asked.

"You accessed the flash drive?" Josie asked.

"Yes, we got the warrant. But I can't tell what the hell any of this is—it looks like a lot of old court documents, even a bank statement, and I don't see the name Pratt in any of these records. Did Colette work in the court system or for a bank?"

"No," Josie replied. "She worked at a quarry. She was in the office—a secretary, I believe. She retired a few years ago. How far back do the documents go?"

"At least fifteen years," Gretchen said. "It's easier if I show you."

Josie glanced at her bedside clock. She was certain the Fraleys would be reminiscing and picking through their family photos well into the night. She could spare some time to meet with Gretchen.

"I'll be there in ten minutes."

Denton's police headquarters was housed in an old, historic three-story building that almost looked like a castle. It was huge and gray, with ornate molding over its many double-casement arched windows and an old bell tower at one corner. It used to be the town hall but had been converted to the police station sixty-five years ago. Josie parked in the municipal lot and made her way through the back door where the holding area was on the ground floor and up to the second floor where the great room was located. It was a large open area cluttered with desks. Josie's, Noah's and Gretchen's desks formed a T in the center of the room. Gretchen already had the PDF files pulled up on her desktop computer. Josie pulled her chair over beside Gretchen's and began scrolling.

"These are sealed court documents," Josie noted. "They're criminal complaints against juveniles."

"Right," Gretchen said. "From what I can see, these documents pertain to three different kids—two boys and a girl—between the ages of fourteen and sixteen."

Josie's eyes skimmed the complaints. "Trespassing, shoplifting, vandalism. None of these are serious offenses. They'd get slaps on the wrists, if that. I'd be surprised if any of these even made it to court. Even a public defender could plead these down to fines or get them off for first-time offenses. These complaints are from 2005. That was thirteen years ago. Did you look these kids up?"

"Yeah, I didn't get much beyond current addresses, but if you keep scrolling you'll see each of them was sentenced to anywhere between six to twenty-four months in a juvenile detention center on the other side of Alcott County," Gretchen said.

"That's a hell of a long time for such minor offenses," Josie noted. She kept skimming over the documents until she found the name of the juvenile detention center. Wood Creek. Something sparked in the back of her mind but as quickly as it flashed to life, it faded. She kept going until she reached the last few pages of the PDF document. "These are bank statements," she said.

Gretchen nodded. "There are two. One appears to be a business account and the other a personal account."

Josie read the names. "Eugene Sanders is the name on the personal account. The address has been blacked out. The business account is for a Wood Creek Associates." The spark in Josie's mind whooshed into a full-blown inferno. "Oh sweet Jesus," she said. "Do you know what this is?"

She turned to see the grimace on Gretchen's face. "I didn't. Not at first. But when I looked up Eugene Sanders and then Wood Creek Detention Facility, I figured it out. It was the Kickbacks for Kids scandal. Sanders was the judge."

"Right," Josie said.

"I was working in Philadelphia back then. I mean, I remember hearing about it on the news, but it didn't really make much of an impression at the time. I had my hands full in the homicide department."

Josie sighed, and pushed her dark brown hair away from her face as she leaned back in the chair. "The Kickbacks for Kids scandal broke just after I joined the force. It happened here in Alcott County. It had been going on for years before a journalist brought it to light in 2010."

"Sanders took money to sentence kids to overly long stays at Wood Creek, right?"

Josie nodded as her eyes tracked down the columns of each bank statement. "Right. Wood Creek was a for-profit, privately owned and run juvenile detention center owned by Wood Creek Associates which was basically a bunch of Sanders' cronies who got together and financed the facility. They built it and then they gave Sanders a fixed amount of money for every juvenile he sent there—the more time on their sentence the better. These kids did completely unnecessary time for minor offenses, and Wood Creek was a shit hole where most of them were abused."

"The men behind the Wood Creek Associates went to prison as well, if I recall," Gretchen said.

"Yeah," Josie said. "Not for as long as Sanders did though. He was the one who handed out all the bogus sentences. He ruined a lot of lives. Here—" she pointed to Eugene Sanders' bank statement. "This is a deposit for $5,000 dated April 20, 2005 and look at the bank statement from the Wood Creek account—same date, a transfer of some kind in the same amount."

Gretchen leaned over Josie's shoulder, peering at the screen. They found two more $5,000 deposits into Sanders' account that occurred on the same dates that Wood Creek Associates transferred $5,000 out of their account. "This was evidence," Gretchen said. "Back in 2005 someone had evidence of what was going on, but the case didn't break for another five years."

"So why on earth did Colette Fraley have this?" Josie wondered aloud.

"And who is Pratt?"

"Let's find out," Josie answered, pulling up the internet browser and navigating to the Google home page.

CHAPTER ELEVEN

"Quinn!" a male voice shouted from behind them, making them both jump.

Josie and Gretchen turned to see Bob Chitwood, their new Chief of Police, hovering over their shoulders. His normally ruddy, acne-pitted face was ashen as he stared past them at the computer monitor. He pointed to the screen. "You get anything from the flash drive you found at the Fraley scene?"

Gretchen nodded. "Yes, and it had the name Pratt written on the outside of it."

"You figure out what it means?"

"No, not yet, sir," Gretchen said.

"Keep looking," he told her. "Quinn, my office. Now."

To Gretchen, Josie said, "See what you can find."

Gretchen nodded and turned back to the computer. Josie followed Chitwood into his office. Sitting in one of the two guest chairs in front of his large desk, Josie noticed he had finally unpacked the banker's box full of personal items he had brought with him when he took over as Chief. Josie looked around at the walls, but he hadn't hung anything up yet. Several frames sat on the floor propped against the wall beside his desk. Not for the first time she wondered what kind of man Bob Chitwood was beneath his bad temper.

"How's Fraley?" Chitwood asked as he closed his office door and walked around to sit behind his desk.

"As good as can be expected," Josie answered, stunned that Chitwood even cared to ask. "Still in shock, I think."

Chitwood sighed. "Well, we're going to need him. Not to work but to answer a lot of questions. You know we work from the family outward."

Josie shifted in her chair, thinking about just how well asking Noah questions had gone for her earlier in the day. "Yeah, I know. Listen, Chief, I think we need Gretchen. She should be the lead investigator on this."

He folded his arms across his chest. "No."

"Sir, she's the most experienced homicide investigator we've got. More experienced than me. You're only keeping her on the desk because—"

He waggled a finger as he cut her off. "Be careful, Quinn. I'm keeping her on the desk because of the shit she pulled with the last murder we had in this town. She should never have been allowed back on the force. You think I don't know you had a hand in that?"

"I'm not interested in talking politics with you, sir," Josie said. "I'm interested in finding Colette Fraley's killer as fast as humanly possible. You and I both know Gretchen is the surest way to do that."

"You questioning my judgment, Quinn?"

"I'm saying this investigation needs Gretchen."

He gestured toward the closed door. "You've got her. There's lots of stuff she can help you with from the desk."

"We need her in the field."

"No."

"Sir—"

"You want to be on leave, too? I'll pull your badge for insubordination, Quinn. This is my department now, not yours. If Detective Palmer shows me that she can stay in her lane while she's on the desk, then I'll put her back in the field. That's my decision. Got that?"

Josie wanted to say more, but she knew she was on thin ice. For Noah's sake, she had to try to stay in Chitwood's good graces. Mettner was good, but someone needed to oversee the investigation. Josie could only do that if she was still in play.

"Yes," she said.

"Good. See what you can get from Fraley," Chitwood told her. "I know he's grieving, but we've got a murder to solve."

CHAPTER TWELVE

Gretchen looked up hopefully as Josie emerged from Chitwood's office. Josie shook her head and Gretchen slumped. Josie squeezed her shoulder as she sat in the chair beside her. "Give it time," she said. "I'm going to keep lobbying to get you back out there."

"Thanks," Gretchen said.

"You get anything on Pratt?"

"No. Unfortunately, Pratt is a pretty damn common name. There are one hundred fifty businesses with the name Pratt in them in Pennsylvania."

"Well," Josie said. "I don't think Pratt is the name of a business in this case."

"There's no Pratt in any of the records on the flash drive," Gretchen said.

"Did you check the names of all the Wood Creek Associates board members?"

"Yeah. No one named Pratt."

"And we know the bank statements didn't belong to anyone named Pratt."

"But the drive either belonged to someone named Pratt or was intended for someone named Pratt," Gretchen said.

"Yeah," Josie said. "I think we can safely assume that."

"Then what was Colette Fraley doing with it?" Gretchen asked.

Josie said, "Let's table that for a second. Focus on Pratt. Let's say you had this evidence of the Kickbacks scandal—"

"You think Colette had this? I thought you said she worked for a quarry."

"She did. I don't know how she got it or why she had it but like I said, let's stick with the Pratt angle. Let's say whoever put this flash drive together—whether it was Colette or someone else completely—they were going to give it to someone named Pratt. What kind of person would you give this to?"

"The police," Gretchen answered easily.

"Let's check County Control for any officer named Pratt. We'll start in Alcott County and work our way outward. Although the Kickbacks scandal took place here in Alcott County, so my best guess is that the Pratt we're looking for is right here."

Gretchen picked up her phone and started dialing their dispatch center. "Do you remember anyone named Pratt on the force here?"

"No," Josie said. "Not since I started. Let me call down to Sergeant Lamay, he's been here longer than any of us."

Lamay, stationed in the lobby, picked up on the second ring. He listened to her question and said, "Let me think." His breath filtered through the line as Josie waited. Dan Lamay had been with the department nearly forty-five years. He had seen the coming and going of five Chiefs of Police—Josie included—and survived a huge scandal. He was now past retirement age, with a bum knee and an ever-increasing paunch. Josie had kept him on as a desk sergeant during her tenure as Chief because his wife was recovering from cancer and his daughter was in college. He had been fiercely loyal to her, helping her when she needed it most. Now she was worried that Chief Chitwood would let him go, but so far, he had stayed off Chitwood's radar, performing his duties quietly and efficiently.

"No," he said finally. "I don't remember anyone named Pratt. My memory's not the best, boss."

"It's okay," Josie said. "Gretchen's on the phone with County Control now to see if they can run it down. I just thought you might remember."

"Sorry, I can't be of more help. But hey, you know, that name does sound familiar."

"Thanks," Josie said and hung up. The name was familiar to her too but she still couldn't figure out why.

After several minutes on the phone, Gretchen hung up with a heavy sigh. "No Pratts in law enforcement in Alcott County—at least not going back as far as the documents on the flash drive."

"We're missing something," Josie said. She took out her cell phone and checked but there were no calls or text messages from Noah. She could still spare some time. "We're going about this wrong."

"The FBI?" Gretchen suggested.

"They do investigate corruption," Josie said. "But no, I think we need to look closer. Think about it: what happens to a case once it leaves the hands of police?"

Gretchen sat up straighter in her chair, her eyes taking on a sparkle to match Josie's. "A prosecutor."

Josie pulled up the internet browser on her own computer and typed the words: Pratt, prosecutor, Alcott County, Pennsylvania. The moment the results popped up, it came back to her.

"Drew Pratt," she said. "He was an Alcott County assistant district attorney. He went missing in 2006. I was in college."

"2006," Gretchen said. "I was working in Philadelphia then."

Josie clicked on the Images tab and photos of Drew Pratt filled the screen. Gretchen leaned in. Drew Pratt smiled back at them, dark eyes flashing with humor. He was nearing sixty with salt-and-pepper hair thinning at the temples as he stood in front of the Alcott County courthouse.

"I remember this," Gretchen said as Josie clicked through several more photos. "He took a ride in his car one day in 2006 and was never seen again, right?"

"Yeah," Josie breathed. "It was one of the most famous missing persons cases in the state."

"It's coming back to me now," Gretchen said. "They found his car, didn't they?"

"Yes," Josie said. "But not him. No body, nothing. People thought—"

She broke off as she clicked on a new photo. Her fingers froze on the computer mouse.

"Is that who I think it is?" Gretchen asked. She put on her reading glasses and leaned in close to the screen. "Zoom in."

Josie clicked until the photo enlarged. It was Drew Pratt standing outside of a federal building with a group of men in suits, together with several men in police uniforms. All were smiling, obviously celebrating some legal victory. Standing behind Drew Pratt, looking two decades younger but no less craggy or thin, was Bob Chitwood.

"Print this out," Gretchen said.

"On it," Josie answered.

CHAPTER THIRTEEN

The Chief was still behind his desk when Josie and Gretchen barged in without knocking. One of his eyebrows kinked upward. "What the hell is this?"

Josie waved the photo in front of him before placing it in the center of his desk. "We think that flash drive was either intended for Drew Pratt or it belonged to him. How did you know him?" she asked. "I thought you were in Pittsburgh before this—that's on the other side of the state."

"You questioning my integrity, Quinn?" Chitwood snapped, giving the photo a cursory glance.

"I'm asking a question, sir," Josie responded evenly. She'd gotten quite used to his outbursts by now, she hardly noticed anymore.

"We worked a drug trafficking task force together. Ages and ages ago. Probably when you were still in diapers."

"What does the Kickbacks for Kids scandal have to do with Drew Pratt?" Gretchen asked.

Chitwood leaned back in his chair and steepled his fingers under his chin. "Sit, both of you," he instructed.

Josie looked at Gretchen who gave a barely perceptible shrug. If Chitwood was willing to talk, they were going to listen. They each took a seat.

Chitwood said, "If you remember the Drew Pratt case, then you probably remember there are about a half-dozen theories about what really happened to him."

Josie had seen a number of specials on Drew Pratt's disappearance over the years. "Yes, I do remember that," she said. "Some said he committed suicide. Others believed he walked away from his life and started a new one under an assumed identity. There were a lot of theories floating around that someone he had prosecuted in the past killed him and hid his body."

Chitwood nodded. "A few years back there was even a convict who claimed to know where his body was—said a gang had killed him and dumped his body in a remote area as revenge for putting one of their members away."

"That turned out to be nothing," Gretchen said. "I remember that being on the news."

"Right," Chitwood said. "The convict in question was trying to get his sentence reduced. There was no body and no evidence at all to support his claim."

It hit Josie then—the Kickbacks for Kids connection. "Drew Pratt had evidence of what Judge Sanders and Wood Creek Associates were doing in 2005, the year before he disappeared. He chose not to prosecute. In 2010 when the scandal broke, people talked about him. His name was back in the press, wasn't it?"

"It was. People thought he walked away from his life because he knew the scandal was coming, and he would be blamed for not prosecuting Judge Sanders earlier. That was a theory. No one could ever prove that he had evidence of the Kickbacks for Kids thing before he went missing. The DA's office didn't have a file. Nothing was ever found in his office or personal effects. This is the first I've heard of a flash drive with documents on it. I knew Drew Pratt. He was a solid guy, and he didn't give two shits who he pissed off. If he had evidence that Sanders was taking money to send innocent juveniles to a hellhole, Drew would have prosecuted, no question."

Josie felt Gretchen's eyes on her. "Chief," Josie said. "There was evidence. We've got it right out there on the computer. The stuff on that flash drive was proof of what Sanders and Wood Creek were doing."

Gretchen added, "And his name was on it."

Again, Josie wondered what the connection was between Pratt, Sanders, Wood Creek and Colette Fraley.

"His name was on it," Chitwood said. "But you can't prove he ever received it or even saw it."

"If his prints show up on it, then we know he had it in his possession." Gretchen pointed out.

Chitwood held up a finger. "That doesn't prove he ever looked at the contents."

Josie was still racking her brain for everything she could remember about the Kickbacks scandal and its connection to the missing prosecutor. "There was another Kickbacks theory," she said. "Wasn't there?"

Chitwood and Gretchen stared at her. She went on. "I'd have to look it up, but I'm certain there was another theory about what happened to Pratt. There was a mother whose son went to Wood Creek for something minor. He was brutalized in there, and never the same once he got out. He eventually killed himself."

Gretchen nodded. "I remember that now. The mother killed one of the Wood Creek guys—someone on their board of directors. Her plan was to kill every person involved in it, but she got caught immediately."

"Yes," Josie agreed. "Then there was speculation that she had killed Pratt all those years ago because he knew what was going on and hadn't prosecuted. There was also a guard who worked at the facility who had committed suicide, and the investigation into his death was reopened after the mother was arrested, because the police were worried that she had been killing people unchecked for years."

"What was her name?" Gretchen asked.

Chitwood answered, "Patti Something... Patti Snyder."

"You knew her?" Josie asked.

"No. I didn't know her, but I had it from several sources that she was looked at hard for Drew's disappearance, especially because in the hours before Drew went missing, he was seen on surveillance footage in a store talking with a woman who vaguely resembled Snyder."

Josie made a mental note to find out everything she could about Drew Pratt's case the first chance she got.

"Do you think it was her?" Gretchen asked.

Chitwood shrugged. "Don't know. Like I said, we have no proof Drew even knew what Sanders and Wood Creek were up to. That's all speculation. Has been for years. Besides, Patti Snyder was just plain crazy."

"Or just grief-stricken," Josie pointed out.

Gretchen said, "Regardless of what this Patti Snyder did or didn't do, regardless of what happened to Drew Pratt—the real question is why did Noah's mother have this flash drive? Why did she hide it, and is this what the killer was looking for?"

"The case already broke years ago," Josie pointed out. "And Pratt has been missing for over a decade. It's not like anything on that flash drive would be so shocking that it would even need to be hidden."

"True," Gretchen conceded. "I'll take a closer look at every person mentioned in those documents and see what I can find out. We need to know what connection Colette had to all of this—if any."

CHAPTER FOURTEEN

The Fraley children had only vague memories of Drew Pratt and the Kickbacks for Kids scandal, things they'd heard on the news or read online. None of them could account for why Colette would have had the flash drive. "She must have found it or gotten it by accident somehow," Laura theorized.

"Yeah," Noah agreed. "I don't know where it came from, but I don't think she had any idea what was on it."

"She knew enough to hide it," Josie pointed out.

Laura laughed. "With two other completely random objects, from what Noah said. You have to understand, Josie, the more the dementia took over her mind, the more strange and inexplicable things she did. God knows where she got those things, but she was probably having one of her episodes and hid them. She's probably got stuff hidden all over that house."

But when Noah did the walk-through with Mettner they didn't find any other hidden items or anything else unusual.

With the funeral looming, Josie had helped Noah straighten and clean up his mother's house before his sister saw it. Laura was entering her last month of pregnancy and Noah was already concerned about the stress that Colette's death had put on her, and didn't want her to see the disarray. Once the house was restored, Laura went through Colette's closet to choose clothes and jewelry for her funeral. Josie did her best during that week to help the Fraley family in any way she could. The days and nights passed in a blur. She had little time to check in with Mettner or Gretchen and, before she knew it, she was walking into the funeral home hand in hand with Noah.

They had arrived well before the viewing was scheduled to begin. A strange, creeping stillness took over them the deeper into the building they went. As her feet, clad in simple black flats, sank into the thick carpeting of the viewing room, Josie couldn't help but flash back to her husband Ray's funeral. All these years later, the grief was still there, the wound barely scabbed over. Josie felt a wave of sadness for Noah. Now he would feel the yoke of loss, forever on his shoulders.

Josie squeezed his hand as the funeral director sailed into the room and beckoned the Fraley siblings into the anteroom where all the photos had been proudly displayed. She stayed behind while Noah, Theo, Laura and Grady went over the final details before the mourners began to arrive. Colette's body lay in a beautiful, shiny rose gold casket at the front of the room, dozens of floral arrangements arrayed around it. Josie read each card. *With Deepest Sympathy*, they read, and below each message was the name of a family. A lump formed in Josie's throat as she realized how many people's lives Colette had touched.

She turned when the Fraley children and Grady shuffled back in. Laura's cheeks were streaked with tears. One hand rested on top of her belly while the other clutched a crumpled tissue. Noah walked over to Josie and took her hand.

Theo looked at his phone. "People will probably start arriving soon. Better get in line."

They took their places along the side of the room, with Theo closest to the casket, then Laura and Grady, and finally Josie and Noah. Laura blew her nose and then leaned forward, looking first in Theo's direction and then in Noah's. "Noah," she said, her voice shaky and shrill. "Josie can sit over there." She pointed to the rows of chairs lined up in front of Colette's casket. For a moment, Josie felt heat rise to her cheeks, but so as not to cause any unnecessary drama, she started to move toward the chairs. Noah didn't let go of her hand.

"Josie's standing in the greeting line with me," he told his sister.

Laura stepped out of the line and pushed past Grady to confront Noah. She poked a finger in the air in Josie's direction. "You're not married. She can't be in the greeting line."

Theo said, "Laura, really. Don't be ridiculous."

Laura shot him a caustic look. "Stay out of this, Theo. You *barely* qualify for the greeting line. When's the last time you even spoke to Mom?"

"Laura, Jesus," Grady said, reaching out to grip her arm. "Stop."

"I will not," she snapped. "This is my mother's funeral."

Noah said, "It's *my* mother's funeral, too and I'd like Josie to stand next to me to support me."

Laura folded her arms over the top of her belly. "I don't want her in the line."

Josie felt both anger and embarrassment. Acerbic words bubbled on the tip of her tongue, but she swallowed them back.

Noah stood his ground. "I want her in the line."

Josie saw a muscle in Laura's jaw begin to throb and tried to pull her hand free from Noah's. "It's fine, Noah," she murmured. "I'll sit."

He didn't let go. With her free hand, Josie reached up and touched his cheek. "Really. It will be fine. I'll sit right there—right across from you. If you need me, I'll only be a few steps away."

Under Laura's glare, he slowly relented, his grip on her hand loosening. As Josie took the chair at the end of the nearest aisle, directly across from where Noah stood, Theo mouthed the word *sorry* at her. She managed a tight smile.

The four of them stood in line with erect posture and tight expressions, the tension among them palpable. It was almost a relief when the mourners started to arrive in a steady stream of faces Josie didn't recognize. They were friends, neighbors and church members, from what Josie could gather by the small talk they made with the Fraley children after shaking hands, hugging and offering condolences. It was apparent from the long line of people that Colette had been well-loved and respected.

A hand squeezed Josie's shoulder gently. She turned slightly to see Gretchen in the seat behind her, and a wave of relief washed over her. "Thanks for coming," Josie said quietly.

"You're not in the greeting line?" Gretchen asked.

Josie shook her head. "Don't ask."

Gretchen leaned in to speak into Josie's ear. "I alibied these guys, by the way. Mettner had me do it over the phone. Theo was in a business meeting in Phoenix. His immediate supervisor was able to confirm that. Laura was heading up a job fair in Bethlehem. Several people were able to corroborate that. The Halls' housekeeper confirmed that Grady was home all day working around the time Colette was murdered."

"That's good," Josie said. "I didn't think any of them had anything to do with her death, but I told Mettner to rule them out anyway."

"Has their father shown up?" Gretchen asked. "Lance Fraley?"

"No. Laura said he wouldn't come. Looks like she was right. Did you talk to him?"

"Not yet. I have a call out to him. Hey, who's this silver fox?"

Josie looked up as a tall, robust man in his seventies with a thick head of striking white hair strode confidently toward the greeting line. He started with Noah and worked his way down, comforting each one of the Fraley children in turn, taking several minutes with each of them while the line of mourners backed up.

"I think that's Zachary Sutton," Josie said. "Colette's old boss. Laura's current boss."

"So the boss comes to the funeral but not her ex-husband—the father of her children?" Gretchen asked.

Josie said nothing. She'd just had the same exact thought. However, she also knew how contentious divorces could be. She wasn't sure that Lance Fraley's absence was that much of a red flag.

Once the line thinned out, Gretchen stood and made her way over to the Fraley children to offer her condolences. Josie noticed several members of Denton PD filing in, including Chief Chitwood. By the time the viewing period was over, it was standing-room only. The warmth of so many bodies combined with collective sadness made what little air was left in the room heavy and cloying. Josie took off the bolero sweater she'd worn over her black sheath dress and shifted her dark hair on her shoulders, trying to cool off. Several people spoke about what a kind and generous person Colette was; how devoted she had been to her children and the church. Then Theo gave a rousing eulogy, and when Josie looked around toward the end of his speech she saw that most attendees were quietly crying.

By the time all the prayers had been said and hymns had been sung, Josie was exhausted, and she hadn't done anything all morning but sit dutifully in her seat. She kept her hand between Noah's shoulder blades as she walked with him out to the chain of cars that would take Colette's body to its final resting place. Laura, Grady and Theo drove in Laura's SUV and Josie drove Noah in her own vehicle. At least there was no bickering over Josie's position in the line of cars. The mood was somber at the cemetery and didn't improve at the post-service luncheon which the family hosted at a nearby restaurant.

Back at Noah's house, Josie followed him up to his bedroom where he collapsed into bed fully clothed. She made a few attempts at conversation, but he told her he was tired and just wanted to close his eyes. She sat beside him in the bed, stroking his hair until he fell asleep. Josie's own exhaustion was bone-deep. She, too, tried to sleep but couldn't settle. Giving up, she got her laptop from her overnight bag and booted it up.

She knew that both Gretchen and Mettner would do everything humanly possible to bring Colette's killer to justice, but still Josie couldn't help but satisfy her curiosity about Drew Pratt. The details she remembered about his disappearance were foggy. Several times during the week she'd started to research it using the browser on her phone but then stopped herself, not wanting to seem rude and insensitive toward Noah and his siblings. After Noah's remarks about wanting her to just be his girlfriend, she didn't want him to feel neglected by her when he needed her most. Even though it was true that she longed to go after Colette's killer, the main reason was that it broke her heart seeing Noah in such pain. She couldn't bear being on the sidelines and itched to get out there and deliver justice to the person who had caused that pain.

Now the funeral was over and Noah was passed out, it wouldn't hurt to have a look.

CHAPTER FIFTEEN

A quick Google search turned up thousands of results, so Josie clicked on a news report from their local television station, WYEP, which had broadcast several years after Pratt's disappearance. Back then, Josie's twin sister Trinity Payne had been a roving reporter for WYEP and in the clip, Trinity stood beside a large television screen in a skin-tight red dress with glossy red lipstick to match. Her long black hair fell halfway down her back in waves that looked as though they had been hair-sprayed into a permanent formation. Josie was astounded by how young Trinity looked. Then again, that had been before the missing girls case and before the Lila Jensen case which had weathered them both.

"In 2006," Trinity began clearly and firmly, "Assistant District Attorney Drew Pratt took the day off from work and took a drive."

Drew Pratt's face appeared on the large screen with the word "MISSING" beneath it. Penetrating brown eyes stared from the photo, and his mouth was set in a grim line. Josie imagined he must have been a formidable opponent in court.

Trinity continued, "He drove from his home in Bellewood to the Susquehanna Craft Fair and Farmers' Market located in Denton."

Next to Trinity, images of the craft fair flashed across the screen. Josie recognized it. There were two bridges in Denton which crossed the Susquehanna River: a little-used one to the south and the more popular Eastern bridge. Near that bridge, not far from the shore of the river was an old barn that had been renovated and modernized inside. The owner rented spaces inside of it to locals who wanted to sell crafts or produce. It was only open a few days a week, but it had been a staple in Denton for as long as Josie could remember.

On screen, Trinity continued, "It wasn't unusual for Drew Pratt to visit the craft fair. As his daughter told us, he liked to support local artists, and most of the artwork hanging in his Bellewood home had been purchased there over the years."

The camera cut to the inside of the converted building, showing the various booths maintained by local artists selling everything from large wall paintings to holiday decorations.

"Pratt arrived at the craft fair around ten a.m. This much police know from surveillance footage taken from inside the building. Pratt can be seen perusing the various stands and then striking up a conversation with a woman. Police say that the footage was grainy so they're not able to pull a still of the woman from it. However, they do say she appeared to be about five foot four compared to Pratt's six foot frame with short, dark hair."

An older Hispanic man with thinning gray hair, wearing a navy blue suit and red tie appeared on the screen. At the bottom of the screen he was identified as Dom Hernandez, FBI agent. "We don't know this woman. We don't know if Pratt knew her or if they had just met. We don't know what they talked about or if they left together. Unfortunately, when the initial investigation took place, the local police didn't place much importance on her, so the fact of her existence was never released to the press. I believe if this detail had been known to people immediately after Mr. Pratt's disappearance, maybe some tips would have come in. Several years have now passed, so who knows who this woman was and where she is now?"

Trinity cut back in. "Police still refuse to release the footage of Pratt and the mystery woman. Pratt's wife died about ten years before his disappearance following a protracted battle with cancer, and his adult daughter tells us that he wasn't dating anyone at the time he disappeared. What we do know is that his vehicle was still in the parking lot of the craft fair building twenty-four hours later when his daughter reported him missing. Back in 2006, Beth Pratt had just graduated from Penn State and returned home to live with her father while she looked for a job. She told police it was extremely unusual for him to be out overnight without telling her where he was going to be."

This time, an Alcott County sheriff's deputy appeared on screen. In the background, Josie could see the river lazing past as he spoke. "The vehicle was locked. Mr. Pratt's keys and cell phone were still in the car. When we got the vehicle open, there was a strong smell of cigarette smoke, but the family told us that Mr. Pratt never smoked. We also found cigarette ash on the passenger's seat so we do believe that at some point before he went missing, another person was in the car with him. Unfortunately, there are no cameras in the parking lot so we don't know who that person might have been. We did print the car, but there were no fingerprints other than those belonging to Mr. Pratt, his daughter, and a few of his colleagues—all of whom have alibis for the day he went missing."

Trinity reappeared. "The only evidence ever to be recovered in Drew Pratt's case is his laptop which washed up on the shore of the Susquehanna River nearly two months later. His daughter says it wasn't unusual for him to take his laptop with him when he went out for a drive as he liked to stop at coffee shops around the county to escape the noisy District Attorney's office. Unfortunately, the hard drive was so badly damaged, nothing could be recovered from it. After the discovery, many in law enforcement speculated that perhaps Pratt had taken his own life by jumping off the nearby bridge into the river. But after weeks of searching the river, marine units found no trace of Pratt."

"It's like he vanished into thin air," said a young woman on the screen beside Trinity. Josie estimated her to be in her early twenties. She bore a striking resemblance to Drew Pratt, and when her name flashed on the screen, Josie understood why: Beth Pratt. "But I don't think my dad walked out on me, and I don't think he committed suicide. He wasn't depressed. He had a very full and rewarding life. He loved his work. He was very dedicated. I think this was definitely a case of foul play. Someone knows what happened to him. They need to come forward."

Trinity's voice cut back in as the screen showed a montage of police vessels searching the Susquehanna River and still photos of Drew Pratt's abandoned car sitting alone in the craft fair parking lot. "Theories abound as to what exactly happened to the popular Alcott County prosecutor. Although Drew Pratt's daughter dismisses the idea that her father committed suicide, Pratt's nephew can't help but be shaken by the familiar facts and circumstances surrounding his uncle's disappearance."

A young man with thick sandy hair appeared onscreen. He looked a bit older than Beth Pratt. The words along the bottom of the screen announced his name was Mason Pratt. He stood in a hoodie, jeans and boots on the muddy bank of the Susquehanna, hands jammed into his pockets. "It's just weird, you know? I mean, really strange. My dad drowned in this same river in 1999. It was almost the same exact thing—he wasn't at home or at work. No one could find him. My mom and I reported him missing when he didn't come home that night. Police found his car out here." Mason waved an arm to indicate the bank. "I mean, this is Bellewood, so we're about forty miles away from where Uncle Drew went missing. Dad's car was parked right here in the mud. His wallet and keys were in the car. Car was locked, but he was gone. A few days later, his body washed up. They told us he committed suicide. He was bipolar, and always had trouble with depression and stuff. I just never thought he would kill himself."

Trinity came back on the screen and beside her flashed more photos of Drew Pratt; some at press conferences and a few personal photos of him and his daughter. Drew's brother's suicide must not have garnered very much press coverage—if any at all—since WYEP had no photos or video to show related to his death.

"Samuel Pratt's son, Mason, isn't the only person who didn't think his father would kill himself. Friends and family members tell us that Drew Pratt always believed foul play was involved in his brother's death."

The screen cut to another prosecutor being interviewed outside of the courthouse in Bellewood. "Yeah, Drew never bought it that Sam killed himself. Unfortunately there was just no evidence that someone else killed him. I know it bothered Drew. He asked police to look into it again every couple of years, but they never did find anything suspicious."

Trinity again: "Two brothers. Seven years and forty miles apart. Both of their vehicles were found near the river with keys locked inside. Samuel Pratt turned up drowned only two days after he was reported missing, but Drew Pratt's body has never been found, and his disappearance remains one of the most puzzling and enduring mysteries in the history of the state."

The broadcast ended with Trinity giving a tip line number and urging viewers with any information to contact police. Josie closed her laptop and set it aside. Her body buzzed with energy, making sleep an impossibility. Beside her, Noah snored on.

Josie grabbed her cell phone from the nightstand and tapped out a text to Gretchen. *I think we need to look into the Drew Pratt case. Remember the mystery woman with him the day he disappeared? Footage was never released to public. Think you can get it?*

Gretchen's reply came back less than a minute later. *Already got it. Mettner pulled it from the file here in cold case storage. Will show you tomorrow if you have time to stop by. Also Mettner set up a meeting with Beth Pratt in the late afternoon if you want to go with? Trying to track down the nephew now.*

This was exactly why Josie had hired Gretchen when she was interim Chief; they were often on the same page. Smiling, Josie tapped back, *Fantastic. Did you get anything from the house? Fingerprints? Fibers? Hairs? DNA?*

Gretchen answered, *Not a hell of a lot. No unidentified prints. No DNA on the body.*

Of course not, Josie thought. She and Noah had ruined any chance of getting whatever DNA might have been left when they did CPR on Colette. In their efforts to revive her they had contaminated—even destroyed—part of the scene.

Gretchen texted once more: *We did find a footprint in the yard. Male, shoe size 10. That's about it. What's Noah's shoe size?*

Josie sighed. *11. That's something. Thanks*, she replied. *See you tomorrow.*

CHAPTER SIXTEEN

Laura stood in the doorway to Noah's kitchen, hands on her hips, and stared at Josie with what could only be described as disgust. "What do you mean you're not coming to dinner with us tonight?"

From where he sat across from Josie at the kitchen table, Noah said, "Laura, please."

"Don't 'please' me, Noah. This is our last dinner before Grady and I go back to Bethlehem and Theo flies back to Arizona. She should be there."

Noah laughed. "Why?" he said. "Josie and I aren't married, as you were so quick to point out at Mom's funeral. They're short-handed at the station now with both of us out. It's fine if she goes to work."

Josie put her coffee mug down and said, "I don't have to go back into work. I'm sure Mettner can handle the interviews on his own. He's more than capable, and Gretchen is working every lead she can from the desk. It's fine. I just thought—"

Laura cut her off. "My mother said you were too focused on work. That's why she didn't like you, you know."

Grady's head appeared over Laura's shoulder, his eyebrows pulled together in a sheepish look. "Sweetheart, really. Calm down." To Josie and Noah, he said, "Pregnancy hormones."

Laura backhanded Grady, striking his chest. "Don't blame this on the pregnancy."

Josie stood up. "I thought your mother didn't like me because I shot Noah."

That silenced all of them. Josie walked over to the kitchen sink and dumped the rest of her coffee down the drain, taking a deep breath.

"What interviews?" Laura asked, changing the subject. "Are you questioning people in relation to our mother's case?"

Josie said, "We're not exactly sure yet. The department is still running down leads."

"What the hell does that mean?" Laura snapped.

Noah said, "Laura, calm down."

"I won't calm down. Did you know one of your detectives called our employers? Mine and Theo's? Not to mention our housekeeper? She wanted our alibis. In my own mother's murder case."

Calmly, Grady said, "I think that's standard operating procedure, sweetheart. Isn't it, Noah? Rule out the family first?"

"Yes," Noah said. "We always check out people close to victims. It doesn't mean anything, Laura."

"The hell it doesn't," Laura snapped.

"Look," Josie said, before Laura could go on. She turned back to them. "I know your mother didn't warm to me, and I'm sorry that we didn't have more time to get to know one another, especially because I genuinely admired and respected her. The last thing I want to do right now is upset all of you more, but I do want to get out there and help find who did this. I want the person who murdered your mother brought to justice. That said, if Noah wants me at dinner, I'll be there. No questions asked."

Silence filled the room. Noah's chair made a scraping sound along the tiles as he stood. He walked over to Josie, gripped her shoulders and pulled her in to him, planting a soft kiss on her forehead. "I love you," he said. "Now go to work."

Josie's eyes filled with tears. It was the first time since they'd found Colette's body that he'd sounded even remotely like the Noah she knew.

Ten minutes later she was back at the station house, squished between Mettner and Gretchen in front of Gretchen's computer, watching the grainy footage of Drew Pratt and the mystery woman the indoor craft fair cameras had recorded twelve years earlier. They walked into the frame side by side and strolled down the wide aisles at a slow pace. Their bodies were close enough and in sync enough to indicate they were definitely together, but only once did their heads turn toward one another. The footage was so grainy, it wasn't even clear whether they were speaking or not. The camera had been set high at an angle that almost looked straight down from overhead.

"I can see why the police didn't bother releasing this at the time," Gretchen remarked. "It's totally useless. All you can really tell is that this woman was shorter than Pratt, relatively thin, and had short, dark hair. This footage isn't even clear enough to guess her age."

"Yeah," Josie agreed. "But if it had been my case, I would have at least notified the public that he'd been seen talking to a short, dark-haired white woman before he went missing and asked that she come forward."

Gretchen sighed. "Yeah, me too. Google enough articles on this case and you'll get to the parts where various law enforcement agencies blame one another for it not being solved. They had local and state police involved, the county investigators from the DA's office, the sheriff and even the FBI all working on this at one point or another."

Mettner tapped away on his note-taking app as the two of them talked. "No one who was at the craft fair that day remembered her?" he asked. "No one could give a composite?"

Gretchen said, "No. I looked over the file. There were lots of notes and interviews. A lot of people came through there that day. No one even specifically remembered Drew Pratt. He was just another customer. Neither Pratt nor the mystery woman was memorable enough for any of the vendors to give a description or a composite. Unless someone who knows something talks, it's not getting solved."

"Maybe, maybe not," Josie said, taking out her phone. She had spent a good deal of the night going through the Fraley family photo albums to find pictures of Colette around the time that Drew Pratt disappeared. She'd then used her phone to snap photos of those pictures which she now showed Gretchen and Mettner. "I thought for a hot minute that Colette might be the mystery woman, but as you can see, she's always had long hair. I couldn't find one single photo of her with short hair."

Gretchen took Josie's phone and swiped through them. "The build is similar though. Maybe she wore a disguise?"

"But why?" Josie asked. "What reason would Colette Fraley have to meet with Drew Pratt? Wearing a disguise, no less?"

With another sigh, Gretchen handed Josie's phone back and used the mouse to close out the video and pull up some photos. "I don't know," she said. "But look—these are photos of Patti Snyder back in 2006."

In her driver's license photo, Patti Snyder's skin was tanned with wrinkles beginning to form at the corners of her blue eyes and around her mouth. Her dark shock of hair was long enough to run fingers through but not long enough to make a ponytail. The sides of it looked as though they'd been shaved close to her head. The other photo they had on file showed her standing beside a Christmas tree with a reindeer antler headband on her head and a long necklace made of glowing Christmas lights hung around her neck. In the background, Josie saw marble floors and glass walls.

"Well there's no denying she had the short hair and a similar build," Josie said. "Did Patti Snyder smoke? Reports say Pratt's car had cigarette ash inside it."

"Not according to the file," Gretchen answered. "Did Colette?"

"Many years ago. I only know that because Noah once talked about how she quit cold turkey and how hard she found it."

"Well," Mettner said. "That's one mark in the Colette column."

"But the short hair puts a mark in Patti Snyder's column," Josie replied. "I assume someone has asked her?"

"The FBI," Gretchen answered. "They shake her down every couple of years. She refuses to talk to any law enforcement about any of it because she says no one listened to her when her son was sentenced to two years at Wood Creek."

"Well," Josie said. "That's going to make things a lot harder when we go to talk to her, isn't it? What's this in the background? Where was she?"

Gretchen said, "Bellewood First National Bank. She used to be a loan officer there."

"So it's possible that the bank statements on that flash drive came from Patti Snyder."

"Yeah," Gretchen said. "And before you ask, Mett and I couldn't find any connection between Colette and Patti Snyder. No common ground at all. They lived nowhere near one another. They didn't go to the same schools, church, doctors—nothing. We even checked to see if there were any connections between her son and Noah and his sister and brother, but we didn't find anything."

"None of this is making any sense," Josie said.

"Right," Mettner agreed. "Even if we say that Patti Snyder created this flash drive and gave it to Drew Pratt, how in the hell did Mrs. Fraley get her hands on it?"

"Not just that," Josie said. "But why? And when?"

Gretchen checked the time on her phone. "I can definitely set up a meeting with Patti Snyder—assuming she'll meet with you and Mettner in prison—but why don't you two go and see Beth Pratt and find out if she's got any relevant information."

CHAPTER SEVENTEEN

Beth Pratt's single-level ranch home sat along a rural route in the mountains surrounding Denton where each home was separated by two or more acres of land and boasted long gravel driveways. Beth's house was small and white with black shutters on the sides of the windows. It sat at least an acre back from the road and was surrounded by tall oak trees. There was no porch, just a small stone step leading to the front door.

Josie parked behind a small red Honda sedan and she and Mettner got out. As they approached, Josie heard the low tones of what sounded like a game show playing on a television. Behind the screen door, the heavy winter door stood open, so Mettner rapped his knuckles against the edge of the door frame and called, "Miss Pratt?"

There was no answer, no sound at all from inside the house other than the television. Josie peered past Mettner into the living room. She didn't have the best angle into the room which was to the right of the front door, but she saw part of a couch, part of a television sitting on top of a small stand, plush beige carpeting and what looked like the sole of a bare foot. Her heart stopped for a beat and then kicked back into motion. Her hand went to her service pistol, fingers deftly unsnapping the holster at her waist, her palm fitting itself around the handle of the gun. "Mett," she whispered. "Something's wrong."

With her chin, Josie motioned toward the living room. The moment Mettner's eyes landed on the foot, he drew his weapon as well. Keeping the barrels of their guns pointed downward, they entered the house, calling out "Police!" in loud, clear voices. No one responded. Mettner moved immediately to the right where a woman's body lay face down on the carpet in front of the coffee table, a pillow partially covering her head. She wore a purple T-shirt and stretchy black pants. Both her feet were bare. One of her arms lay at her side and the other was bent, palm reaching over her head. Near her feet, a mug lay on its side next to a dark brown stain. A few feet away from that was a television remote and a copy of *People* magazine. Across the room at the foot of an empty bookcase lay piles of paperback books and photo albums which had been torn from the shelves.

Mettner squatted down and took one hand off his weapon to feel the woman's neck for a pulse. He met Josie's eyes. "She's gone." His hand gently touched the woman's arm. "Cold." Which meant she had likely been dead for some time, and they would not be able to bring her back.

Josie nodded toward the hall leading to the back of the house and Mettner followed. They fell into a formation with Josie leading, clearing each room and the back patio before returning to Beth's body. The scene was eerily similar to Colette Fraley's house except that whoever had ransacked the house had done so more hastily, leaving much more of a mess. Kitchen drawers had been pulled from their homes and tossed onto the tile floor, their contents spread all over the room. Papers, pens and other office supplies covered every surface in what looked to be a home office. In the master bedroom, every dresser drawer lay on the floor on top of a pile of discarded clothing. The closet doors stood open, and its contents were in a pile on the floor. Even the bathroom had been torn apart, items from the medicine cabinet and under the sink hurled onto the floor.

"Someone was looking for something," Josie muttered.

With the house cleared, they moved outside to the yard beyond it but found no one nor any traces of anyone. Holstering their weapons, they returned to the body. Josie took out her phone and called dispatch. "We're going to need the ERT and the medical examiner," she said. "Better write up some warrants, too. It looks like we've got another murder on our hands."

CHAPTER EIGHTEEN

An hour later, Josie and Mettner stood in Beth Pratt's living room watching the medical examiner, Dr. Anya Feist perform a cursory examination of the body. The medics helped her turn Beth Pratt onto her back so they could hook her up to the AED machine to ensure there was no cardiac rhythm, but it quickly became obvious there was no need for the machine. Livor mortis blackened the skin of Beth Pratt's arms where they had touched the floor. Dr. Feist sighed. "I'd guess she's been dead about two hours."

Mettner tapped notes into his phone. Josie grimaced; if only they'd got here sooner.

"She's definitely the homeowner?" Dr. Feist asked, looking up at them both.

Josie said, "Yes. The killer dumped her purse onto the dining room table—at least, we assume it was the killer who did it by the way everything was tossed onto the table. Her driver's license was there." With gloved hands she pulled out her phone and brought up the picture she'd snapped. Dr. Feist took the phone and studied Beth Pratt's smiling face, looking back and forth from the phone to the dead woman before her. It was difficult to tell from the body before them with its waxy, lifeless face, but from her photo ID, Josie could see that Beth had her father's square jaw, thin lips and dark hair. She knew from her research that Drew Pratt had been over six feet tall but Beth, at only around five foot two, would have had difficulty fighting off a larger, aggressive attacker.

Dr. Feist handed the phone back to Josie with a sigh. "I'd say that's a positive ID, all right." Pulling a small flashlight from her jacket pocket, she shone it into Beth Pratt's glassy eyes. "Petechiae here as I would expect. I'll know more when I get her on the table, but my initial impression would be death by asphyxiation." Gently, her gloved fingers probed Beth Pratt's lips, pulling them away from her teeth methodically. She then pressed a finger to the middle of Beth's chin to draw her mouth open so she could examine inside with her flashlight.

"There are cuts on the insides of her lips and what looks like carpet fibers on her tongue, suggesting someone held her face down against the carpet." Dr. Feist pointed to the pillow near Beth's head. "They probably used that to hold her down and keep her quiet."

The entire scene sent a chill down Josie's spine.

Mettner said, "It looks like there was somewhat of a struggle with all this stuff knocked onto the floor."

"So, let's imagine she was probably sitting on her couch," Josie agreed. "Reading a magazine, having a cup of coffee, waiting for us to arrive."

Mettner pointed toward the large front window of the living room which overlooked the driveway, now filled with police vehicles, Dr. Feist's van and an ambulance. "The killer pulls up. She probably had her heavy door open because she was expecting us."

Josie said, "The screen door isn't damaged. Maybe she even went over and opened it when he got here?"

Mettner walked over to the front screen door and pushed it open as though he were letting someone in. "By the time she realizes her visitor is not with Denton PD, it's too late, he's already standing in the open doorway. He comes right in."

"Or," Josie proposed, "she was still on the couch, waiting for him to knock, but instead he tried the door, realized it was open and came right in. Took her by surprise and attacked her then and there. They struggled. He got her face down on the carpet, put the pillow over her head and suffocated her."

"Then he goes through the house."

"And we have no idea if he found whatever it was he was looking for," Josie said with a sigh. "When Gretchen talked to Beth on the phone, do you know if she mentioned whether she lived with anyone else?"

Mettner said, "Gretchen told me that she broke up with her live-in girlfriend three months ago, so she lived alone."

"That's not that long ago," Josie said. "First thing: alibi the ex-girlfriend. If she clears, maybe then she can have a look around and tell us if anything is missing." To Dr. Feist, she said, "You think this is the work of the same guy who killed Colette?"

Dr. Feist stood and peeled off her gloves, stuffing them into her jacket pockets. "Clinically, I can't really say. Once I get her on the table, I'll know more. I think the cause of death is going to be the same—asphyxiation—but you know as well as I do that doesn't mean the same person did it."

Mettner stepped back into the room. "The scene looks damn similar. A single woman, living alone. No forced entry, the victim suffocated in a pretty brutal way, the house ransacked but no valuables taken—that we can tell at this point anyway."

"Right," Josie said. "Exactly what I was thinking. There's a lot of jewelry in Beth Pratt's bedroom, a lot of electronic devices throughout the house, and about three hundred dollars in her wallet. So whatever the killer was looking for was something very specific, valuable only to him."

"Exactly like Colette's," Mettner said.

"We have no way of knowing what he was looking for at Colette's, but let's assume it was the bag of items we found in her sewing machine," Josie said. "In that bag was a flash drive which led us to Drew Pratt and then his daughter. I don't think her murder is a coincidence."

"Me neither," Mettner said with a grimace.

Dr. Feist went to the door and called for the paramedics to come in and take Beth's body for transport to the morgue. Josie and Mettner gave them a wide berth, retreating to a corner of the living room near the stripped bookshelves. "So what did Beth Pratt have that was worth being murdered for?"

Mettner shook his head. "What could she have? She couldn't have evidence of what happened to her dad. No way she would sit on that all these years."

Josie looked around the room—an otherwise bright and cheery place now marred by violence. "Maybe she had something important, but she didn't know it was important. Or maybe the killer just thought she had something relevant."

"Like the flash drive that Colette had? There is nothing even remotely worth killing over on that flash drive."

"Not to us, maybe," Josie said. "We're missing something. Something big. Who is Beth's next of kin?"

"Mason Pratt," Mettner said. "Samuel Pratt's son. He and his mother are her next of kin—at least the closest around here. Beth's mother's family lives in Texas. I already had Gretchen put a call out to Mason before we got here."

"Maybe we need to pay him a visit," Josie said. She checked the time on her phone. "Hummel's just coming on shift. Call him and tell him to pick Mason Pratt up. We'll meet him at the station."

As Mettner made the call, Josie studied the floor where the paperback books and photo albums lay in heaps near their feet. One of the albums was open and from where she stood, Josie saw what looked like photos of Drew Pratt's wedding. She squatted down to have a better look. They were candid photos taken by friends or other family members, old and yellowed. She scanned a few of them until she spotted one with what had to be Drew Pratt and his older brother, Samuel. Both were dressed in dated, blue tuxedos, smiling at the camera. Samuel looked older with a neatly trimmed goatee. His eyes were brown like Drew's but closer together beneath bushier eyebrows. The shapes of their chins and noses were the same, as was the dark brown of their hair. Samuel was a few inches taller than his brother.

"Maybe Mason can tell us more about his father, too," Josie mumbled as Mettner finished up his call. She turned some pages in the album, finding more photos of Drew and his wife, then a small swaddled baby between them in nearly every photo. When she came to the end of that album, Josie picked up another one. Gone was baby Beth and her mother in this album. Instead there were photos of Drew and a teenage Beth alongside Samuel, looking much older, and a teenage boy who was clearly Mason Pratt. Occasionally, a woman joined them in the photos. Josie assumed she was Samuel's wife. But most of the time it was the two brothers and their teenage children—hiking, canoeing, white-water rafting and embarking on all kinds of outdoorsy adventures. Samuel Pratt's wife only appeared in their less physical activities like a visit to New York City where they stood outside a Broadway theater and a trip to Disneyworld.

"Hey," Josie said, waving Mettner closer. "Look at this."

Mettner squatted beside Josie, taking the open album into his hands. "What am I looking at?"

Josie pointed to a photo of the two Pratt brothers and their children standing on the summit of a mountain, all in hiking boots with backpacks on, sweaty, red-faced and smiling in the sunshine. "That's Samuel Pratt, I think."

"Stands to reason," Mettner agreed.

Josie pointed to his right hand where a small light-colored object was clutched in his fist. "What is that?"

Mettner squinted. "I can't tell."

Josie reached over and turned a page, pointing to another photo of the four of them standing on a riverbank, two canoes behind them. They had their arms around one another. Samuel Pratt's left arm was slung over his son's shoulder, but his right hand hung at his side, his fist again closed around something, part of its pale surface just visible.

Mettner quickly turned more pages of the album. "He's holding it in almost every photo."

"Yes," Josie said. "Except this one." She turned back several pages to one of the canoe photos. In it, Drew and Beth stood on the bank in front of a campfire, the canoes now to their right. To their left, Samuel Pratt sat on a camping chair, peeling an apple with a paring knife, eyes focused on the task at hand. He hadn't been part of the photo, just picked up in the background. Josie pointed to his lap. Against the navy blue shorts he wore rested the small, pale object.

Mettner brought the photo closer to his face. "Holy shit," he said. "Is that—"

"It's kind of blurry," Josie said. "But it looks like an arrowhead, doesn't it?"

CHAPTER NINETEEN

Back at the station house, Bob Chitwood waited for them, standing behind Gretchen, who was seated at her desk with a phone receiver pressed to one ear. His arms were crossed over his narrow chest. His natural crimson flush had returned, making his scattered white facial hair stand out against his skin. "Quinn," he shouted as they approached. "Are you kidding me?"

"Sir?" Josie said, tossing her keys onto her desk. She gave Gretchen a small wave.

Chitwood pointed a finger at her. "You and Mett just caught Beth Pratt's murder? Beth damn Pratt? Do you understand how high-profile this case is gonna be? The press is still talking about her father's disappearance twelve years later. This is gonna be a real shitstorm, you know that?"

Josie put her hands on her hips. "Yep."

"That's it? Yep? You better be ready for this, Quinn. I don't know what the hell is going on around here, but you better get to the bottom of it like your job depends on it, because it just might. I'm gonna try to keep this out of the press as long as possible."

Ignoring his tirade, she said, "Sir, this might be a good time to reinstate Detective Palmer. Put her back in the field."

"Don't even try it, Quinn."

"Sir," Josie protested.

Chitwood's shout stilled every sound in the room. "Dammit, Quinn, I said no. Palmer is on the damn desk, and that is my final word on the matter."

Mettner cleared his throat from behind Josie. "Sir," he inter-jected. "We've got someone downstairs we need to interview. Hummel brought him in and put him in the conference room."

"I heard," Chitwood said. "Mason Pratt. You think he's a suspect?"

"No," Mettner replied. "Not at this time."

With one last glare, Chitwood retreated to his office muttering something about people dropping like flies and the damn Pratt family.

Mettner looked relieved, but Josie and Gretchen suppressed their smiles. "Let's go talk to Mason Pratt," Josie told Mettner.

"I'll be here at my desk," Gretchen said with a sigh.

Mettner said, "Can you see if the Evidence Response Team turned up anything on the footprint found at Colette Fraley's house?"

Gretchen nodded and picked up her phone. "Great idea," she told him. "I'm on it."

Josie gathered the Colette Fraley file and a couple of notepads and pens and walked downstairs to the conference room where Mason Pratt sat before an untouched cup of coffee, his sandy hair covered with a ballcap and his eyes red-rimmed from crying. Hummel had told them that he had picked Mason up where he worked at a local tractor and feed supply store. Mason's boss confirmed he'd been there since six that morning. He wore a dark green hoodie and beneath the table, Josie could see he had jeans and boots on. He stood when they walked in and shook both their hands. Both Mettner and Josie offered their condolences.

"Thank you," Mason said. "I just can't believe this is happening."

"Has anyone notified your mother?" Mettner asked. "Have you had a chance to tell her?"

"I haven't had a chance to get over to see her. I just found out when your officer came to get me. My mom lives at Rockview," Mason said. "The nursing home?"

"I know it," Josie said. "My grandmother lives there too."

"Were you and Beth close?" Mettner asked.

Mason took off his ballcap and pushed a hand through his hair. "Yeah, pretty close, I guess. I mean first my dad and then hers. That kind of thing—not many people can relate to it, you know? But Beth and I—" he broke off, his gaze dropping to his lap. "Jesus, I'm starting to think my family is cursed."

"This is a lot to take in," Josie said. "And you've been through a lot. We hate to have to do this, especially now that you've had such a shock, but we need to ask you some questions about Beth, your Uncle Drew and your dad. Would that be okay?"

He nodded. "What do you want to know?"

Mettner began, "Do you know of anyone who would have any reason to hurt Beth?"

Mason shook his head. "No. I can't think of anyone. I mean, she was stubborn and strong-willed like Uncle Drew, but she didn't have any enemies. Not that I know of. She worked at the college. Did you know that?"

"Yes," Mettner said. "When Detective Palmer called her to set up today's meeting she mentioned that. She worked in the registrar's office, is that right?"

"Yeah. She loved her job. Loved her co-workers. I can't imagine anyone up there having any reason to kill her. Did you talk to her girlfriend—I'm sorry—*ex*-girlfriend?"

"Our team is tracking her down now," Josie said. "When's the last time you spoke to Beth?"

"About a week ago maybe? I've been calling to check on her since the big break-up. She was taking it kind of hard."

Josie pulled out a photo of Colette Fraley she had copied from the Fraley family photos and showed it to Mason. "Do you recognize this woman?"

A blank look came over his face. "No," he said. "I've never seen her before. Who is she?"

Josie said, "She was murdered about a week before Beth. We're just exploring the possibility that the deaths are connected."

"Maybe my mom might know her?" he suggested.

Josie put the photo away. "We'll check." She took out her phone and brought up some of the photos she had snapped pictures of at Beth Pratt's residence. She swiped through them for Mason's benefit and pointed to what looked like an arrowhead in the last one. "Can you tell us what your dad is holding in these photos?"

A small smile played on Mason's lips. "Yeah," he said. "It was this dumb arrowhead. You know what those are, right?"

"Yes," Mettner and Josie answered in unison.

Josie asked, "Did the one in these photos have some kind of special meaning for him?"

"Well, yeah," Mason said. "You know my dad was an archaeologist, right?"

"No," Josie said. "We weren't aware."

"Yeah, he was a professor at Denton University. Anyway, archaeology was his passion. Before I was born, he traveled all over the world on digs."

Mettner asked, "Is that where he got the arrowhead? On a dig?"

"No. He got it here in Pennsylvania. When he was growing up he used to go out into the woods to play, and he would pretend to be some world-famous archaeologist. Well, one time he actually found this arrowhead. It wasn't worth anything, but it meant a lot to him. When he went off on digs he would carry it with him to remind him of home. To keep him 'grounded' he used to say. Later, when he settled here and started teaching, he carried it around in his pocket and when he started to feel anxious or nervous he'd take it out and run his fingers over its edges."

Josie's heart did a little double tap as she thought of the smoothed edges of the arrowhead they'd found in Colette's sewing machine. "How old was your dad when he died?" she asked Mason.

"Fifty-nine."

"He had this arrowhead since he was a child?"

"Yes. Maybe since he was nine or ten."

That was roughly fifty years of rubbing the hard edges of the arrowhead's surface. Plenty of time to smooth it down.

"Do you know what happened to it?" Mettner asked.

"Nah," Mason said. "I mean my mom and I assumed it was in his pocket when he went into the river, and it went down with him. He never went anywhere without it, and it wasn't in his car."

Josie said, "Can you tell us about the day your dad went into the river?"

Nineteen years had passed since the trauma of losing his father, and Mason's words were matter-of-fact, almost emotionless, like it was a story he had told hundreds of times. Josie guessed he had. "I was still in high school. Back then we lived between here and Bellewood—outside of Bowersville. He went to work that morning and taught his nine o'clock class. He walked over to the cafeteria to get a coffee after that, just like he did every day. He was on camera there. Then he walked out and no one saw him for two days. My mom reported him missing that night when he didn't come home for dinner, but the police wouldn't start looking for him until twenty-four hours had passed. The next day the state police found his car on the bank of the Susquehanna River down in Bellewood. It was locked. His keys, phone, wallet, everything was still in the car. Except for him."

"Had he been depressed?" Josie asked.

"My dad was always depressed. Well, I mean, he struggled his whole life. He was bipolar. So he was either on top of the world or he was ready to check out, but none of us ever thought he actually would."

"He never expressed any suicidal ideations?" Mettner asked.

"Not in a way that made us think he would ever really hurt himself. When he was in one of his down cycles, he would just be very sad and morose, sleep a lot. Sometimes he'd say something like, 'I'd be better off dead,' but he never seemed like he was planning to kill himself. He had a therapist and he saw a shrink for meds.

My mom was really on top of him about it because she said if he wasn't vigilant then he could spiral out of control. Even after his body washed up, she didn't believe he killed himself. But there was no proof that he didn't."

"What did you believe?" Josie asked.

"I don't know. I used to think my mom was right but as I got older, I wasn't so sure. Now, I don't know what to think. I mean, don't they say that people who are going to kill themselves don't talk about it beforehand, one day they just up and do it? I've read a lot of stuff on the topic of suicide since then. Maybe he just decided to do it. The police said he didn't have any marks on his body—well, there was some bruising on his back, shoulders and arms, but they said it likely came from his body smashing against rocks and tree branches in the river and near the shore. They couldn't prove that he had been in a struggle."

"Was he a good swimmer?" Mettner asked.

"Passable."

"What did your uncle think?" Josie asked.

"That he went there to meet someone and that person either killed him and dumped his body in the river or held him down and drowned him."

"The cause of death was drowning, wasn't it?" Mettner asked.

"Yeah."

"Who did your uncle think he was going to meet?" Josie asked.

"Don't know. We never could figure that out. My mom and Uncle Drew checked his emails at work and at home, his offices at work and at home, talked to his assistant, his colleagues, his students, looked through his phone. From what I remember, they didn't find anything out of the ordinary. I mean, if they did, they didn't tell me. What I always wondered was, like, if he was going to meet someone, wouldn't there be some record of it? A phone call? An email? Something?"

"You would think," Josie said.

She thought of the mystery woman Drew Pratt had met with at the craft fair on the day he disappeared. There hadn't been any indication that Drew had meant to meet up with anyone either. Had he known the mystery woman before he went to the craft fair? Had he gone there with the intention of meeting her or had he just run into her? Regardless, it was doubtful that the mystery woman had killed Drew Pratt. Both the Pratt brothers were over six foot. It would have taken someone either very strong, very skilled, or both to overpower them. Even if she had found a way of killing them that didn't involve the need for brute strength, like poisoning them, she would have needed help disposing of their bodies.

The rustle of a paper evidence bag brought Josie's attention back to the table. Mettner snapped on gloves and reached inside, bringing out the plastic bag they'd found in Colette's sewing machine, minus the flash drive, which had been sent off to be tested for fingerprints after the contents were downloaded. Mettner held it out for Mason to see, instructing him not to touch it, and smoothing the plastic so he could get a better look at it. "Does this look like your dad's arrowhead, by any chance?"

Mason squinted at it, standing up and leaning over to get a closer look. "Where did you get this?"

"We recently found it at the scene of a crime," Josie said. "We can't get prints from it because of its uneven surface. Even though it's pretty smooth, it's got enough edges to make it nearly impossible to lift from. We're trying to figure out its significance."

Mason pointed to the bag. "Can you turn that over?"

Mettner turned the bag over in his hands and held it out for him to see. Mason pointed to the bottom edge. "Right there," he said, his voice a gasp. Josie leaned in and saw a faint black mark along the bottom of the edge of the arrowhead that she hadn't noticed before. Mason repeated, "Where did you find this? What crime scene?"

"Is this your father's?" Mettner said.

Tears welled in Mason's eyes. "Yes, I think it is. He was painting the outside of our house one summer—I was just a kid, maybe ten or eleven—and he had left it sitting on the table on the porch. I thought I'd help him by painting the siding out there, but I ended up spilling this dark blue paint on his beloved arrowhead. I thought he was going to kill me. He was so upset. He got most of it off. All except that one little fleck. It always bothered him."

Josie and Mettner looked at one another, eyes wide. Colette Fraley had been in possession of two personal items belonging to two men—one dead, the other missing for twelve years. The words went unspoken between them, but Josie knew Mettner was thinking the same thing she was: *what the hell was Colette involved in?*

CHAPTER TWENTY

"Does the name Colette Fraley mean anything to you?" Josie asked Mason Pratt.

He shook his head. "No, I've never heard of her. Who is she?"

Josie said, "She was the woman who was murdered last week. The crime scene and circumstances were very similar to Beth's. We found your father's arrowhead hidden inside her house."

"With this belt buckle," Mettner said, shifting the bag in his hands so Mason could have a look. "Do you recognize it?"

He leaned further across the table, craning his neck to get a better look. Mettner turned it over in his hands a few times so Mason could study it. Finally, Mason said, "No. What's this got to do with Beth—or my dad?"

While Mettner placed the baggie back into the evidence bag, Josie said, "There was another item in that bag. It was a flash drive with the name Pratt written on it. We believe it belonged to your uncle Drew."

His brow furrowed. "My uncle Drew? What was on it?"

"Legal documents," Mettner said.

"But nothing that tells us anything about what happened to him," Josie added. "We were actually on our way to speak with Beth about her dad's disappearance when we found her."

"Why?" Mason asked. "You're the police. Don't you already know everything there is to know about his disappearance?"

"We do have a file here," Josie said. "Because he vanished within the city limits, but a lot of agencies have worked his case over the years and that means that our file could be incomplete. Also, it happened long before either one of us came to this department.

We wanted to hear from some of the people who knew Drew back then directly. Tell me, Mason, did Beth believe any of the theories that abounded after he went missing?"

Mason dragged both hands up and down his cheeks, looking more exhausted by the second. "Beth believed that her dad was dead. But not by suicide. She always believed someone murdered him. It was just a matter of finding his body."

Mettner asked, "Did she have any thoughts as to who killed him or why?"

"She thought the most obvious explanation was probably the right one."

"Which was what?" Josie asked. "That his murder had something to do with someone he prosecuted?"

Mason nodded emphatically. "Exactly. That's where your mind goes first, right? Successful, respected assistant district attorney who's been doing his job well for decades? Uncle Drew put away illegal arms dealers, drug traffickers, and lots and lots of gang members from biker gangs to white supremacist gangs. Even that Latina gang—you know, the 23?"

Josie felt a jolt of recognition. "Yes, I know the 23. Some of them were involved in a shoot-out on the interstate right here in Denton a few years ago." In fact, it had been that shoot-out that had plunged Josie directly into the dark depths of the missing girls case that had rocked not only the city, but the entire nation.

Mason scratched behind his ear. "Yeah, I think I remember that. Anyway, Uncle Drew put away a shit-ton of bad guys, you know? Beth always believed it was someone from one of the organized crime outfits that did him in."

"Not Patti Snyder?" Josie asked.

Mason raised a brow.

"She was—" Josie began, but he cut her off.

"I know who she was—is. Believe me, Beth and I know all the players in every scenario the press has vomited up the last twelve years. I can see why a lot of people bought into that, but there was never any proof that Uncle Drew knew anything about what was going on with the Kickbacks for Kids scandal. So no, Beth never believed that Patti Snyder killed her dad."

"Some investigators over the years have suggested that Patti Snyder was the woman talking to Drew Pratt at the craft fair the day he died," Josie pointed out.

"Yeah, yeah. I know."

Mettner asked, "Did Beth have any theories about that woman?"

"She didn't think it was Patti Snyder. She thought whoever that woman was—she was there to lure Uncle Drew to his death. She was one of the last people to see him alive, to talk to him. If she wasn't involved, then why hasn't she ever come forward? Plus, if it was Patti Snyder and she knows what happened to him, why wouldn't she use that for leverage—you know, for a reduced sentence or something?"

"Good point," Josie said.

"Also there was that two or three week period where Uncle Drew was—" Mason stopped abruptly, a hint of panic flashing across his face, as though he'd said too much.

Softly, Josie said, "Where your Uncle Drew what?"

"Beth never told anyone because she thought that the cops and the press would immediately cry suicide, but for the two or three weeks before he went missing, she says Uncle Drew was in a bad way."

"In what way?" Mettner asked.

"She said he wasn't eating or sleeping; he was snappy and just out of sorts."

Josie asked, "Was there anything that precipitated this?"

"He wouldn't talk about it. Beth asked him many times, but he blew her off and said he was just stressed about work."

"But his work files were studied thoroughly after his disappearance," Josie said. "He had no major cases pending. It was only minor stuff."

Mason said, "Yeah, Beth really pressed the police on that after Uncle Drew went missing, and they told her there wasn't anything really stressful going on at his job."

"But she still believed that he was killed by someone he prosecuted?" Josie asked.

"Yes. She thinks maybe he received some kind of threat a few weeks before he went missing."

"But there was no evidence of that," Josie said. "Investigators went over every inch of his life."

Mason threw his hands in the air. "I know. I'm just telling you what Beth believes—believed. My God, I can't believe this. I can't believe she's gone. Who would do something like this? Why?"

Josie felt her stomach drop as tears streamed down his face. He'd lost his father, then his uncle and now his cousin—all under strange and suspicious circumstances. She wished she had more answers for him.

Mettner said, "That's what we wanted to ask you. Beth's house looked as though someone had gone through her things, as though they were looking for something. Can you think of anything she might have had that someone might want?"

He shook his head. "No, not that I can think of—nothing worth killing over."

CHAPTER TWENTY-ONE

They took a break, leaving Mason alone in the conference room to go to the first floor break area to get themselves cups of coffee and a bottle of water for Mason. Josie put a fresh filter into the coffeemaker, scooped coffee grounds into it and then poured new water into the receptacle. "He should be in protective custody."

Mettner laughed. "Do we have that in Denton?"

"You know what I mean. We should at least put a unit on him. I mean don't you think this is strange? Colette had something that belonged to both Drew and Samuel Pratt. She ends up murdered. We track down Drew's daughter but she's dead. What if Mason is next?"

"It's not a bad idea," Mettner said. "But no way is Chitwood going to approve the overtime for putting a unit on this poor guy."

Josie inspected the coffee mugs on the draining board next to the sink and plucked two for her and Mettner. "Sure he will. If he wants to keep this Pratt situation from getting any worse. He's already worried about the press finding out that Drew Pratt's daughter was murdered."

"Okay, so we put a unit on Mason Pratt till we get a handle on things. I'll go over to Rockview and talk to his mother, see if she knew Colette Fraley."

"I think we should talk to Patti Snyder," Josie said. "Or at least try."

"You think she was the mystery woman on the video?"

"I don't know what to think, but I'd like to find out if she knows anything about the flash drive that Colette had," Josie pointed out.

Hummel poked his head into the break room. "Boss," he said. "Mett."

Josie said, "Just Detective Quinn, now."

Mettner said, "Yes?"

"We got something back on the flash drive. A partial thumb print."

"A partial?" Josie said. "How many possible matches?"

"Five," Hummel replied. "But Drew Pratt is one of them. Detective Palmer has the report."

Josie abandoned the coffee. Mettner handed a bottle of water to Hummel as they passed through the doorway and told him to deliver it to the guy in the conference room and tell him they'd be back in ten minutes. Once in the stairwell, they raced up the flight of steps, bursting into the large room side by side. Gretchen was at her desk, a report in her hands, scanning the list of names. "I don't recognize anyone else on this list," she said as they approached.

Josie and Mettner read the names over Gretchen's shoulder. "The only one that matters is Drew Pratt. I'd say this pretty conclusively proves that he saw the contents of the flash drive," Josie said.

"No," Gretchen disagreed. "All it proves is that he held it. We don't know for sure whether he ever viewed the contents of the drive."

"Hmmm," Josie murmured. "That is true. Or maybe this is what put Drew Pratt in such a dark mood before he went missing. I mean, let's say he received the flash drive before he disappeared but hadn't yet acted on it."

Gretchen handed the list to Mettner so he could look it over. "He would have known from the contents of the drive that he needed to prosecute—or at the very least, investigate. Maybe he was mulling it over when he disappeared. But we still can't say that the flash drive had anything to do with what happened to him."

"Right," Josie said. "We *can* safely say that at some point this was in his possession and then Colette Fraley came to have it. We just don't know how or why."

"We're going to have to start looking into the belt buckle, too," Mettner mumbled.

Josie felt a cold prickle of fear along the nape of her neck. "I'm afraid of what we're going to find."

"Yeah," Gretchen said. "Me too." She picked up another set of pages and handed them to Josie. Immediately, Josie recognized photos of the footprint found at Colette's murder scene. There were additional photographs of the cast the team had taken together with a report on the Evidence Response Team's findings.

"What've you got?" Mettner asked.

Josie said, "The footprint was a size ten—which we knew—but this says, given the impression in the dirt, the owner of the print was likely between 180 and 200 pounds. The more definitive outline near the front of the foot suggests he was leaning down, putting most of his weight onto the ball of his foot."

"Which he would have had to do to kneel and straddle Colette," Gretchen remarked.

Josie continued, "The tread was matched to a very common brand of men's sneakers which can be found in just about any store in the country that sells men's sneakers."

"Well, that narrows it down," Mettner said.

"Yeah," Josie sighed. "I'm not sure this takes us very far."

Gretchen pointed at the clock on the wall which read 11 p.m. "Why don't you go home and check on Noah? I'll write up all the reports from today, and you and Mett can hit this hard tomorrow."

CHAPTER TWENTY-TWO

Noah's house was dark when Josie slipped inside. Her skin pricked as she moved from the foyer, past the living room and into the kitchen. They had been attacked in these rooms only months ago. It was still difficult for her, but he refused to move. They'd been spending most of their time at her house, but not since Colette's death. Josie flicked on the kitchen light and saw the note he had left her on the fridge. *Got you something to eat. Exhausted. Went to bed. N.*

She opened the fridge and smiled, a bit of relief pushing aside the sadness weighing her down since Colette's murder. Noah always made sure she ate. The delicious smell of perfectly grilled steak wafted from a takeout container on the top shelf. Josie sat at the table and wolfed it down before heading up to Noah's bedroom. She still had clothes there so she changed into sweatpants and a T-shirt, brushed her teeth and slipped into bed beside him. As her eyes adjusted to the darkness, she watched his bare chest rise and fall. She ran her fingers through his hair and planted a kiss on his cheek, but he didn't stir.

Exhaustion made her limbs heavy but after minutes tossing and turning, she knew sleep was beyond her. She snatched up her phone from the nightstand and texted her sister, Trinity. *You up?*

Trinity's response came back a few minutes later. *Always for you, sister. What's going on? How's Noah?*

Devastated, Josie tapped back. *Hey, you covered the Drew Pratt disappearance when you were still a local reporter. Do you remember?*

Only one of the biggest cases in PA. Of course. Has there been a development?

Sort of, Josie wrote back. *I can't say right now. Just wondering what you think happened to him.*

There was a delay. For a moment, Josie thought perhaps Trinity had fallen asleep, but then her response popped up. *I think someone killed him. Someone Patti Snyder either knew or hired. You know who she is?*

Yes, Josie typed back. *Well aware. Why do you think it was Snyder?*

It's the only thing that makes sense given the mystery woman. The police let me see the video when I did my story for the local news station. I think Snyder told him what was going on and when he chose not to pursue it, she had him killed. She'll never talk though. Then she'd have to give up the killer.

Well, thanks, Josie responded.

I want to know if there are any developments!!! Trinity texted back almost immediately. Then: *FIRST.*

Josie chuckled and put her phone back on the nightstand. She lay back on her pillow next to Noah, inhaling his familiar, comforting scent. Her mind swirled with questions. After twenty minutes more of tossing and turning, sleep eluding her, she picked up her phone again and googled Patti Snyder. The woman had been a single mom working as a bank teller and raising her only son when in 2002 he was arrested for simple assault after getting into a scuffle with another teenage boy. The fight had happened on the football field during a game between rival high schools and was part of a larger brawl among the players. It had been caught on tape which someone in the press dug up after the Kickbacks for Kids scandal broke, and from what Josie could see from the grainy, far-off footage—the fight between Snyder's son and the other boy was highlighted with a circle of light—there wasn't anything particularly brutal about it.

However, Judge Eugene Sanders sentenced Patti Snyder's son to nearly two years at Wood Creek. His public defender had tried to enter a plea deal, but Sanders had rejected it. Snyder's son did his time at Wood Creek and, according to his mother, came out a shell of the person he'd been when he went in. He never fully recovered, Snyder said at her trial. Nothing lifted him out of his depression, and she was teetering on the edge of bankruptcy trying to get him the help he needed. Then one day in 2005 while she was at work, he hung himself in their backyard. At her trial, Patti Snyder described finding him and cutting him down. There wasn't a dry eye in the courtroom.

But she still got life in prison without the possibility of parole.

Patti Snyder had suspicions about Wood Creek pretty early on. The investigating she did at the bank where she worked—which was illegal—turned up what she believed was confirmation. She claimed that she had tried to blow the whistle on the operation multiple times, but that no one would listen to her. Then when the story broke in 2010, all the men involved got high-priced attorneys. There was talk in the press that most of the men involved were going to take plea deals to avoid prison time. Snyder went to the home of one of the Wood Creek Associates' financiers, knocked on his door, and when he answered, she shot him in the chest and left him there to die.

Noah shifted onto his side, the sudden movement startling Josie. Her phone fell from her grip and into her lap. She dug it from the covers and put it back on the nightstand, hooking up the charger. It was enough for one night. Tomorrow, Gretchen would work on getting an interview with Patti Snyder, and hopefully, the woman would shed some light on just how much Drew Pratt knew about the Kickbacks scandal before his disappearance—and if she was the mystery woman who spoke to him at the craft fair or not.

Josie fell into a fitful sleep and woke a few hours later to daylight shining around the edges of Noah's shades and his arm slung across her waist. His body fitted snugly against hers, spooning her. When she stirred, so did he. Their hands sleepily explored one another, bodies warming with need and urgency, finding a sweet release in one another that left them both breathless and sweaty. Josie was just dozing in Noah's arms, ready now to sleep for several solid hours, when a knock at Noah's front door startled them both.

They waited, bodies tensing, to see if the knock would come again and it did.

"I'll get it," Noah told her. "Stay here."

Josie watched as he threw on some clothes and disappeared into the hall. She listened to his footsteps and the sound of his front door creaking open. Then a female voice. Josie stood and pulled on her own clothes, padding downstairs after him. By the time she reached the foyer, he had closed the door. In his arms was a large casserole dish with a card taped to its lid.

Noah smiled at her. "A lady from my mom's church," he explained. "They thought I might need some nourishment."

Josie followed him into the kitchen. "That's so nice."

"She said to put it in the oven for twenty-five minutes at 350 degrees," Noah mumbled as he found a place for it in his freezer. He came to the table with the card in his hand, tearing off the envelope and opening the card. He read it quickly and then handed it to her before heading back to the fridge to look for something to make for breakfast. "They're really good people," he said over his shoulder.

"Yes, they are," Josie agreed as she read the card. It was a pretty standard sympathy card. Rather than having the congregants each sign it, someone with flowery script had written: *Please let us know if you need anything. Keeping you in our prayers. Your family at St. Mary's Episcopal.*

"I thought you said your mom was Catholic," Josie said.

"What's that?" Noah said, closing the door to the fridge with only a carton of orange juice in hand.

"I thought your mom was Catholic. She went to an Episcopal church?"

He took a swig of the orange juice, directly from the carton, and said, "So?"

"So an Episcopal church is not the same as a Catholic church, and there are four Catholic churches in Denton, one of which is closer to her house than St. Mary's Episcopal," Josie pointed out.

"Josie, who cares what church my mom went to?"

"How long did she go to St. Mary's?"

He gave a sigh of frustration and said, "I don't know. She always went there."

Which meant as long as Noah could remember. Josie rose from the kitchen table and went to the counter where his coffeemaker sat, getting the filters and coffee grounds from the cabinet above it. "Noah," she said. "Those things we found in your mother's sewing machine—"

The orange juice carton slammed onto the kitchen table. Josie turned and stared at him. "Why do you keep going on about those things? I told you, it's some kind of mistake. They're not important. A couple of old trinkets and a flash drive some lawyer had."

Josie turned her entire body toward him. "Not 'some lawyer', Noah. Drew Pratt. The assistant district attorney who disappeared twelve years ago. Yesterday, Drew Pratt's daughter was murdered. In very similar fashion to your mother. Suffocated in her own home. Whoever did it was looking for something because her house had been ransacked. We had to talk to her cousin, Mason, after she died. Mettner showed him the arrowhead, and he says it belonged to his dad."

"So what?"

"So his dad is dead, too."

Josie could see some of the irritation in Noah's tense shoulders bleed away. "What?"

She gave him a brief rundown of everything she, Gretchen and Mettner had learned about the Pratt brothers.

"My mom didn't know those men," he said.

"How do you know she didn't?" Josie prodded. "You couldn't have known everything about her."

"I knew enough about her. I'm telling you, she didn't know those men."

"Then how did she get their possessions?" Josie asked.

"It's some kind of a mistake," Noah said, his voice rising.

"I'm sorry, Noah, but I don't think it is. Two men, one dead and one missing—brothers, no less—and your mother had their personal property hidden in her house. You don't think she was hiding something?"

He walked toward her, stopping so close that Josie could see the rapid rise and fall of his chest. "Like what?" Noah asked. "What could she possibly have been hiding?"

"That's what I'm trying to figure out."

He pointed a finger at her chest. "You're trying to figure out what my mother was lying about when you should be trying to figure out who killed her."

Josie placed a palm on her sternum. "Because I think whatever she was hiding is what got her killed, Noah."

"What could she possibly be hiding? What? You think she was some kind of serial killer? Drowning men in rivers? Making it look like they killed themselves? Is that what you think?"

Josie's back slid along the counter as she inched away from him. "I never said that. But Noah, she had secrets. Surely you recognize that."

His face twisted into an expression that was unrecognizable to her. When he unleashed his next words she realized why; he'd never once been cruel to her. Then again, he had never been this traumatized, this off-kilter. He said, "I know you were raised by a woman who might as well have been Satan's sister, and she's the only example you have, but *normal* mothers don't keep secrets, and my mom was *normal*. You have no frame of reference for normal, so maybe that's why you don't get it, why you're not listening to me. With my mom, what you saw, you got. She wouldn't have gotten caught up in anything like what you're talking about. I don't know where those things came from or how they got into her sewing machine, but she didn't do anything wrong."

Josie kept her voice calm and reasonable. "Noah, I didn't say she did something wrong. I just said there were some things she was keeping secret. Those secrets may have gotten her killed."

"My mother didn't have secrets. I know that you and your grandmother and that evil bitch who raised you all had more secrets than you could keep track of, but—"

Josie cut him off. "What's that supposed to mean?"

"It means you were raised by a pack of liars. Everything about your life was a lie. Now you see things through that filter. You see things that aren't there. Not every person is lying and devious like what you're used to. My mother was—"

Josie couldn't keep her anger in check any longer. She stepped toward him and thrust her chin forward. "Your mother was what? A perfect saint? You think she never told a lie in her entire life?"

"Don't talk about my mother," he shouted.

Josie didn't back down. "Noah, another innocent woman is dead. Like it or not, there is a killer loose in this city. We need to find him."

He turned away from her.

"Where are you going?" she asked.

He paused at the doorway but didn't look at her.

"Why are you doing this?" Josie said, the words slipping out high-pitched and filled with emotion before she could snatch them back. "Why are you acting like this?"

"Like what?"

"Like you don't care that someone killed your mother?"

He turned back, tears in his eyes. "Of course I care that someone killed her. It's all I can think about. But please, I'm begging you, don't shit on my mother's memory."

"Oh, Noah, I would never—"

He held up a hand to silence her. "I don't want to talk about this anymore. Maybe you should go home."

Tears stung the backs of her eyes, but she bit them back. Afraid anything else she said would only lead to more fighting, she murmured, "If that's what you want."

He said nothing. She stood frozen in the kitchen, listening to him move around the house. She heard the jangle of his keys and then the front door close. When his car roared to life out front, she let herself cry.

CHAPTER TWENTY-THREE

"It's like I don't even know who he is anymore," Josie complained to Gretchen. The two sat across from one another at a table inside Komorrah's Koffee, which was just a few blocks from the police station. Josie finished off her third cheese Danish and sipped her coffee.

Gretchen picked up a pecan-crusted croissant and put it on the plate in front of her. The moment Gretchen saw Josie, she had decided it was a dozen-pastries type of day and promptly ordered an entire box for them to share. "Well," Gretchen told her. "People process grief differently. You and I—we lock it away, push it down, and throw ourselves into work."

"True," Josie said.

"Some people become very depressed and stop functioning. Some people get angry and lash out. Sounds like Noah is just lashing out."

Josie put her coffee down and sighed. "But it's so unlike him. He's always so... even-tempered and reasonable."

Gretchen laughed. "Oh, I know. When everyone else is losing their shit, he can walk into a room and diffuse things pretty damn quick."

"It's his gift," Josie agreed. "I wish Chitwood would let you off the desk. Then I could be home with him more and it wouldn't necessarily have to be me asking the tough questions."

Gretchen took a bite of her pastry and chewed slowly, her expression thoughtful. After she swallowed, she said, "I don't know that anyone else asking the questions would make it easier on him."

"You're right," Josie said.

"My third or fourth year in homicide, I caught a case where a woman's grandson was shot to death. He was only a teenager. She was raising him so it was just the two of them. She was devastated, that was obvious, but she didn't want to know anything about our investigation. Not until we caught the killer and even then, all she wanted to know was that he was behind bars. Most families are calling six times a day for updates. But there were always one or two who needed to distance themselves from all of it—the murder, the details, the investigation. It's too much, too painful. That's where Noah is at the moment. The pain is too big for him right now."

"He's so angry."

"It's not at you," Gretchen assured her. "He's angry at the whole horrible situation. He's just taking it out on you."

"Great," Josie said drily. She picked up her fourth cheese Danish and took a big bite, thinking she'd need to take a run later to burn off all the calories she was consuming. Since she stopped drinking, she'd been doing a lot of stress-eating.

"He's never lost anyone really close to him, has he?" Gretchen asked.

Josie shook her head. "No, he hasn't."

"Well, there's no blueprint for these things—you know that. He's going to be in pain for a long time."

"Do you know if Mettner talked to Mason Pratt's mother?" Josie asked, changing the subject. Gretchen was right. When she was hurting, work made it better.

"Yeah, she's never heard of or seen Colette Fraley."

"So that's a dead end."

"Afraid so. I put in a request to the prison where Patti Snyder's incarcerated, but the warden warned me that she never talks to cops or reporters."

"Sounds promising," Josie muttered.

The door at the front of the coffee shop swooshed open and then came the sound of Chief Chitwood's voice booming across the dining area, making them both wince. "Quinn! Palmer!"

Gretchen gave a small wave and he strode over toward them. He looked at the table. "What the hell is this?"

"Sir?" Josie said.

"I thought they had cheese Danishes here? What's this crap? Pecan?"

Josie glanced across the table at Gretchen who fought to keep a smile from breaking across her face. "Don't," Josie said under her breath.

Gretchen blurted, "Quinn ate them all. They're her favorite."

Chitwood gave Josie a look. "No shit. Well, we have something in common."

"Shocking," Josie muttered.

"Move over," Chitwood told her, squeezing his tall, thin body into the booth beside her before she even had a chance to move. His bony elbow knocked against hers as he picked up one of Gretchen's pecan-crusted croissants and sneered at it.

"Sir," Gretchen said. "Would you like me to get you something from the front? Coffee? Cheese Danish?"

"No," Chitwood said. "Thanks."

Gretchen said, "You didn't come here for a cheese Danish."

Chitwood rubbed at the spotty facial hair on his chin and gave Josie a sideways glance. "No, I'm here because Patti Snyder, who hasn't talked to anyone in law enforcement the entire time she's been in prison, has agreed to talk to Quinn."

"What?" Josie and Gretchen said in unison.

Chitwood turned his head and gave Josie a long, penetrating look. Josie made sure he looked away before she did. "Quinn, do you know this woman?"

"No, sir. Never met her."

"She specifically said she would only talk to you. Not Mettner. You. Why the hell is that?" Chitwood's voice held more wonder than contempt, which was a welcome change.

Josie said, "I don't know, sir."

Chitwood put the croissant back on the plate in the center of the table and sighed. "It doesn't much matter, does it?" His face twisted into a grimace, as though what he had to say next pained him deeply. "Good job, Quinn. She can see you this afternoon. I set it all up with the warden. Muncy prison is about two hours from here so you better get going. We need to get a handle on this Pratt thing yesterday. I'll only be able to keep the press off this for a short time, and there are spies in the Department of Corrections. Soon as word gets around that Snyder met with a cop after all these years, the vultures will be circling."

Gretchen's phone chirped. She pulled it out and looked at it. "Mettner's headed over to the morgue for Beth Pratt's autopsy. I'm going to work on the alibi for her girlfriend. We'll meet and regroup when you get back."

CHAPTER TWENTY-FOUR

Three times on her way to Muncy prison Josie glanced at her cell phone and then tossed it onto the passenger's seat of her Ford Escape, but there were no calls or texts from Noah. She thought about what Gretchen had said—about the way people dealt with grief. She understood that losing his mother had spun Noah into entirely new territory; that the loss was too raw and too big for him to handle; and that he had lashed out at Josie because she was close, but she still wondered if she was supposed to be pushing back or not. This was new territory for her as well.

Muncy State Correctional Institute was the only maximum security state prison for women in Pennsylvania. Josie knew this because Lila Jensen, the woman who had torn her family apart and destroyed her childhood, was currently serving life without parole there. Josie had hoped she would have passed away from the cancer that had been eating her insides for several years now, but she was still hanging on.

Located in a lush valley of Lycoming County, at first glance, Muncy SCI looked more like a college campus than a prison. A large, tree-lined road led from State Route 405 to the prison grounds. Josie parked in the visitors' parking lot outside the barbed wire fence, behind which was a stone building with a white clock tower—the centerpiece of Muncy's sprawling grounds. Its perimeter circled thirty acres but beyond it was over seven hundred fifty acres of dense wooded area. Josie knew there were over seventy buildings within the fenced perimeter, nearly twenty of which housed the inmates.

She went through processing at the front gate. Then she was shuttled to the visitors' center by one of the correctional officers who waited for her at the warden's instructions. At the visitors' center she checked her weapon and followed another correctional officer down a lengthy maze of hallways until finally she was deposited into a beige room with a long metal table in its center. She sat facing the door while one of the guards brought Patti Snyder in. The guard uncuffed her and left the room, standing just outside where a large glass window allowed him to keep careful watch on Snyder, although Josie had been told that she'd been a model prisoner since her incarceration. Josie had only seen photos and video of Snyder right after her capture and during her trial. Back then, Patti had been slightly overweight with a soft, round face and long, lank brown hair that showed strands of gray. The woman in front of Josie now was lean muscle and hard angles. Her brown hair had been shorn off, leaving behind a shapeless cut that didn't leave anything for anyone to grab onto. There was a hardness about Patti Snyder that hadn't been there before.

Patti folded her hands on top of the table and gave Josie a long look. "You're smaller than I thought you'd be."

Not what Josie was expecting. "You've seen me on the news, I guess."

"A few times."

Silence descended between them. Josie waited a beat to see if Patti would offer anything but she didn't. Josie got right to the point. "I need to ask you some questions about Drew Pratt."

Patti's gaze drifted to the window where the guard stood watching, arms crossed over his burly chest. Slowly, her head swiveled back to face Josie. "Do you know what killed my son?"

Josie took only a few seconds to mull over her answer. She knew Patti wasn't speaking in a literal sense. "Greed."

A smile broke across Patti's face. "Close. Very close. Greed had a hand in it, but that's not what killed my son. Corruption killed him."

"I can see that," Josie agreed. The men on the board of Wood Creek Associates had been greedy, sacrificing teenagers to line their own pockets, but the judge had been the one to buy into the scheme. The judge was supposed to be fair and impartial. Instead, he had passed sentences that were far in excess of what was warranted, ruining the lives of countless children to fatten his own bank account.

"I knew that you would understand. You've seen corruption up close, too, haven't you?"

Josie swallowed. She knew at once that Patti was talking about the missing girls case that had catapulted her into fame around Denton. "Yes."

"Corruption killed your husband, didn't it? Never mind what happened to all those girls and the old Chief…"

"You could say that," Josie answered.

"I'll never trust a cop or a lawyer or a judge again after what happened to my son, but I'll talk to you. Today only. This is your one shot, so ask all your questions, and I'll answer them honestly, but if you try to use anything I say to screw me over or get me tangled up in something I got no business being tangled up in, I'll deny everything."

Josie bobbed her head toward the glass window. "This is being recorded, Patti."

Patti shrugged. "Don't mean nothing. People make stuff up all the time. Maybe I'll tell you anything you want to hear cause I want to meet a hometown celebrity." With that, she winked, and Josie had the sense she would tell the truth. Depending on what Patti knew, that could be a good thing or a bad thing. If she told Josie something terribly incriminating, Josie wouldn't be able to use it—or, at the very least, it would be difficult to use—but if she knew something that could prove important or useful to the Colette Fraley and Beth Pratt cases, then this whole game would be worth playing.

Josie said, "Did you kill Drew Pratt?"

Patti laughed and gave Josie an admiring glance. "Well, you sure as shit don't mess around, do you? No. I didn't kill Drew Pratt. He would have been on my list, but by the time I got around to making that list, he was gone."

"Do you know what happened to him?"

"No. I do not, and that's the God's honest truth."

"Did you meet with him on the day he disappeared?"

"No, I did not."

"Did you give him a flash drive with evidence of what Sanders was doing?"

Patti's brown eyes went wide with shock, but she quickly got her expression under control. "Yes," she said. "I did."

"When?" Josie asked.

"About five or six months before he went missing."

"You sure about that?"

"Yes. Drew Pratt used to eat breakfast at the counter of this diner in Bellewood almost every morning."

"The one across from the courthouse?"

Patti nodded. "That's the one. My boss had a crush on him. Pratt was single—or widowed, or whatever—and she had it bad for him. Eligible guy with a good job, well-respected in the community, not too old. She was over there almost every morning too before the bank opened. That's where I got the idea to try talking to him."

"Did your co-worker set it up?"

"No, she never even knew. She was off on Thursdays so I gathered what I could and one Thursday, I went and had breakfast at that diner. Sat right next to him at the counter."

"What month was it?" Josie asked.

"Early December," Patti answered. "It was after Thanksgiving but before Christmas. I know that because I was struggling. It was my first ever holiday season without my son."

That lined up with what Patti said about it being five or six months before Drew's disappearance. He'd gone missing in April.

"Did you tell him what was on the drive?"

"No. I didn't want anyone overhearing us. I just told him there was something he should have a look at on there."

"Did he look at it?"

"Not at first, I don't think," Patti said. "I found him in the diner on a Thursday about a month later. It was tough even waiting that long, but I didn't want to come on too strong or for other people to see us together too close in time and get ideas. Back then it seemed like those Wood Creek men had so much power. So much power. I didn't know if it was dangerous for me to try blowing the whistle or what."

"But he looked at it eventually," Josie prompted.

"I met him in the diner again in February, right before Valentine's Day. He told me to take a walk with him, and I did. He said nothing that I gave him was admissible or even really proved anything. That he couldn't indict Sanders based on a few banking statements anyway." She blew out a breath of frustration. "I was devastated. But he said we shouldn't give up. I was supposed to meet him two months later—give him some time to do a little investigating on his own."

"Then he disappeared," Josie filled in.

"Yes, then he went missing."

"But there was no investigation," Josie said. "I've been over the police files. Drew Pratt's life in the months before he went missing was combed over repeatedly. There's no mention of Sanders or Wood Creek in any of his personal notes, on his computer at home or at work."

"Well, I can't speak for what he did after we talked in February. I can only tell you what he told me at the time."

"Do you think Sanders or any of the Wood Creek guys had anything to do with his disappearance?" Josie asked.

"I don't know. If they did, it wasn't one of them that did the dirty work."

"You're right," Josie agreed.

"Drew Pratt's been missing twelve years. It took you guys this long to figure out what was on the flash drive?"

"No. We just found it," Josie said.

"That's why you're here?"

"No, I'm here because Beth Pratt was murdered."

"What's that got to do with me?" Patti asked.

Josie sighed. "Nothing, it seems. But she was murdered right after we found that flash drive which led us to look more deeply into what happened to her father."

"Well, it's a damn shame."

"Yes," Josie said. "She was very young."

"No," Patti said. "It's a shame that Drew didn't live long enough to know what it feels like to lose a child."

CHAPTER TWENTY-FIVE

Back at the station house, Josie sat at her desk, typing up a report on what she had learned from Patti Snyder. She smelled the comforting scent of coffee even before Gretchen walked up and deposited a cup of it in front of her, the words Komorrah's Koffee wrapped around the midnight blue paper cup. For just a moment, Josie felt a small ache in her heart. It was usually Noah who kept her caffeinated and shored her up during a big investigation. He hadn't called or texted all day.

"Mettner's on his way up," Gretchen said as she sat at her own desk.

A few moments later, Mettner appeared, looking pale, his brown hair in disarray.

Josie said, "You were at the autopsy?"

He nodded.

"Takes a while to get used to," Gretchen offered.

He didn't look at either of them. Instead, he took out his phone and started skimming over his notes, reporting what he had learned from Dr. Feist. "Nothing surprising about the autopsy. Beth Pratt was suffocated to death after a brief struggle. I interviewed a bunch of Colette Fraley's friends and a bunch of people she knew from church. No one had anything helpful to offer. I then cross-checked all those people to see if I could find any connections between them and Drew Pratt. Nothing. Then I went out to the quarry office and talked to her boss and co-workers. Nothing helpful there either, and none of the people I talked to have any connection to Drew Pratt. Also, I don't know what the hell to do about that belt buckle.

Can't get prints. I don't even know where to start looking for men who wore gaudy belt buckles in 1973."

Josie laughed.

"Maybe we should put it out in the press," Gretchen suggested. "Or at least social media. Ask for the public's help."

"No," Josie said. "I don't think we can risk that right now. Someone is obviously looking for this stuff. For some reason, it's important. I don't want to tip our hand to the killer."

"If this stuff is important, then wouldn't its meaning be more obvious to us?" Mettner joked, finally meeting her eyes.

Josie smiled. "You would think. It's never that simple. Start with Google. Then eBay. Also, have Hummel take it around to both pawn shops and antique places to see if anyone recognizes it."

"Good idea," Mettner said, tapping out a note on his phone. He looked at Gretchen. "You get anywhere with Beth Pratt's girlfriend's alibi?"

Gretchen said, "Yes. She cleared. She was at work and I verified that with three of her co-workers."

"How about Noah's dad?" Mettner asked. "Did you have a chance to talk to him?"

"I alibied him. He was in New York City. I got confirmation from the hotel he was staying at, and he had tickets to a Broadway show. He sent me photos of the stubs."

Josie said, "What did he say? About Colette, I mean?"

"He was sad, but he said they hadn't seen one another in over ten years. There was no reason to—Noah was their youngest and he was eighteen when they divorced. He said he had no idea who would want to hurt her. Even though their marriage didn't work out, she was a good person, he told me."

"What about the kids?" Josie asked. "Did he ask about them?"

"He didn't ask about them, but he did say that he tried over the years to reach out to them, but they were so angry with him for leaving that they didn't want to talk to him and eventually, he just gave up. He said it would have made it worse for them if he'd come to the funeral."

"Yeah," Josie said. "I got that sense from Noah and his sister."

Mettner said, "I think we should keep looking at the Pratt brothers because that's what we've got to go on and because another Pratt has just been murdered. Let's go down that rabbit hole and see where it leads for now."

"Fair enough," replied Josie.

Mettner asked, "How'd it go with Snyder?"

Josie sipped the coffee, feeling its warmth spread throughout her body and the mental fog of fatigue lifting. She gave Mettner and Gretchen a rundown of her meeting with Patti Snyder.

"Do you believe her?" Gretchen asked.

"I'm not sure," Josie said. "I mean she had nothing to hide so why would she be so secretive all this time? Why not just come out and say that yes, she had given Drew Pratt the drive, but he never did anything with it?"

"Because that just makes it look even more like she was involved," Gretchen said. "Before today, we had no firm connection between the two, only speculation. Now we know they did meet, and they did talk, and she gave him evidence of what Judge Sanders was doing. If the public knew that all along—she'd be the main suspect in his disappearance. The Patti Snyder theory would go straight to the top of the list. Although from reading the files, I know she was investigated anyway, and no law enforcement agency could find any evidence that she had an associate who possibly killed Pratt for her."

"True," Josie conceded.

Mettner said, "Regardless of whether she killed him or not, now we know Pratt definitely saw the contents of the drive and didn't investigate."

Gretchen said, "I can check out Judge Sanders and the Wood Creek guys to see if there's any connection to Drew Pratt, but if they were involved in his disappearance, they've successfully kept it hidden this long. We may not find proof."

"I'm not sure the Kickbacks thing had anything to do with it." Josie looked up at Mettner. "Remember what Mason said? Drew started acting strangely two or three weeks before he went missing. He'd already known about the Kickbacks thing for months before that. So what did he find out, or what happened in the two or three weeks before he disappeared to make him so distraught?"

"How the hell could we know, if his own daughter couldn't figure it out?" Mettner groused.

"It's worth trying," Josie said. "Sometimes a fresh set of eyes makes all the difference."

Mettner slid his phone into his back pocket. "How would we go about figuring out what Drew Pratt was so distraught over right before he died?"

Josie shrugged. "I don't know. Maybe we can take another look inside Beth Pratt's house? Start there? We can talk to Mason again, too. Maybe he can tell us if Beth kept any notes or documents that belonged to her dad before he went missing. She might have kept some of her dad's personal effects—maybe all of them. I'd also be interested to see if Drew had notes on Samuel's death. He was a prosecutor who asked police to take another look at his brother's death every few years, there's no way he didn't maintain some personal file on Samuel's death."

"You think that's something Beth Pratt would have had?" Gretchen asked.

"I think it's worth looking into," Josie answered. She looked at the clock. It was already evening. "We'll get started on it tomorrow. First thing."

CHAPTER TWENTY-SIX

Josie drove past Noah's house after leaving the station. His lights were off, there was no sign of his car and no response when she pulled over to text him. Heading home, she slowed down as she passed the liquor store, every cell in her body longing to stop and buy a bottle of Wild Turkey to drown out all her insecurity over what was happening between Noah and her. She felt the hot burn of alcohol searing her throat just thinking about it, but she had promised herself she wouldn't do that anymore. *It would be so easy*, a voice in her head told her. *Just a few hours of numbness.*

"No," she muttered out loud, pressing her foot heavily onto the gas pedal and white-knuckling it all the way home.

Once there, she was suddenly relieved that she hadn't given in as she recognized the cars of both her mother, Shannon Payne, and her friend, Misty Derossi, in her driveway. As she paused just inside her front door, the sounds of female voices and laughter floated toward her from the kitchen. She took a few steps forward and looked in to find not just Shannon and Misty, but also her grandmother, Lisette Matson, at the table. Spread out before them was a vast array of cosmetics—mostly nail polishes and various manicure tools.

"Jo! Jo!" The sound of two-year-old Harris Quinn's voice startled her. Looking down, she saw him race across the kitchen toward her. Opening her arms, she caught him expertly and scooped him up.

"Hi honey," she said, planting a kiss on his cheek. All the dark, cloying feelings that had assaulted her in the car were swept away when Harris's little arms tightened around her neck.

He loosened one of his arms and pointed toward the table. "Girls night!"

Then it came back to her.

"You forgot, didn't you?" said Shannon, reading the shock on her face.

"No, I didn't—"

"She forgot," Lisette announced. "It's okay, Josie. We debated on whether or not to cancel because of everything going on with Noah, but then we thought it might do you some good."

Misty waved a hand, a nervous smile on her lips. "It was my turn this month, so I chose spa night."

"Next month we're doing book club night," Shannon put in.

They'd been meeting on every second Tuesday of the month for a while now—this strange but wonderful Frankenstein of a family that had formed itself around Josie—and took turns choosing a theme for their gathering. They'd extended an invitation to Gretchen, but she'd declined, so it was the four of them. Lisette had wanted a game night, Josie had chosen a movie night, Shannon always did book club and Misty always did something that involved self-care. Josie couldn't remember whose idea it had been, but she enjoyed it more than she could ever dare to admit.

Josie had been raised by a woman who had kidnapped her as an infant and didn't meet her biological mother, Shannon, until she was thirty years old, so they were still getting to know one another. Misty had been dating Josie's late husband Ray after Ray and Josie had separated and had given birth to his son, Harris, shortly after his death. Lisette had been the one and only constant in Josie's life and remained so, even though they now knew that they were not related by blood.

"This is good," Josie said, shifting Harris on her hip and walking to the table. "Shall we order food?"

Two hours later, their nails were painted, their bellies full and their cheeks hurt from laughing. Harris slept peacefully in the Pack 'n Play in Josie's living room.

"Do you need to get back to Noah?" Lisette asked.

"He doesn't seem to want me around right now," Josie muttered.

"Nonsense," Lisette scoffed. "He needs you. He just lost his mother. Who else does he have?"

No one, Josie thought. "I went to his house before I came home, but he wasn't there," she said.

"Well, where else would he be?" Shannon asked.

*

The lights were on at Colette's house, and there was Noah's car in the driveway. The door was unlocked so Josie pushed it open and called out his name. She found him eventually in his mother's sewing room where he had pushed her sewing table to the side of the room and spread several photo albums and documents on the floor. Beside him sat three portable plastic file boxes. He didn't look up when she came in, but he said, "I'm trying to find a connection between Mom and the Pratt brothers. I'm telling you, Josie, it's not here."

Josie sat down cross-legged in front of him. "I know," she said. "We're not finding it either."

He shuffled some photos around on the floor. "What if this is all a mistake? What if she found that stuff somewhere when she was having one of her... less lucid moments, and she didn't know what to do with it?"

"So she hid it? Noah, if she had picked it up somewhere during one of her episodes, at some point she would have been lucid again and realized she had no idea what it was. If that happened to me, I'd probably just throw it away, or I'd go on social media and share it and ask the owner to claim it."

He pushed a hand through his thick locks. "I guess you're right. What if—what if someone gave it to her, and told her it was really important, and so she hid it?"

"Who?" Josie asked. "Mettner has interviewed everyone she knew, and Gretchen did background checks on them as well. No connection to the Pratts."

"There has to be something," Noah said. "None of this is making sense."

"You're right," Josie said, looking down at some of the photos. In one, Colette stood at the doors of the Episcopal church in a poofy wedding dress, the groom on her arm the spitting image of Noah. "Is this your dad?"

"Yeah," Noah said. He took the photo from her and set it aside, shuffling through more until Josie spotted one of Colette as a young girl in a Catholic schoolgirl uniform. Josie estimated her to be about eleven or twelve years old, fresh-faced with shiny dark hair that caught the sunlight. There were a few other photos of her and other children in Catholic school uniforms.

"Was the Episcopal church your dad's church?" Josie asked. "Is that why your mom switched?"

For the first time, Noah met her eyes. "What? No. My dad was an atheist. He put up with my mom's faith. He only got married in the church because she insisted on it."

Circles of red rose up on his cheeks. She had more questions, but he was talking to her again and she didn't want to ruin that, so she changed the subject. "What else did you find? In the other file bins?"

Noah tapped on the lid of one of them. "Nothing, really. Old bills. The title to the house. Warranties for household appliances, cards from her co-workers from when she retired. Marriage certificate, divorce decree. Some old planners. When her mind started to go, she went out and bought one. She said it helped her stay on top of things. There's one from this year and last year."

"Can I see them?"

"Sure, I guess." He pushed one of the file bins toward her and she opened it, digging out the two small weekly planners. She paged through them but didn't find any unusual entries. Nothing that stood out to her, just church, her children's visits and a few doctor's appointments.

Her cell phone sounded. She pulled it from her pocket. "It's Mettner," she told him. "I've got to take this." Pressing the answer icon, she said, "Quinn."

"Boss," Mettner said, sounding slightly out of breath. "Beth Pratt's house is on fire."

CHAPTER TWENTY-SEVEN

Mettner and Josie stood along the side of the road, across from where Denton firefighters fought the blaze that used to be Beth Pratt's home. The night was alive with flashing emergency lights, and the heat and light from the fire made it feel like an afternoon in August. Beads of sweat formed along Josie's upper lip and she swiped at them with the back of her shirtsleeve. "Where's Mason Pratt?" Josie asked.

"He's home. I've checked with the unit three times already."

"I want someone inside the house with him."

Mettner raised a brow. "Not sure he'll allow that, but we can try." He took out his phone and made some calls.

Josie watched the firefighters dragging more hose from a second truck that had pulled up right onto Beth Pratt's front lawn. Flames shot out of the windows and ripped through the roof. Glowing orange embers floated above the entire area, and Josie felt a thin slice of fear, hoping they wouldn't set the surrounding trees on fire.

Mettner hung up. "We'll have two units on Mason Pratt, and one of the officers who is already there is going to wake Pratt up and see about getting one of our guys inside at least for tonight."

"Thank you," Josie said.

A blast of gray smoke whooshed in their direction, and as they both coughed and wiped at watery eyes one of the firefighters yelled at them to get back. They walked a little further up the road, out of the direction of the wind, where the cooler air was a relief.

A dark-colored four-door sedan rolled down the road, slowing in front of them. Josie was getting ready to tell the driver that he or she couldn't make it through right now, but when the driver's side window opened, she saw it was Chief Chitwood. "Beth Pratt's house? Are you shitting me?" was all he said.

Chitwood swiped at his thinning hair. "I had to come by and see it for myself. For the love of all that is holy, this is a disaster. I'm not going to be able to keep this out of the press. You realize that, don't you? This is gonna be a real shitstorm. You put extra units on the other Pratt kid?"

"Yes, sir," Josie said.

"Why the hell is Beth Pratt's house burning down, Quinn?"

"I don't know, sir. Maybe the killer didn't find what he was looking for the last time he was here and thought torching the entire place would get rid of it once and for all."

Chitwood said, "You think Beth Pratt had something the killer didn't want anyone to see? Like what?"

"We don't know, sir," Mettner said.

"Maybe, whatever it was, Beth Pratt didn't realize it was important," Josie suggested.

Chitwood opened his mouth to speak but Mettner's cell phone rang, interrupting them. "Mettner," he answered. Then, "Oh shit. Yeah, we'll be right over."

Josie and Chitwood stared at him as he ended the call. He said, "Mason Pratt was attacked in his home about twenty minutes ago."

CHAPTER TWENTY-EIGHT

Mason Pratt sat in the back of an ambulance in his driveway, an ice pack pressed to the side of his head. The moment that Mettner and Josie arrived they had all emergency units turn off their lights; the attention that Beth Pratt's murder and the arson of her home would bring was bad enough, they didn't need the attack on Mason to become more grist for the neighborhood rumor mill. Mettner ducked into the back of the ambulance and sat on the vinyl bench next to the gurney that held Mason. Josie climbed in behind him.

"I was asleep," Mason told them before they even had a chance to ask questions. "I thought I was dreaming at first."

"What happened, exactly?" Josie asked. "What do you remember?"

"I sleep on my stomach. So I started to kind of wake up to this pressure on my upper back and then my head. When I got fully awake, I realized someone was on top of me, pushing my head into the pillow. I could barely breathe."

Josie felt a tiny shiver. "Did he say anything?"

Mason brought the ice pack down, shook his head, and placed it back on the side of his skull with a wince. "No. He never said a word. As soon as I realized that it was real, that it was really happening, I started to fight. It felt like it took forever. He was really strong. Like, even for me. I used to wrestle in high school, but still this guy was everywhere at once. I managed to get him off me and then I rolled off the bed and hit my head on my nightstand."

He brought the ice pack down again and turned his head, using his fingers to brush back some of his hair. Josie could already see a large purple lump rising from beneath his locks.

"You should get that looked at," Mettner said. "Maybe get a head CT."

Mason sighed. "Whatever. I just can't believe this shit is happening. First Beth, and now this—and the police told me about her house." Tears leaked from the corners of his eyes. "Man, it doesn't stop. I mean what the hell is going on?"

"We're trying to figure that out," Josie assured him.

Mettner said, "What happened after you rolled off the bed?"

"He was still there, like, standing over me. He went to bend down, like he was going to straddle me, and then we heard a knock on my front door. Not just a knock, but like a pounding. Real hard. It spooked him and he ran. I think he went out the back door. Next thing I know there's police in my bedroom, and everyone's shouting, and one officer goes running out the back after the guy."

Josie and Mettner already knew from having spoken with their colleagues on patrol that they hadn't apprehended Mason's attacker. One of the uniformed officers had given chase but lost him in the maze of backyards behind Mason's house. Another unit was still driving around the neighborhood looking for the guy—or anyone who seemed suspicious. But Josie had a feeling he was long gone. He would have had some precious time to get a head start before the Denton officer gave chase. If he'd been parked on an adjacent street, he could easily have hopped a few fences, gone through an alleyway and been back on the road in his vehicle before anyone even noticed.

"I'm so sorry you're going through this," Josie said. "I know this isn't the best time, and I agree with Officer Mettner that you should get to the hospital, but we'd like to ask you a few more questions."

"It's fine," he said, leaning back against the head of the gurney, his face sagging with exhaustion and pain.

"Did you get a look at this guy at all?" Mettner asked.

"No, I'm sorry. It was pitch black in my room. He had just woken me up. Then I hit my head. I was disorientated. He was just this big shadowy figure."

"Can you think of anything at all distinguishing?" Josie said. "Or could you tell if he had a weapon?"

"No," Mason replied. "Nothing distinguishing and no weapon that I could see."

"Listen," Mettner said. "We think whoever is doing all of this is looking for something. Or he thinks that you either know something or have something important, something incriminating."

"Incriminating? Like what?"

"We don't know," Josie said. "Something that could possibly reveal what happened to your uncle. Maybe even what really happened to your dad."

Mason's eyes widened. "You think my dad was murdered?"

"We don't know," Josie admitted. "But whatever this person is after, they're willing to kill for it—or to keep it hidden. We had been hoping to visit Beth's house tomorrow morning and check out everything she had or might have had that belonged to her dad before he went missing. We were thinking she must have kept some of his things."

"She did," Mason said. "She thought he was dead, but she couldn't bear to get rid of his stuff. You think this killer is looking for something that belonged to Uncle Drew?"

"That's the only thing that makes sense at this point," Josie said. "It may be something that doesn't seem significant or important, but that's just because we don't have all the pieces that this killer does."

"Or the pieces are scattered, and he doesn't want us to put them together," Mettner said.

"Right," Josie agreed.

"In the morning, I can show you Uncle Drew's possessions," Mason said eagerly.

Josie and Mettner exchanged a skeptical look. Did he have a concussion, Josie wondered?

Mettner said, "Mason, there is nothing left of Beth's house. We were just there. I don't think they'll be able to salvage anything."

"I know," he said. "But Beth didn't keep her dad's things at her house. There was too much, and it was too painful for her to have all that stuff around."

"What are you saying?" Josie asked.

"I'm saying she rented a storage unit. And I have the spare key."

CHAPTER TWENTY-NINE

Josie wasn't willing to leave Beth Pratt's storage unit unattended even for the night—not after everything that had happened in the past twenty-four hours. The killer they were hunting was as bold and as brash as any criminal Josie had ever pursued. For all they knew, he'd found evidence of the storage unit inside Beth Pratt's house before he burned it down. Josie sent a unit over to the address Mason provided to check on it and then guard it for the night. She couldn't go home and sleep until she heard from them that the unit was safe and undisturbed. It was after one in the morning, but she was encouraged by her earlier encounter with Noah—at least he hadn't ignored her or pushed her away—so she texted him to see if he was awake, but she got no response.

The next morning, Josie and Shannon had a quick breakfast before Josie met Mettner and Mason Pratt at Lux Storage, a large, flat, blocky building near the entrance to the interstate in South Denton. It was gray cinderblock with bright yellow double doors at the entrance to each unit.

The storage unit Beth had rented was near the back and out of sight of the road, for which Josie was grateful. They could poke around at their leisure and not have to worry about anyone asking questions. They pulled up behind Mason's truck and got out. Mason hopped out too, looking exhausted. Josie wondered if he'd even had a chance to sleep. They'd sent him to the ER while the ERT dusted his bedroom and back door for prints. That had only been four or five hours earlier.

He greeted them with a half-hearted wave and fished a set of keys out of his jeans pocket. A moment later they were inside the unit, and Mason flicked on an overhead light which cast a harsh glare over the room. Several rows of plastic bins, stacked shoulder-high, sat on a concrete floor. It smelled musty, and the air was cold.

"I'm really not sure what she kept in here, specifically," Mason said, tapping a palm against the nearest stack of bins. "But you're welcome to look as long as you like." He tossed the key toward Mettner and he caught it. "I'm going home to sleep," he added. "Just get that back to me when you're done."

"Mason," Josie said as he started to walk back to the truck. "I'd like to have one of our officers inside your house and a unit outside for now, if you don't mind."

He scratched his forehead. "I'm not gonna argue, especially after last night."

They thanked him and got to work. Mettner started looking through the bins on the far left, and Josie checked the ones on the far right. They worked their way toward the middle, finding old clothes, sports memorabilia, kitchenware, some photo albums, Drew Pratt's framed college degrees and dozens of notebooks filled with Pratt's handwriting that were obviously notes he had taken on his various cases as an ADA.

"Good lord," Mettner said, swiping his forearm across his upper lip. The air outside was cool, but the longer they worked in the small storage unit, the warmer and sweatier they became. "It will take us ages to go through all these, and we don't even know what we're looking for."

"Set them aside," Josie said. "We can have a closer look at them later."

"What are we looking for?" Mettner asked.

"I don't know, but I think we'll know it when we find it."

They found a collection of shoes and ties, several bins of books, some blankets and sheet sets, and an old tool box.

"Well," Mettner said. "I know Mason said that Beth thought her father was dead, but it looks like she kept everything he owned."

Josie felt a small tug at her heart. "There was probably always a part of her that still hoped he would come walking back in through the front door."

"Check this out," Mettner said, tugging a small brown box out of one of the plastic bins. On the top, in thick black marker, was the name: Sam. Mettner carried it to the front of the storage unit where the daylight was strongest and the air was coolest. They both knelt on the floor and Josie opened the box. There was a notebook, which looked like an old daily planner, and several loose papers.

"This looks like Drew Pratt's unofficial 'file' on his brother's death," Josie said. She tried to imagine what it had been like for Drew Pratt to lose his brother under such odd circumstances; to have grown up with someone and know them intimately and then have them do something so unexpected. Josie had known her husband, Ray, since childhood. They had been best friends, then high school sweethearts and then husband and wife. How would she have reacted if one day Ray had walked off, driven forty miles to a river bank and disappeared, only to wash up a few days later, dead? Like Drew Pratt, she would never have believed it was a suicide. Like Drew Pratt, she would have conducted her own investigation. She would not have been able to let it go.

Mettner leafed through the loose pages. "You're right. Here's the autopsy report, and there are some police reports, too."

"What's that?" Josie asked, pointing to a stack of typed pages that had been bound together with a thick rubber band.

Mettner pulled them from the bottom of the pile he had taken and riffled through them. "Academic papers written by Samuel Pratt."

He handed them to Josie. The archaeological terms in the text and titles were foreign to Josie, but she gathered that the papers appeared to have been written about digs Samuel Pratt had done in various countries: Egypt, Italy, Bosnia Herzegovina, China and even a few places in the United States. Josie set them aside and pushed a few more items around inside the box. There was a stapler, a tiny cylinder filled with paper clips, and a desk nameplate that read: Dr. Samuel Pratt. "Some of this is stuff from Samuel Pratt's office," Josie said. "The last place he was seen alive."

Josie picked up the notebook and started flipping pages. There were notes upon notes in Drew Pratt's crowded scrawl about his brother's case. Most of it was questions in black ink which Pratt had later answered in blue ink.

Did he get any calls that day at the office?
Secretary reported only one call from department chair about summer class schedule.
Did anyone stop by his office that day?
Secretary reported one student stopped by to leave an overdue paper.
Did anyone at the café actually see him?
Barista reported Sam came at his usual time, ordered his usual drink and seemed normal.

Over Josie's shoulder, Mettner gave a low whistle. "This guy sure was thorough. If there was anything suspicious to find, he would have turned it up."

Josie turned more pages, eyes skimming the notes as quickly as she could while still taking in their import. Finally, at the end, something unusual caught her eye.

Who/What is C.F.?

Drew Pratt had answered below it with several possibilities: *Conference? Sam was set to travel to a conference the week after he died. Café? No, Sam went to the café daily. Students? Sam had two current students with those initials but both were in class all day. Chronic Fatigue? Cystic Fibrosis? Was he having some serious medical issue?*

Would it have shown on autopsy? Colleague? Sam had one colleague with those initials but he was having surgery that day. Affair?

No answer was written beneath the word "affair".

"Where did he get those initials?" Mettner asked.

Josie's fingers shook slightly as she dug out the planner she had seen when they first opened the box. "From here," she said. "What's the date that Samuel Pratt went missing?"

Mettner took out his phone and scrolled through the entries in his note-taking app until he found the note. "April 14, 1999."

Josie opened the planner. In the front was Samuel Pratt's name, his Denton University office address, and phone number. She turned to April. A few things were marked—some office hours, a paper deadline, faculty meetings, the conference at the end of the month and then on April 14th there was only one notation. Two letters.

C.F.

"Colette Fraley," Josie said.

CHAPTER THIRTY

"I thought Colette Fraley and Samuel Pratt didn't know each other," Mettner said.

The two of them had cleaned up the unit, put all the storage bins back in place and taken the box marked "Sam" with them after calling Mason for his permission. Now Mettner drove back to the police station while Josie sat in the passenger's seat with the box balanced on her knees.

"Who else would C.F. be?" Josie countered. "Drew Pratt spent years trying to figure out what or who those initials belonged to. Maybe he never got it because he had no idea who Colette was. I mean, we haven't been able to find a connection between her and either Pratt brother."

Mettner frowned. "So we might be talking about an affair. You know that, right? Nineteen years ago, Noah would have been in middle school. When did you say his parents got divorced?"

Josie said, "When he was eighteen. In April of 1999, he would have been about thirteen years old. So yeah, Colette would have been married."

"An affair might explain why Sam drove all the way to Bellewood. I mean they both lived here in Denton, and yet Samuel Pratt's car was found forty miles from here," Mettner said.

Josie felt her heart sink, a cold stone descending into the pool of her stomach. "Back in 1999 probably neither one of them would have had a cell phone. Even email wasn't that prevalent back then."

"They wouldn't have subpoenaed his home or office phone records if it looked like suicide," Mettner added. "There is a possibility that he and Colette could have been in touch for some time and no one ever found out."

Josie flipped the box open and took the planner back out. She combed over the entries between January 1st and April 14th. There was only one other entry with the initials C.F. and that was about three weeks prior to the April 14th entry. "I don't think it was ongoing," Josie said. "Or at least, it didn't go on very long. There's only one other entry here, a few weeks before Samuel Pratt ended up in the river. But if it was an affair, what happened?"

Mettner said, "What do you mean?"

Josie closed the planner and put it back in the box. "One day she meets him at the river and she convinces him to drown himself? Have you seen photos of Samuel Pratt? He was huge. No way someone Colette's size held him under water till he drowned."

"Maybe she broke things off with him, he didn't take it well, and killed himself."

"That's a possibility," Josie agreed. "Especially with his mental health issues."

"Or maybe Colette had a jealous lover—someone else—or maybe her husband found out, lost it, and killed him."

Josie hadn't known Colette Fraley for long, and she hadn't known the woman that well, but she had a difficult time imagining her as a young temptress carrying on multiple extra-marital affairs. "But then what about Drew Pratt?"

"What about him?"

"Colette had his flash drive, which means she was very likely the mystery woman from the craft fair. How else would she have gotten it? She hid it together with Sam's arrowhead. There was a connection there. Did she start an affair with Drew as well?"

"Hmmm," Mettner said. "That seems unlikely. Although even if seven years after Samuel drowned, she met with his brother and they did have an affair, she was divorced by then. Drew Pratt was single. So we can probably rule out the husband as a jealous killer.

There would have been no reason for secrecy either. But I don't think she was having an affair with Drew."

"Right. I don't think so either. Maybe you're right, she dumped Sam and he killed himself, and she felt guilty about it. Or she knew who killed Sam, and she was trying to come clean to Drew, although why would she just tell him everything after all those years? It makes no sense," Josie said.

"Not necessarily," Mettner said. "Maybe she couldn't live with the guilt of having driven Sam to suicide any longer and needed to make amends with his family. Or let's say she had another lover who got jealous and killed Sam. Maybe Colette either knew or at least suspected that her jealous lover was behind his death. Maybe she couldn't live with the guilt any longer, and she decided to approach Drew. He was a prosecutor. Maybe she thought he could help her—although it doesn't account for what she was doing with his flash drive."

"True. Maybe that's why Drew Pratt was distraught in the weeks leading to his death—not because of anything to do with the Kickbacks scandal, but because he had finally found out what happened to his brother," Josie theorized. "Then she ended up luring Drew to his death, just like Sam; perhaps not intentionally, but it happened just the same. And yet like you said, why did she have Drew Pratt's flash drive? Why did she have personal effects from each of them? Why keep them? And who does the belt buckle belong to?"

Josie could see Mettner's frown, even in profile. "It is disturbing, isn't it? I mean usually only serial killers keep trophies, right?"

"Right. I can't see Colette as some kind of killer, but anything is possible, I guess." She sighed. "Noah's not going to like this line of questioning one bit."

"We're going to have to have a more in-depth conversation with Noah's dad," Mettner said.

"Noah's not going to like that either."

"I'm sure he won't," Mettner said. "But there's a killer on the loose, and he's escalating."

Josie swore she could still smell the smoke in her hair from the fire at Beth Pratt's house the night before, even though she had washed it twice. She said, "I know."

CHAPTER THIRTY-ONE

Back at the station house, they updated Chief Chitwood and Gretchen, and then ordered takeout. Josie checked her cell phone, but there were no messages from Noah. She tried calling him but got no answer. She sent him a text threatening half-jokingly that she was going to send a unit to his house to check on him if he didn't let her know he was alive. It took ten minutes, but finally, he texted back, *I'm alive. Packing Mom's house today*. Josie felt part relief and part anxiety. She was happy he was responding, of course, but she missed the genial and even flirty nature of their usual exchanges. He used to end nearly every text to her with a series of smiley faces or a '*love you*'. Inwardly, she chastised herself. Noah had just lost his mother in a horrifically violent way. The least of his concerns was making Josie feel reassured. She felt selfish for even thinking about it. She turned her mind to another worry—would Noah be safe alone at his mother's house? They still didn't know what the killer was after, and in only a matter of days Beth Pratt had been murdered, her house burned to the ground, and Mason Pratt had been attacked in his sleep.

She picked up the phone and dialed dispatch to see if Officer Hummel was still on shift then called his cell phone and asked him to run checks on Colette's house.

Without looking up from her computer screen, Gretchen said, "Good call."

When Mettner appeared next to her desk, it was a welcome relief. He handed Josie a list of what looked like antique dealers and pawn shops. "I had Hummel work on this today. He got nowhere with your belt buckle."

With a heavy sigh, Josie studied the list. "We're going about this the wrong way."

Gretchen looked up from her computer. "What do you mean?"

"The year has to have some significance. It was forty-five years ago." She looked at Mettner. "Have someone go over to Rockview."

"The nursing home?" Mettner asked.

"Yes," Josie said. "Get someone to talk to the residents. Show them the photos of the belt buckle. Many of them would have been young to middle-aged in 1973. Someone might have an idea as to its significance or where it came from."

"You got it," Mettner said, walking off.

Gretchen stood, stretched her arms over head, and called after him. "Don't go too far. I got you two a meeting with Lance Fraley."

Chitwood appeared in his open doorway. "Palmer can go," he said.

Mettner, who was almost at the steps, froze and looked back at the Chief.

Gretchen's face filled with hope. "I'm off the desk?"

Chitwood raised a brow. "No, not entirely. But we've got two murders—and I consider Beth Pratt's to be pretty damn high-profile—and now an arson and another Pratt in danger. So Palmer can help *very quietly* with some of the leg work. Quinn, you'll take Palmer to see Lance Fraley. Mettner, you track down that belt buckle yourself. I've already got the ERT working overtime to process the evidence from the Pratt murder scene, and now the Pratt arson scene plus Mason Pratt's house. I have more crimes than I have people. But Palmer, I swear to God, if you step out of line even one time, even just a little bit, your ass is on the desk until you retire."

Gretchen could barely contain her grin as she answered, "Yes, sir."

CHAPTER THIRTY-TWO

Noah's dad lived about two hours away from Denton in a town near the northern border of New Jersey and the southern border of New York state. Gretchen called him before they left to make sure he would be home. They spent the drive discussing Gretchen's adult children with whom she had just been reunited—she had spent a lot of time with them during her months off, and things seemed to be going well. It was one more thing they had in common; reconnecting with family after decades without them. As they pulled up in front of Lance Fraley's house, Josie wondered if Noah would ever reconnect with his dad.

When she saw two boys playing basketball in the driveway, she realized why that was not likely. Both boys were tall, perhaps thirteen or fourteen years old, dressed in oversized T-shirts and loose-fitting shorts. They both had shaggy brown hair and looked like miniature Noahs, except without the resemblance he bore to Colette. As Josie and Gretchen got out of the car and started walking up the driveway, one of them hollered, "Dad! Your friends are here!"

They kept playing as though Josie and Gretchen weren't there. Edging around the one-on-one basketball game, Josie and Gretchen made their way to the front door. The house was a large two-story with eggshell white siding and bright red trim. Carefully tended flower beds surrounded the perimeter. The porch had a bench swing and several potted flowers hanging from its small roof. A small brown carpet in front of the door announced: The Fraleys.

Josie felt her heart stop momentarily when a pretty blonde woman, who could not have been much older than Josie herself, answered the door. She smiled brightly at them, drying her hands off with a dishtowel before opening the screen door. "You're the detectives, right? Come on in."

She waved them past her into a bright foyer area with hardwood floors and a small cherry table that held a pile of mail and a bowl of keys. "Andi Fraley," the woman said, extending a hand toward them. Gretchen shook it first and then Josie, who was so dumbstruck, she couldn't speak. Luckily, Gretchen introduced them both and then gave Josie a nudge as Andi Fraley led them into a spacious living room with a large, taupe-colored sectional sofa and a matching area rug over the gleaming hardwood floors.

"Can I get you anything? It must have been a long drive. Water? Coffee?" Andi asked.

Gretchen said, "Coffee would be great." When Josie didn't respond, her gaze traveling the room, Gretchen added, "Detective Quinn would love some coffee as well."

Andi shot them another megawatt smile and said, "Sure thing. I'll get Lance. He's in his office."

The moment she was gone, Gretchen hissed, "Quinn, snap out of it."

Josie motioned toward the far wall where a large bookcase stood, its shelves dotted with happy family photos. They showed Andi, the two boys from the driveway, and what was obviously Lance Fraley. Noah looked nearly identical to him. Noah's sister had a pretty equal mix of both their parents and Theo looked almost entirely like their mother, but Noah was a near clone of his father.

And Lance Fraley had left his wife of thirty-four years and started a whole new family.

"He started over," Josie said. "Completely."

Gretchen whispered, "That is typically what people do when they get divorced."

"Well," Josie answered. "There has to be something more. Maybe he didn't try to reach out to them as much as he said he did."

Josie could see now why Noah and his siblings were so bitter over their father's absence. Josie wondered if what Lance had told Gretchen about making an effort with his adult children was really true. The Noah she knew was kind, forgiving, even-tempered and fair. It was hard to imagine him turning his father away; choosing not to have any type of relationship with him at all. Given what she knew, it made more sense that Lance's "efforts" had been so minimal as to be non-existent. Then, given the age of his children with Andi, it was quite possible he had already been seeing his new wife when he was still married to Colette. Even if he had made some efforts to stay in his children's lives, the fact that he had left their mother for another woman and started a whole new family would have been extremely painful for all of them. Gretchen was right. It was what people did—get divorced and start over—but if Lance had been as absent as the Fraley children claimed after the divorce, she could see why they were still so angry with him. She wondered what it would be like to have a real father your whole life—someone who was caring and doting and attentive, someone who was there—and then one day have that person walk away from your family and more or less not look back.

Before she could speculate more, Lance Fraley came in with Andi trailing behind him. She carried a small tray with cups of coffee on it, two spoons, a squat little carton of milk and a bowl of sugar. Lance shook their hands while Andi set the tray onto the coffee table. Josie studied him as they sat down. He was much taller than Noah and his hair was gray, but it was thick like Noah's, and their faces were almost identical in person as well as in the photos she had seen.

With another sunny smile, Andi left them alone in the living room. Lance sat diagonally from them on the other part of the sectional, his large hands on his knees. His smile looked more like a grimace. It was the same look Noah got when he knew he had to do something, but was dreading it. "What can I do for you ladies?" he asked.

Josie regained her voice. "We need to talk to you about your ex-wife."

The grimace morphed into an expression of sadness. "I'll do what I can," he said.

Gretchen pulled out her phone and swiped to a photo of the three items they had found in Colette's sewing machine. She showed them to Lance, but his expression remained the same. "Do you recognize any of these items?" she asked.

He shook his head. "No, I'm sorry, I don't. What does this have to do with Colette?"

"Maybe nothing," Josie said. "Where did you and Colette meet?"

"High school," he answered easily. "We were high school sweethearts."

"What was your marriage like?" Gretchen asked.

He frowned. "I'm sorry, I don't see the relevance of—"

Josie cut him off. "We need to know if Colette ever had an affair—or multiple affairs—that you know of."

At this, Lance laughed. "Is this a joke? This is a joke, right? Did the kids put you up to this? Yes, I was having an affair with Andi while I was still married to Colette. Yes, Andi got pregnant, and I left. I know it wasn't an ideal situation, but it's been years. They really need to move past this."

Josie put sugar and cream into her coffee and took a sip, using the mug to hide the shock on her face. There was more bad blood than she had thought between Lance and his adult children.

Gretchen raised a brow. "We're here on behalf of the Denton Police Department investigating a series of murders, Mr. Fraley, so no, no one is 'putting us up to' anything."

"A series?" he said, face paling.

"Yes," Josie said. "We have reason to believe that the person who murdered Colette also murdered another woman, and attempted to kill a third person. We're trying to get as much background on all the victims as we possibly can. If we can find connections among them, it might help us find the killer."

"Oh, I see. Sorry, I—I just… listen, I haven't talked to Colette since our divorce was finalized."

"Not even about your kids?" Josie said, setting her mug back onto the table. She recalled the photos she had seen from Noah's college graduation. His father hadn't been in any of them. She wondered if he even knew that Noah had been shot a few years back. She knew divorced parents of adult children wouldn't have much reason to keep in touch, but for the big things—graduating from college or a medical crisis—it seemed like they could at least communicate then.

Lance said, "No, our kids were grown up. There was no need to discuss them anymore."

"Oh, so once they grow up, there's no need to concern yourself with them?" Josie blurted, for which she caught a sharp elbow in the ribs from Gretchen. She clamped her mouth shut and let Gretchen take over the questioning.

"Mr. Fraley, I think what my colleague is trying to say is that we understand you also had little contact with your children after the divorce. So it's probably safe to say you had no contact with Colette in recent years either directly or indirectly."

Lance shifted uncomfortably but said, "Yes."

"So with that in mind, we'd just like to ask some background questions. You were married to Colette for over thirty years. It stands to reason that you knew her pretty well during that time, wouldn't you say?"

"Of course."

"I don't like asking uncomfortable questions any more than you like answering them, but it's necessary for our investigation. We do have to exhaust every line of inquiry. I hope you understand."

"Of course," Lance said.

Josie watched as Gretchen weaved her spell, all professionalism and sympathy. Gretchen continued, "So to your knowledge, did Colette ever have an affair?"

"No, not that I know of, and truly, I don't think she ever did. She just wasn't that type of person. She was very devoted. To tell you the truth, I wasn't so keen on getting married. I—I kind of wanted to break up after high school, but then she got pregnant with Theo. You know, back then, not getting married wasn't an option."

"Was Colette happy when she found out she was pregnant?" Gretchen asked.

"Thrilled, yes. She wanted to marry right away. We planned a quick wedding. Moved in together. Had more kids. It wasn't always easy, but we made it work. Well, until the kids got older and I met Andi…"

He trailed off, his eyes staring at a point over their heads. After a few seconds, he said, "I know I hurt her. I know I hurt the kids. I deeply regret it, but I just couldn't keep going on like that… Noah was about to go off to college. It would have been just the two of us. You know, we really didn't have much in common. When you meet in high school, it's not really—"

"I married my high school sweetheart," Josie said.

"I'm sorry," Lance said. "I didn't mean—I mean some people are perfectly happy—"

Josie managed a smile. "It's okay. It didn't work out. We… grew apart."

This admission seemed to loosen Lance's posture. He returned her smile. "Yes, I think that's what happened with us. We were interested in our children, and then when they weren't there to bond over any longer, we just got so distant. Then I met Andi and everything changed."

"And I bet it was still hard to let go of something you'd been in for so long," Josie went on. "Especially when you knew all of each other's secrets."

Lance was nodding as she spoke.

Josie said, "Although from what we've gathered so far, Colette wasn't really the type to harbor secrets."

"She wasn't, that's true," Lance said. "What you saw was what you got with her. There was really only this one time that I saw her…"

He broke off.

"Saw her what, Mr. Fraley?" Josie prompted.

He waved a hand. "It was nothing. I don't even know why I'm bringing it up."

"It couldn't be nothing if it stood out to you enough that you remember it all this time later," Josie pointed out.

"One time I saw her talking to another man, which in itself wasn't that unusual. She talked to lots of people. She was friendly with people at her church and at work. The butcher at the grocery store just loved her. But this was… I don't know, different."

Both Josie and Gretchen had moved to the edge of the couch. "In what way?" Gretchen asked.

"They were in the park," he said. "You know, Denton's city park?"

"Yes," Josie and Gretchen said in unison.

"We used to have this little dog, when the kids were teenagers—well, Laura and Noah—Theo had already moved out by then. You know, the older they got, the less they wanted to spend time with us. We thought if we got this dog, it would bring something to the family. So anyway, Colette always took the dog for walks after dinner. Noah was, oh I don't know, maybe thirteen at the time? He had a friend over and they were horsing around. Noah fell and smashed up his nose pretty good. I figured I'd take him to the ER, swing by the park to let Colette know I was taking him on the way there. Well, we were driving down that road alongside the park, and I saw her standing under a tree with the dog, talking to this guy. He was big, burly, and bald. But not like he lost his hair, like he shaved his head on purpose. Tough-looking. At first, I thought maybe he was threatening her because he looked like the type, but as I got closer, it looked like they were talking. They were standing close. He was leaning down into her. Then she—she put her hand on his chest."

"Like she was pushing him away?" Josie asked. "Or more of an intimate gesture?"

"It was definitely more of an intimate thing," Lance said. "Noah didn't see anything cause he had his head leaned back with a big old ice pack on his face. I kept driving. The whole time at the ER, I was wondering what the hell was going on. I mean I really thought she was seeing this guy. I thought maybe all those walks with the dog were just a ruse to go meet her lover."

"Did you confront her?" Josie asked.

"Yes, of course. That night after the kids were in bed, I told her that I'd seen her with a man in the park and she said, 'Oh, that was Ivan.' Like it was nothing at all. I said, 'Who the hell is Ivan?'"

"And who was Ivan?" Gretchen asked.

"She said they went to grade school together and that back then they were very good friends. Like brother and sister, she said. I told her, 'If you were like brother and sister, why is this the first time I'm hearing about him?' And she said it was because he moved away from Denton a long time ago, and he only comes back to town every few years and they had grown apart during that time."

"Did she say if she had just run into him at the park that day or if it was planned?" Josie asked.

"She said she ran into him but I'm not so sure."

"And that was it?" Gretchen asked.

He shrugged. "I pressed her on it. Damn near came out and accused her of cheating with this guy but she scoffed, laughed it off. Said the whole idea was absurd. It was the way she dismissed the idea that made me think she was telling the truth. Colette was a terrible liar to begin with. I felt very confident that she was telling the truth about the whole thing."

"But that's what came to mind when we asked you about extra-marital affairs?" Gretchen said.

"Yeah. It was something between them. Like you said, an intimacy. A level of comfort I saw between them just in those few seconds from far away. I know it sounds stupid, but it really struck me at the time."

"Did Colette have siblings?" Josie asked.

"No. It was just her and her mom. Her dad died when she was eight."

"Did her mom remember Ivan?" Josie asked. "Did you ever bring it up with her?"

"Colette did," he said. "The next time we went to her house for dinner. Right there at the table she said, 'Mom, you remember that boy Ivan from school? I ran into him in the park in April.'" He laughed. "Then her mother said yes, she remembered him. He had been an altar boy before he started getting into trouble—kid stuff, she said, like vandalism and such. The family pulled up stakes and moved after he was expelled from the school."

"Wait a minute," Josie said. "When you and Colette met in high school, was she still going to Catholic church?"

"Well, we didn't even notice one another until we were seniors in high school," he said. "By that time, she was going to the Episcopal church."

Josie said, "You know, we found rosaries buried in her backyard."

Again, he laughed and his expression held a sort of nostalgia. "Oh yes, she kept her Catholic customs. In the house we raised our kids, there's probably two dozen rosaries buried in that backyard as well. Colette was big on saying the rosary."

"Did she ever tell you why she switched to Episcopalian but continued to observe her Catholic rites?" Josie asked.

Another shrug. "When we got married, her mom wanted her to get married in the Catholic church. You know, her mom worked for the priests in the rectory almost her whole life. She cooked and cleaned for them. I mean she had another job, too, but the work at the rectory kept them afloat after Colette's dad died. Anyway, Colette absolutely refused and said she'd never set foot in that church again. Then her mom said she could pick a different Catholic church. It didn't have to be the one she grew up attending. There was a nice one in Bellewood that would have allowed us to wed there, but Colette was adamant. She said as far as she was concerned, there was no Catholic church any longer. She and her mother fought over it. It was the only time I ever saw her scream at her mother, and one of the few times I ever saw her upset enough to cry."

Gretchen said, "Is there a possibility she was… abused there?"

Lance thought about it for a second, his lips bunching up as he mulled it over. "No, I don't think so. I mean I asked her about it when the whole wedding controversy was going on because I had never seen her so upset about anything before. It was creating so much tension between her and her mom, too. I asked her point blank if one of the priests had ever done anything to her, and she said no. She said that she would not talk about it but all I needed to know was that she had witnessed things that were not very Christian. So she switched to the Episcopal church, and she was happy there."

Josie wondered if Colette's anger toward her old church and Ivan were connected in any way. There was no way to know without tracking down this Ivan person, and she wasn't sure Colette's switch from Catholic to Episcopalian was really relevant to the issue at hand, which was finding Colette and Beth Pratt's killer. On the other hand, it couldn't hurt to talk to Ivan. Colette had been seen talking to him when Noah was around thirteen years old which would have been the same year that Samuel Pratt died. It was too coincidental.

"Did she or her mother ever tell you Ivan's last name?" Josie asked.

"No," Lance said. "He never even came up again after that."

"What about anyone named Pratt?" Gretchen asked. "Did she know anyone by that last name? That you're aware of?"

He shook his head. "No, doesn't sound familiar."

"How about her work schedule?" Gretchen asked. "She worked for Sutton Stone Enterprises for a long time, didn't she?"

"Yeah, she got that job when she was about twenty-two and it was a godsend at the time because I was unemployed. They were good to her there. She seemed to love it, and it was easy work—typing letters and answering phones, making appointments. She was in their secretarial pool at first and then got promoted eventually to assistant to the big guy."

"So she basically worked nine to five every day?" Gretchen probed.

Josie knew she was trying to establish how flexible Colette's work schedule had been; would she have had time to slip away during the day and carry on an affair with Samuel Pratt?

"Yeah, for years and years," Lance answered. "Decades, really. Like I said, they were good to her there. She got bonuses each year and a good pension. Back when pensions were a thing."

They asked him a few more questions before leaving, and Josie was struck by the fact that as perfect and lovely as his new home life seemed, he hadn't once expressed concern about his other kids now that Colette was dead. She wondered if he even knew that he was about to be a grandfather.

As they left Lance Fraley's home in the rearview mirror, Josie couldn't help but feel even more sad for Noah than she had before. She texted him to see how he was doing, but he didn't respond.

CHAPTER THIRTY-THREE

It was dark by the time they made it back to the station house. Gretchen booted up her computer to start looking for the mysterious Ivan while Josie tracked Mettner down to update him and see if he had gotten anywhere showing photos of the belt buckle to the residents at Rockview. Josie found him in the break room, seated at one of the tables eating a greasy slice of pizza. "Hey," he said around a mouthful of food. "The old-timers at Rockview were pretty helpful."

Josie raised a brow. "They're residents, Mett. Not old-timers."

He bobbed his head and swallowed. "Sorry, boss. Residents."

She sat across from him. He motioned to the box of pizza between them, but she shook her head. "What'd you get?"

He wiped his fingers on a napkin and took out his phone, scrolling and tapping until he found what he was looking for. "A couple of the guys there said that back in the seventies there used to be shooting clubs around here. All around the state, actually."

"Shooting clubs?"

"Yeah, like target shooting. They had competitions. There were at least a half dozen, they said. The guys in them would compete with rifles and pistols for speed and accuracy. Mostly outdoor ranges."

"Like a league?" Josie asked. "Like they have with bowling?"

"Yeah, exactly. I mean, it was just a bunch of local guys getting together, hanging out and competing. Anyway, for a few years they actually had championship shooting matches. All the clubs would enter their best shooter, and the last guy was the champion. He's the guy that got the belt buckle."

Josie felt a small thrill of excitement set off butterflies in her stomach. Finally, a lead on the belt buckle. "So that belt buckle belongs to the 1973 shooting champion?"

"That's what they think, yeah. In rifle shooting, on account of it having two rifles on it," Mettner said.

"So how do we track down these clubs? Did anyone have a name? Anything?"

Mettner shook his head. "No, but they said sometimes in the local papers they would report stuff about the competitions, and I'm talking the local papers, you know? Like the ones that don't exist anymore. I don't know if the local library would have them or not."

"They do have them," Josie said. "I know exactly where to look. Thanks, Mett!"

"What happened with Lance Fraley?" he asked.

Josie gave him a run-down of the interview with Noah's dad.

"Gretchen's working on locating this Ivan guy?" he asked.

"Yes. I'm going back upstairs now to write up some reports."

Back at the desk, Gretchen was having no luck finding a white male, approximately sixty-five years old, named Ivan. "I might have to go over to the Catholic church tomorrow, see if they kept records," she said.

Josie told her what Mettner had found out. "So you'll go to the church, and I'll go to the library."

"Yes," Gretchen said. "As long as Chitwood doesn't change his mind. But it's late so it'll have to wait till tomorrow."

"First thing," Josie agreed. "I'm going to get out of here now. I feel like I haven't seen Noah in weeks. I need to check on him."

CHAPTER THIRTY-FOUR

Josie went to Noah's favorite barbecue restaurant and got his favorite meal. It was what he would have done for her—what he had always done for her in times of great stress. He made sure she ate and got enough rest even when those were the last things she wanted to do.

She found him at Colette's. Every light in the house was on. The front door was unlocked. As she moved through the house calling his name, she saw boxes stacked in each room. Noah was in Colette's bedroom, throwing clothes from her dresser into an open box on the bed, sweat pouring from his temples down the sides of his face. His dampened T-shirt clung to his torso. His movements were frenetic. Once the box was full, he punched the clothes down inside it, taped it shut, and grabbed another box from the floor.

"Noah," Josie said as she set the takeout bag on the empty dresser.

"Hey," he said. He gave her a glance and kept going, yanking clothes off the hangers in the closet and stuffing them into the new box.

"You've been at this all day?" Josie said. "Have you eaten?"

"No," he said. "I just want to finish."

Josie took another step into the room and grabbed another empty box from the floor. "Let me help you," she said.

He didn't protest. They worked in silence until everything in the room was packed into boxes. Noah collapsed onto the edge of his mother's bed, shoulders slumped. His skin was pale, and dark circles smudged the skin below his eyes. Josie gave him a moment to catch his breath, sitting next to him and lightly stroking his back. "I brought you something to eat," she said. "Let's go down to the kitchen, okay? You need to eat."

He pointed at the bag. "Is that from Talulah's?"

"Yes," Josie said.

When he smiled at her, her heart skipped a beat. "Thank you," he said, reaching for the container, opening it, pulling out the sandwich and eating it where he sat. His movements gradually slowed from the manic pace of earlier, and Josie was surprised when, between mouthfuls, he asked her if there were any new developments. She started to tell him about her and Gretchen's day, but when she got to the part about interviewing his dad, Noah turned to stare at her, his mouth hanging open, a lump of half-chewed beef brisket visible. A red hue crept from his collar to the roots of his hair. He said, "You talked to my father? You went to his house? Behind my back? Without even talking to me?"

Josie stood up from the bed. "I didn't do it 'behind your back,'" she said, perplexed. "Noah, you know this was a legitimate line of inquiry."

"We're talking about my dad here," he said, his voice nearly a shout. He tossed the remains of his sandwich into its takeout container and paced the room.

"Yes, but to us he was a family member of one of our victims who might have had knowledge that would help our investigation. Noah, you know this."

"He's not a family member," Noah snarled. "He is not family to me. He abandoned my mother. He cheated on her, and then he walked out and never looked back."

Josie stood and tried to take one of his arms, but he swatted her away and continued to pace in the small area. "I'm sorry, Noah," Josie said. "I'm sorry that your mother died. I'm sorry we've had to speak to your father. I can't even imagine how painful this must be for you, but please know that Mettner, Gretchen and I are trying to find the person who killed your mother. That's all."

"What did he tell you?" Noah asked. "What did he say about her?"

"That she was a devoted wife and mother," Josie said. "He admitted to the cheating. He told me a story about you and a friend horsing around and you breaking your nose. He said he took you to the hospital."

Noah scoffed. "Yeah, only cause my mom was out."

"You were thirteen?" Josie coaxed.

"Yeah. Mom was so upset. Way, way more upset than any of us thought she'd be over a broken nose. I mean, one time Laura and I were fighting and we knocked over her curio cabinet, broke everything in it and fractured Laura's wrist. She was twelve. Needed three surgeries and a bunch of physical therapy. Cost my parents a fortune. Mom wasn't even that upset when that happened, but when I broke my nose… I don't know, maybe because it was on my face? I remember we were supposed to get our pictures taken for the baseball team—they made these frames for the pictures that made them look like fake baseball cards. Anyway, I looked like someone beat me up."

"It was spring?" Josie said.

"Yeah. Theo's birthday is April 28th. It was right before that. I remember because he came home to visit us and my mom was still pissed about the whole thing so she was in a really terrible mood the whole weekend, and Theo joked that I ruined his trip by getting mom so worked up." At this, he laughed. Then his brow kinked and he said, "Why would he tell that story? He wanted you to think he was this great, caring dad?"

"Wasn't he?" Josie asked, genuinely curious. "I mean, for the most part?"

"Well, yeah, I guess. I mean, until he walked out. But that's just it. How much could he have possibly cared? He started a whole new family," Noah said. "He spent thirty-four years with my mother, and then he walked away from her and started all over again. Discarded us like we were nothing."

Josie said, "I'm so sorry, Noah. He said he made efforts to reach out to you, Laura and Theo."

He snorted. "Efforts. He called me once. One time. Said if I ever wanted to get together, to just give him a call. That was his *effort*. He's a liar and a piece of shit. He didn't care about us or my mother. He hasn't been in our lives in almost fifteen years. You didn't need to talk to him. If you wanted to know about him, you could have asked."

"Noah, we go where the investigation takes us. You know this. Do you think I enjoyed it when my personal life—every horrible thing that ever happened to me in childhood— was picked apart last year? It was devastating. But I dealt with it—in part because you were there for me. I'm trying to be there for you."

"No, you're trying to solve a case."

Josie threw her arms in the air. "Yes, that too! I'm not trying to hide that. When I close my eyes at night, I still see your mother's face, just like you, and I see *your* face. I see the pain this has caused you, and I want to stop the person who did this and make them pay."

"You didn't need to go there today. Gretchen could have gone on her own. You could have asked me what happened with my dad, but instead you went there without even consulting me first. Did you get what you wanted?"

"What I wanted? I don't know what you're—"

Her words were cut off by the sound of glass breaking somewhere in the house. They both froze, meeting one another's eyes for a split second before rushing out the bedroom door and down the hall. The smell of something burning filled the air. Noah was in front of her, heading toward the stairs. Josie clamped a hand down on his shoulder. "Noah, he's here."

Billows of thick gray smoke snaked up the stairwell and licked the ceiling of the hallway.

"Get down," Josie said, tugging Noah down to the floor.

On their hands and knees, they crawled to the top of the steps, but the smoke was too thick for them to make their way down.

Josie's eyes watered; the fumes seared and scratched the back of her throat. Sweat slicked her skin, making her clothes feel heavy against her. She grabbed at Noah's calf to stop him from going any further. He looked over his shoulder at her, but his face was barely visible through the thickening smoke. Josie knew that with fires, inhalation was the main cause of death. She pointed toward one of the doors in the hall. "The bathroom!" she shouted.

They crawled down the hall toward the bathroom, Josie closing the door behind them and leaning against it, her breath coming hard, chest burning. Boxes lined one wall of the narrow, cramped space. Noah tore one open and pulled out towels which he wet under the tap. He handed her one and she swiped at her face, the cold feeling like heaven against her flaming skin.

"I think the downstairs might be fully engulfed by now," Josie said. She took out her cell phone from her back pocket and dialed 911, asking the dispatcher to send the fire department and an ambulance immediately. A cough erupted from her chest as she pocketed her phone. Noah pried the bathroom window open and punched out the screen, extending his head outside.

Josie stood. "How far down is it?"

He brought his upper body back inside and motioned for her to look. From the window, Josie could see dark smoke pouring from the downstairs windows of the house. Directly below was a sheer drop into one of Colette's perfectly pruned flower beds. They were high enough to break something should they have to jump, but not enough to kill themselves. Josie turned back to see smoke filtering under the bathroom door and grabbed one of the wet towels, pressing it tight against the gap.

Noah said, "We can't wait. We're going to have to jump. Another five or ten minutes and the upstairs will be engulfed as well."

"You're right," Josie said, coughing again.

Noah tore the shower curtain down and twisted one corner of it around his left hand and wrist. "I'm going to hang this out the window and hold onto it. If you slide down it, you can drop to the ground without getting hurt."

"What about you?" Josie asked.

"I'll be fine."

Josie motioned to the window. "No, you won't. Noah, you're going to get hurt if you jump."

"Then I'll get hurt. Josie, we have to get out of here. Now."

He pushed her toward the window. Josie climbed out and let her body slide down the siding, her palms hanging onto the window sill. Once she was suspended there, heat and smoke blowing up from beneath her, Noah leaned out, throwing the shower curtain out beside her. Using one hand, Josie grabbed a handful of the vinyl material. It wouldn't hold for long, but it would be enough for her to slide down and soften her fall. Once she had a firm grip on it with her right hand, she transferred all her weight to the shower curtain and took her left hand from the window sill and wrapped it around the curtain. Above her, Noah's face reddened and dripped with sweat from exertion. "Go," he told her.

Little by little, she slid down the curtain until there were only inches left. She had no choice but to let go. With a glance down, she saw that she had gotten much closer to the ground. Maybe only five or six feet separated her feet from the dirt below. With one last look at Noah, she let go, her body sliding down the exterior of the house, and her feet landing hard in the soil below. A shock went through her heels up to her thighs, and her knees buckled, sending her flat on her ass. But she was safe and nothing was broken. The shower curtain flew away from the house, and Noah's legs appeared in the window—first one, then the other—until he was dangling from the window just as Josie had just been.

She heard the crack of bone breaking as he landed. He writhed on the ground, clutching his leg. Josie knelt beside him, watching his mouth yawn open to scream out in pain, but as he struggled for breath, no sound came. She didn't know if the fall had knocked the wind out of him, if the pain was making it difficult to take in air or if the toxic smoke they'd inhaled made it hard for him to breathe, but there was nothing she could do but wait for his breath to return. When it did, she helped him up, fitting her body under his left arm. He kept his left foot up off the ground as they hobbled together away from the house. Josie heard sirens in the distance. As she deposited Noah onto the neighbor's front yard, she glanced around to see many of the street's residents had turned their lights on and come outside. The fire, now fully engulfing Colette's home, lit up the entire street. Josie's eyes tracked the various vehicles parked in driveways. No vehicles were parked along the street. Then she saw a crumpled form in the middle of the road. "Wait here," she told Noah. "And don't move."

Josie unsnapped her holster as she raced toward the figure, but as soon as she got to him, she realized he wasn't a threat. It was an older man, probably in his seventies, judging by his thinning white hair and wrinkled, age-spotted face. Curled on his side, he groaned. Josie knelt down and touched his shoulder gingerly. "Sir," she said. "Are you okay?"

"He hit me," the man rasped. "Son of a bitch hit me."

Gently, she turned him onto his back. "Where did he hit you?"

Sweat poured off Josie's brow, and her chest felt heavy. The man pointed to his stomach. "Here," he gasped. "Hit me hard, too. I went right down."

"Who hit you?" Josie asked, pressing two fingers against the inside of his wrist to check his pulse, which was strong and steady.

"The guy burning Colette's house down," he said. "Help me sit up."

Josie slid an arm under his shoulders and lifted him to sitting. "You saw someone? What did he look like?"

"Big. Burly. Dressed all in black. He had a ballcap on. I live over there—" He turned slightly and pointed to the house directly across from Colette's. "I saw Noah come in this morning. Talked to him. I've seen you here a few times so when you pulled up, I knew it was okay."

Josie wondered whether he had been watching Colette's home this closely before her murder. As if reading her mind, he said, "I only started paying attention after Colette was killed over there. It's terrible. A terrible thing. These things don't happen around here."

Josie glanced back at Colette's house where two fire trucks and an ambulance had just shown up. She watched as two paramedics rushed over to where Noah lay on his neighbor's grass. "I know," she said. "They shouldn't happen anywhere. What happened? You saw him coming out of the house?"

"I saw him go in. He came walking from down there." He pointed down the street from Colette's house. "Then I waited a few minutes. I noticed what looked like fire in the downstairs window. Came out to the end of the driveway. Still wasn't sure what I was looking at. Heard some commotion in there so I came out here to the street. Then I saw smoke coming out the windows and I knew. I was going to go back inside and call 911, but then he came running out from behind the house, right in my direction."

"Did you see his face?" Josie asked.

The man shook his head. "Not really. He had that cap on. It wasn't as bright out here as it is now. It looked like he had dark eyes—beady, like a rat, and a flat nose like it was broke a few times. That's all I can tell you." He groaned and held his stomach. "It hurts. He hit me hard. I told him to stop. He never even said anything. Just punched me in the gut and ran off."

"I know you're in pain right now, but can you estimate height and weight?"

"Maybe five foot ten?" he said uncertainly. "Two hundred pounds?"

"Boss!" It was Mettner rushing toward her from his patrol car. Behind him trailed paramedics from a second ambulance, rolling a gurney with them.

As the paramedics lifted the elderly neighbor onto the gurney and took him off to the ambulance, Josie gave Mettner all the information she had as quickly as possible, including a description of the man seen fleeing Colette's home. "I want units out looking for this guy," Josie said. "He was on foot so he may have parked not far from here. Get someone to canvass residents on the neighboring streets to see if they saw any strange cars, strange men or anything unusual."

"You got it, boss," Mettner said, jogging off.

Josie stood alone in the middle of the street, staring down the small hill in the direction the arsonist had gone. She glanced back to where Noah was being loaded into an ambulance. The firemen were already blasting their hoses at what was left of Colette's house, trying to contain the fire. As the ambulance with Noah in it pulled away, Josie sprinted down the hill.

CHAPTER THIRTY-FIVE

As she ran, lungs burning, Josie mapped the neighborhood in her mind. Colette's home was the last one at the top of the hill before it crested and went downhill in the other direction. Her house backed up to a short span of woods that led to a rockface. The development had basically been carved into the side of a mountain. The killer wouldn't have gone through the back because there was nowhere to go. He could have gone through the backyards but most of them had high privacy fences and had he made a lot of noise in someone's backyard, he might have been easily spotted back there and perhaps even trapped. If he had wanted to draw the least amount of attention after setting a fire, simply running down the street in one direction or the other would be most effective. It was still risky because he would be in plain view, but it was more direct and posed fewer potential pitfalls than trying to navigate the series of backyards that terminated at the foot of a rock wall. Also, he would be moving under the cover of night, which gave him an advantage.

He had to have parked nearby. When Josie got to the first intersection at the bottom of the hill, she turned right. Here it was darker although many houses began lighting up, probably in response to the commotion at the top of the hill. Josie ran down the street, her gaze panning right to left and left to right for anyone or anything out of place. There was nothing. The street was silent and still. Only four cars were parked on the street. She checked them all, glancing inside for any figures and then feeling their hoods to see if they were warm. Nothing. A moment later, one of Denton's units rolled past her. She gave them a wave and kept jogging until her lungs erupted into a coughing fit that nearly made her vomit. After working through seven or eight of the surrounding city blocks and finding nothing, she took out her cell phone and dialed Gretchen.

"Come get me," Josie told her. "I don't think I can walk all the way back."

*

Josie was beginning to hate Denton Hospital. She only had one good memory of the place and that was the night she had saved baby Harris Quinn from drowning. All her other memories of the hospital were traumatic. Her mind catalogued the last several visits as she lay on a bed behind a curtain waiting for Gretchen to return with news of Noah. Josie had looked frantically for him when they arrived, but he had been taken up to surgery. His leg break was worse than she'd thought.

"Honey, you should keep this on," said a nurse, flitting around the bed and tucking the nasal cannula from the oxygen tank into Josie's nostrils. She slipped a small clip onto Josie's index finger and wrapped a blood pressure cuff around her upper arm—for the third time since Josie had arrived.

"I'm fine," Josie said.

"Well," the nurse said as the cuff squeezed, squeezed, squeezed and slowly released, "We'll let the doctor be the judge of that. Your oxygen saturation is good, actually, considering what you've been through, but your blood pressure's up a bit, hon."

"That's from stress," Gretchen said, pushing the curtain aside and stepping up to Josie's bedside. "Noah broke the shaft of his fibula."

"Ouch," Josie winced.

"Yeah, it was displaced. They had to do surgery to realign it. Should be a few hours. Want me to call his sister?"

"No, but I guess we have to," Josie said. "She'll want to know. Especially with all that's happened."

Josie pulled Laura's number up on her cell phone, but Gretchen took the phone from her. "I'll handle that," she said. "You just rest a bit."

Gretchen stepped out of the room, returning a few minutes later with a grimace on her face. She handed Josie her phone. "She and her husband will be here in a few hours."

"I guess no one found anything—the guy running from the fire wasn't located?" Josie asked.

"Sorry, boss," Gretchen said. "Nothing."

"Well that's just great," Josie said. "Listen, I know this is a stretch, but it's the only lead we've got—I think we need to work harder at tracking down this Ivan person."

"You think Colette's friend from grade school is running around killing people and burning their houses down?" Gretchen asked.

"Before the fire broke out, Noah confirmed what Lance said about breaking his nose when he was thirteen—in April—the same month that Samuel Pratt died. According to Noah, his mom's reaction was disproportionate to what happened. Evidently, he and Laura roughhoused a lot and she had had a much more serious injury before that, but Colette didn't get upset back then. But when Noah broke his nose…"

"You think she wasn't actually upset about Noah's broken nose," Gretchen said.

"Right. I think whatever she discussed with Ivan that day was the thing that upset her. It just happened to coincide with Noah's broken nose and Samuel Pratt's death," Josie said. "The timeframe fits."

"So who the hell was Ivan to her really?" Gretchen asked. "Do you think they were lovers? Are we back to the jealous lover theory?"

"She was seeing Ivan and Samuel Pratt and Ivan killed Pratt out of jealousy?" Josie said. "I'm not entirely comfortable with that theory, but I think Ivan is involved. It's the only lead we have."

It was only the whisper of a lead, and a real stretch at that, but Josie was desperate to stop the slaughter in Denton as quickly as possible, especially with Noah in harm's way.

"There's also the belt buckle," Gretchen said. "So our plan is the same—you see what you can find at the library, I visit the church. If Chitwood will let me. Maybe if I tag along with Mettner, he'll okay it."

"You and Mett should go," Josie agreed. "First thing in the morning. But I also think we need to talk to everyone Colette knew again to see if anyone else remembers this guy or anything else that raises red flags. Anyone we can find who goes back the last twenty years. Maybe they know something and they don't know that they know it."

"So church folks and co-workers," Gretchen said. She took out her notebook, flipping back several pages. "Mettner told me that there were a handful of each who knew her going back that long. Not many, but a few. We can split them up. Mettner and I will take the church folks, you take Sutton Stone Enterprises?"

"You saw Colette's boss at the funeral. He was obviously very fond of her, given the way he fawned over her children. I think I can get him to help."

The nurse came back and checked Josie's vitals once more, again pushing the nasal cannula deeper into Josie's nostrils. She fussed over her for a few minutes before bustling off. Once she was gone, Josie said, "You have to get me out of here, though. I need to be there when Noah gets out of surgery."

CHAPTER THIRTY-SIX

Josie slept fitfully in a vinyl chair next to Noah's hospital bed. He woke a few times during the night, groggy and dazed. Each time she took his hand and spoke softly to him, assuring him that everything was fine, which felt like a lie. His mother had been murdered; her house had been burnt to the ground, and Josie and Noah had nearly perished in the fire. In his anesthesia-induced stupor, Noah accepted her words, giving her hand a squeeze before drifting back off to sleep. She studied his pale face with the dark circles beneath his eyes, her gaze traveling down to the IV feeding pain medication into the crook of his right arm and down to the long cast wrapped round his leg, elevated on pillows. He looked small somehow, as though the last couple of weeks had sapped something vital from him and shrunk him down.

By the time the daylight streamed through the large windows, every part of Josie's body ached. Her eyes burned with fatigue, and her chest still felt heavy. The taste of soot and smoke coated the back of her throat. Noah's chest rose and fell evenly. Josie went into the bathroom and splashed her face with cold water, then sucked some of it down her throat, drinking directly from the faucet. There was a small tube of toothpaste along with several items in a small plastic yellow bin on one of the bathroom shelves. She used her index finger to rub some of it along her teeth.

She emerged to find Laura standing over Noah's bed, holding one of his hands and stroking his hair, her giant belly pressed against the bedrail. She looked up when Josie came in. "You're here."

"I've been here all night," Josie said, trying not to sound defensive.

"What the hell is going on, Josie?" Laura asked. Tears glistened in her eyes.

Before Josie could answer, Grady walked in with a cup carrier filled with four paper coffee cups, and sugar and creamer packets stuffed into the center. Immediately, he approached Josie, pecking her on the cheek and handing her a cup from the carrier. "I'm so sorry to hear what happened," he said. "We're so glad you two are okay." He looked at Noah as he set the rest of the cups down on the tray table. "Well, not completely okay, but alive."

Tears streamed down Laura's face. "I can't do this. Whatever this is, whatever's happening, it needs to stop."

"We're trying to get to the bottom of it," Josie assured her.

The coffee was a salve to Josie's exhausted and frayed nerves. Grady encouraged her to fix it as she liked it, and she did, guzzling it down. The three of them talked about what had transpired the night before while they waited for Noah to wake. Laura was intermittently hysterical and stoic with Grady calmly managing her rollercoaster of emotions. Josie was relieved that he was there. He sat on the other side of Noah, sipping his own coffee and watching his wife pace before him.

"Laura," Josie asked, once all their questions about the fire had been answered. "Do you remember your mother ever meeting with or keeping in touch with anyone from her Catholic elementary school?"

Laura stopped walking and pressed two fists against her lower back. "What? What do you mean?"

"Was there anyone that you remember your mother keeping in touch with from Catholic school? Specifically, a man."

Laura shook her head. "I don't think so. No. I don't remember anyone."

"Does the name Ivan mean anything to you?"

Her fists dug deeper into her sacrum, and a grimace spread across her face. "Who?"

"Ivan," Josie said. "Do you know anyone named Ivan? Did your mother know anyone named Ivan?"

"No, I don't think so. I definitely don't know anyone by that name. Why?"

"It was a name that came up when we spoke to your father," Josie said. "We're trying to figure out the significance."

"You talked to our father? Does Noah know?"

"Yes, I talked to him about it."

"And he was okay with it? That's hard to imagine." It sounded like an accusation.

Josie kept her voice even. "He had to be interviewed as part of the investigation. It's pretty standard stuff."

Laura opened her mouth to snap back, but the sound of Noah groaning stopped her. All three of their heads turned to stare at him. His eyelids fluttered open. He looked around slowly, blinking away his fatigue. "What the hell happened?" he croaked.

Josie was at one side of his bed, Laura on the other, both of them talking at once. He held up a hand to indicate for them to stop. He looked at Josie. "Are you okay?"

She smiled. "Yes, I'm fine."

"How bad is my leg?"

"It was a clean break but displaced. They had to do surgery to realign it, but you'll make a full recovery. The doctors don't anticipate you having any problems with it once it heals."

"But you're going to have to stay off it for a while," Laura told him. She shot a glance at Josie. "I'm his next of kin. I spoke with the doctor before I came in."

Josie said nothing.

"It hurts like hell," Noah said.

"I'll ask if they can give you more pain medication," Josie said.

Laura said, "They're going to discharge you tomorrow. I think you should come home with me and Grady."

"What?" Josie blurted.

"I'm fine," Noah said. "I just need some crutches."

"You need care," Laura said.

"I'm fine," Noah repeated.

"And yet you're here in the hospital with a broken leg after barely escaping a fire," she pointed out. "You're not fine. I don't know what the hell is going on in this town, but I think you need to get out of here for a while. You're under enough stress as it is. You need a support system."

But Noah was already dozing off again. Josie bit back the words itching to burst from her mouth. Starting a war with Noah's sister was the last thing any of them needed. Plus, as much as Josie hated to admit it and hated the thought of being separated from Noah even more, Laura was right. He would be safer two hours away with her and Grady.

Laura squeezed Noah's forearm until his eyes sprung open again. "Baby brother," she said. "Promise you'll come home with me."

He looked at her and then his head lolled to the other side, his eyes meeting Josie's. She managed a tight smile.

Laura pressed on. "Do you know anyone named Ivan?"

"What?" Josie said.

Laura ignored her, leaning down into Noah's face. "Josie was asking about someone named Ivan. She thinks our mother was somehow involved with someone named Ivan when we were kids."

"What are you talking about?" Noah asked, his eyes clouded with fatigue and confusion. He turned back to Josie again. "Who is Ivan?"

Josie folded her arms across her chest. "Just someone your dad mentioned. He said he saw your mom with a man the day you broke your nose. Your mom said the guy's name was Ivan, and they went to school together. We're are running it down as a potential lead."

Laura laughed. "So every person my mother ever talked to now is a potential killer? I'm sorry I brought it up. Noah, you don't remember anyone named Ivan, do you?"

Josie wondered why she had brought it up. She seemed determined to drive a wedge between her and Noah, but Josie couldn't fathom why. Colette hadn't warmed to Josie, but she had never actively tried to keep them apart.

Noah still looked stunned, but he shook his head. "No, I've never heard of anyone named Ivan. Don't remember Mom having any male friends by that name." He closed his eyes but kept talking, his voice raspy with exhaustion and pain. "Josie, you can't believe anything my dad says. He's a liar."

"We don't need to talk about this now," Josie pointed out.

"I don't want to talk about it ever," Noah said. "Please. You knew where I stood with my dad, and you went to see him anyway."

"Noah," Josie said. "I was doing my job. I don't think you're thinking clearly right now. You've been through a lot."

"I need some time," Noah mumbled. "Time alone."

"Time alone?" Josie echoed, cheeks stinging with heat. "What are you—what are you saying?" She couldn't help but wonder if he meant time away from *her*. Temporarily, or permanently, asked a quiet voice in the back of her head. Had the rift between them really grown that large?

"Yes," Laura interjected. "I think time alone is exactly what you need." She looked pointedly at Josie. "Time away from all of this drama, all of these ridiculous questions."

Josie was certain Laura really meant time away from her. "Well," Josie said to Laura. "He doesn't need to answer any questions right now. He just needs to rest and heal."

Laura crossed her arms over her belly. "He can do that with us, right Grady?" She looked beyond Josie to her husband.

Grady's expression was pinched as he stood up and clapped his hands together. "Uh, sure," he said. "Noah's always welcome." He offered Josie a tight smile. "And you can come by anytime to see him."

"Grady," Laura snapped. "Do you really think that's a good idea?"

"What?" Josie asked.

Laura pointed a finger at Josie. "Every time you're around, something dreadful happens. I'm just trying to protect my baby brother. I think you two need a break from one another."

"I don't—" Josie was at a loss for words. Well, there were many words she wanted to say to Laura in that moment, but she didn't want to upset Noah or cause him any more stress. The strain on him already was beyond what she could bear to see him endure. Even if she wasn't welcome at Laura and Grady's home, Noah staying there would put him out of harm's way, and that was what mattered most.

She looked down at Noah's face. "Is this what you want?" she asked softly.

His gaze flitted to his sister and then back to Josie before he nodded and closed his eyes.

"Okay," Josie muttered, willing tears not to form in her eyes. "Go with Laura and Grady. I'll work with Mettner and Gretchen to make this right."

CHAPTER THIRTY-SEVEN

The Denton Library was a two-floor stone building designed by a local architect in the early 1900s in neoclassical style, complete with a grand staircase and large Doric columns. Josie had spent many hours as a teenager tucked away among the shelves, studying in the reverent hush that presided over the massive collection of books. In the intervening years, much of the building had been modernized, upgrading from tables to computer stations and expanding into conference and activity rooms. But even the beloved building failed to cheer her up as she trudged inside. Fatigue burned through every cell in her body. She felt as though she was weighed down by an invisible cloak. She couldn't shake her sadness over the disconnect between her and Noah. That's what it was, Josie had realized on her way from the hospital to the library: a disconnect. They'd been side by side almost every day for the last four years, moving through their personal and professional lives together with a natural ease. They had fallen in love and after many false starts, begun their romantic relationship. Josie thought they'd been tested in the past by some of their more shocking and difficult cases, but it was only now, only with this particular case, that she felt herself unmoored from Noah in a way she didn't like at all.

As Josie approached the information desk, she wondered if there was something fundamentally wrong with her that she couldn't be there for the significant other in her life. But that wasn't true. She'd seen Ray through many things before he'd died, and there had been a serious relationship—an engagement—to a state trooper named Luke Creighton after Ray. She had faithfully cared for him for over a year after he was shot and lost his spleen. So why was she getting it so wrong in her attempts to be there for Noah?

"Miss? Can I help you? Miss?"

Josie blinked and gave her head a quick shake, trying to focus on the task at hand. She explained to the librarian what she was looking for, and the woman led her to a computer station on the second floor. Josie was already familiar with the electronic database, but she was too tired to stop the woman from giving her a spiel. She didn't listen to much of it, only the part where the woman suggested that the items Josie was searching for were most likely in either the *Denton Tribune* or the *Bellewood Record*, but since the *Record* was a smaller paper, something like the results of shooting club competitions would have been more likely to be printed in it.

Josie thanked the woman for her assistance and started with the *Bellewood Record*, searching back to the early seventies for shooting clubs, shooting competitions and gun clubs. There were listings of the dates, times and locations of several competitions in the back of the *Bellewood Record* between 1970 and 1975 in the same area where the local churches listed their food drives, Easter egg hunts, potluck dinners and other services. She checked the papers in the days after each competition, but no results were listed. She expanded her search parameters to include the 1980s but still found nothing. She switched over to the *Denton Tribune* where she found a small article from 1976 in the bottom corner of the "Local" section titled: "Tri-County Shooting League Disbanded".

In the late sixties, Brody Wolicki and a couple of his friends were having a few beers after their weekly target practice when they got into a friendly argument about who was the most accurate shot. The next week, they had an informal competition at the outdoor range in Bellewood, and Wolicki lost. He wanted another chance, so the next month they competed again. From these informal competitions came the idea to form a target practice club so there would be more shooters to compete with. Within a couple of years, target practice clubs had popped up in Alcott County and two of its neighboring counties. Wolicki saw an opportunity for fun and the expansion of his favorite hobby. He formed the Tri-County Target Practice League and organized tournaments where the clubs could compete for most accurate shooter. Competitions were held four times a year with a final championship meet held every fall. Wolicki collected dues from each club which he used to fund the meets and prizes for best shooter. "We started out with trophies," Wolicki said. "Then someone got the idea for belt buckles, and people liked that better."

For six years, shooters participated in Wolicki's annual league tournament, the champion shooter earning the respect and admiration of his fellow league members as well as a nice bauble to wear to show off their accomplishment.

"But then people didn't want to pay," Wolicki says.

Membership in the Tri-County League dropped off, which Wolicki says wasn't enough to endanger the league. "It was when members started questioning why they needed to pay membership dues. What do these guys think? All of this is free? Someone has to pay for range time, the refreshments and the prizes. It can't all come out of my pocket."

So this year will be the last target practice championship for the Tri-County League. "Makes me sad to disband the league," Wolicki says. "But I don't have much choice. You need shooters to have the tournaments. If shooters don't pay, they don't join the league. No league, no competitions."

Wolicki has no plans to give up his own hobby. "I'll keep shooting," he says. "I love getting out there on the range, but it's time for someone else to take up the reins if people want to compete."

Josie read the article twice and then scoured both newspapers for more stories about the target practice league from 1965 through

1977, but she found nothing. The league had only been in existence for six years. Why was there no mention of the champions' names?

"Because that would be too easy," she muttered to herself.

She printed the article, scooped it out of the nearby printer, and left the library. If Brody Wolicki was still alive, maybe he would know the name of the winner of the belt buckle in 1973.

CHAPTER THIRTY-EIGHT

With a sudden surge of energy from having found a clue to the belt buckle, she decided to drive right to Sutton Stone Enterprises headquarters to talk to Zachary Sutton. Mettner had done some initial research into the company before he interviewed Colette's old co-workers, which he had shared with Josie. So that's how Josie knew that the company headquarters were located forty-five minutes southeast of Denton in a remote, mountainous rural area. The headquarters building was a tall, modern glass edifice perched on the edge of the original Sutton family quarry which had been founded by Zachary Sutton's great-grandfather in the late 1800s. The quarry was miles from any town, although a tiny hamlet called Mount Haven twelve miles away had claimed it as part of their postal area.

Zachary Sutton had taken over the business as a young man under his father's tutelage in the 1960s and expanded the company to other areas of the state, buying up more land and opening more cracks in the earth. Zachary Sutton had also expanded their product line to include more than just bluestone and marble, offering aggregate, which was a coarse particulate material used in construction projects the world over, as well as soil and turf products. Josie knew that he had initially paid Laura Fraley-Hall big bucks to manage the entire company's public relations department. Colette had often bragged to Josie about how one of the first things Laura had done as the director of PR was community outreach in the towns in which Sutton's quarries were located, building goodwill among local citizens and buffing Sutton Stone Enterprise's reputation to a perfect shine. She had done so well that she easily moved up the ranks until she reached her current position of vice president of the entire company.

Josie's ears popped as she drove a winding mountain road to the quarry entrance. Tall foliage rose up on either side of the road, making her feel closed in and yet, as she crested the hill and the Sutton Stone Enterprises building gleamed and flashed in the spectacular sunlight, she felt like she was on top of the world. She parked in the visitor lot and walked toward the entrance. A glimpse of the quarry below gave her a bit of vertigo. Trucks, heavy equipment, and piles of stone were toy-sized in the bottom of the huge crater in the earth, devoid of anything but ribbons of various types of stone. She clasped a nearby railing to steady herself. Around the edges of the quarry was forest, stretching as far as the eye could see.

Inside the double doors was a reception desk, manned by a gray-haired lady in a pink blouse. Josie presented her credentials and asked to speak to Mr. Sutton. The woman tutted but picked up the phone and dialed Sutton's extension. She seemed surprised when he told her to send Josie right up to his office, speaking loudly and clearly enough for Josie to hear through the receiver. The receptionist gave her directions and she followed a winding set of stairs up two stories to a glass balcony that overlooked the lobby. Josie saw Zachary Sutton's large office immediately. Double glass doors enclosed it, but beyond the large desk and guest reception area in the center of the room, was a wall of windows; the daylight streaming through nearly blinding. Josie wondered if it would be steaming hot inside, the way a greenhouse was, but when Sutton met her at the doors and ushered her in, it was surprisingly cool.

In front of his desk was a low, white, modern coffee table surrounded by four coral-colored chairs. "Have a seat," Sutton said, smiling. "I remember you from Colette's funeral. We didn't have a chance to officially meet, but Noah did point you out to me. You're his lady friend, correct?"

"Uh, yes," Josie said, perching on the edge of one of the chairs. "Noah and I work together at the Denton Police Department."

Sutton sat across from her and rested his left ankle on top of his right knee. He wore khaki pants with loafers and a blue collared shirt, open at the neck, no tie. His hands, large and veiny, rested on the shin of his left leg. "I suppose you're here as an officer of the law then. I heard from Laura this morning about the fire at Colette's house. Horribly tragic, especially after her death. I'm sorry to hear about Noah's leg, but I am quite glad no one was killed."

"Me too," Josie said.

"What I can help you with, dear?" Sutton asked. "Your colleague was here last week and interviewed nearly everyone here."

"Mettner is very thorough," Josie said. "We just had some follow-up questions. You knew Colette for decades."

Sutton nodded, a look both sad and wistful passing over his lined face. "She was in her early twenties when she began working here, I believe. She was in the secretary pool. She was very good at what she did. Eventually, my father promoted her to his assistant, and when I took over three years later—in 1980, I believe—she came with the office."

"So you worked closely with her for many years," Josie said.

"Oh, yes. Many years. We saw each other through many things. Ups and downs at the company, the births of her children, the deaths of her mother and my father, and the dissolution of her marriage."

"It sounds like you were very close."

"Well, as close as a boss and employee could be, I suppose. As close as two people like us could be." A little laugh accompanied this statement.

"What do you mean?" Josie said.

"The reason Colette and I got on so well for so long is because we were very similar. Private, reserved, stoic; not given to dramatic displays of emotion. You know, when her husband left her, she came into my office and said, 'My marriage is over. I'm struggling a bit and may need to use some of my personal days,' in the same tone she used to read off my schedule for the week."

"Matter-of-fact."

"Yes."

"Did you ever see her cry?"

One bushy white brow kinked. "Yeah, I guess. Maybe once when one of her kids broke their nose?"

"I heard that story, too," Josie said. "It was Noah. He had to have pictures taken right after that, and he looked like someone had beaten him."

Sutton laughed. "Boys will be unruly. I told her not to worry. The swelling would go down, and the bruises would fade, and her son would be as handsome as always."

"How about you? Do you have children?" Josie asked.

He waved a hand. "No, not me. Never married. No children. This company is my baby. My labor of love."

Josie glanced at the bank of windows which showed a sheer drop into the depths of the quarry. "It's quite an empire you've got here. What will happen when you retire? If you don't mind me asking."

He winked at her. "Everyone wants to know that. Because I have no heirs. Well, if I tell you, don't you have to keep it a secret? Being an officer of the law?"

Josie smiled. "I think you're thinking of a priest or a lawyer. No, I have no confidentiality requirements, but I promise not to tell anyone of consequence."

Sutton raised a hand and waggled an index finger, a small smile on his face. "Not even Noah?"

Josie smiled tightly, thinking that Noah wasn't in any shape to talk with her so it wouldn't make any difference. "Not even Noah," she said.

"I'm grooming Laura to take over. She's the best fit. I've already made arrangements, although I haven't told her yet."

"Laura Fraley?" Josie asked, momentarily shocked though she shouldn't have been. She knew how dedicated Laura was to Sutton Stone Enterprises and how much she loved her job, and she was already the Vice President.

He nodded.

Josie said, "Mr. Sutton, I have to ask you some questions that might make you uncomfortable. About Colette. I don't like doing it, but it has to be done."

"We never had an affair," he said easily. "That's what you think, isn't it? Besides her mother, husband and children, I was in Colette's life the longest. I was very good to her, and now her daughter will become the president of this company. It's only natural to make that assumption. I think many people have over the years—people in the company, at any rate—the big business owner always... romances his secretary, right?"

Josie stared at him. "I don't know that that is an assumption every person would make. But it's an avenue of investigation I can't ignore."

"I understand."

"Do you know if Colette ever had affairs with anyone else?"

"I don't think so. If she had, I don't think she would have told me. We didn't have that kind of relationship."

"Did she ever mention anyone named Ivan?"

He raised a brow. "That actually sounds familiar."

Josie said, "We believe they were school mates."

He snapped his fingers. "I think that was the young man she asked me to hire!"

"She asked you to hire someone?"

"Decades ago. I think that was his name. It was an unusual name, and I do remember her telling me she had gone to school with him," Sutton explained.

"How long ago was this?" Josie asked, feeling excitement spiral up from her stomach.

Sutton rubbed his chin as he thought about it. "I had just taken over from my dad. I know that because she asked me to hire him, not my father, which means I had to have taken over by then."

"What did she want you to hire him to do?"

He shrugged. "As I recall, anything. She said he was in a bad way, but he was a good person and needed work."

"Did you hire him?"

"I did, as a laborer, if memory serves." He looked her in the eye. "Detective Quinn, you must understand this was quite a long time ago. My memory isn't that good. I wouldn't take this as gospel. This young man could have been named anything."

But Josie was sure he was named Ivan.

"How long did he work here?" Josie asked.

"Oh it wasn't that long, I don't think. A few years, perhaps? I've had many employees, detective. I can't remember them all."

"Do your personnel records go back that far?" Josie asked hopefully.

He smiled. "They just might, but those records—if we still have them—would be at an off-site storage facility. I do maintain my own storage though so I can call over there and have my staff take a look. You know, the wonder of technology—I can even have them scan whatever they find and email it to you. Isn't that miraculous?" he laughed.

Josie couldn't help but smile. "It is, I suppose."

"Oh, it is. You're too young to remember a time before all this technology was at our fingertips. It is truly amazing."

"Do you think I could have any personnel records you have going back to the time Ivan would have been hired? We're trying to track down anyone Colette might have been close to so if there were employees who worked with her for a long time, we would want to track them down and speak to them."

He stood and walked over to his desk. "Let me write this down, dear." He picked up a pen and scribbled on a notepad. Then he opened one of his desk drawers and pulled out a business card. Josie stood and walked over to take it from him. "My direct line is on there," he said. "If you give me your card, I'll pass your contact information to my staff and have them get you whatever you need. But you keep my card in case you have any issues."

Josie fished her own card out of her jacket pocket and gave it to him. "I really appreciate this, Mr. Sutton."

The skin around his eyes crinkled. "Of course, dear. Colette was a lovely person. I hope you'll find her some justice."

CHAPTER THIRTY-NINE

Josie trudged into the great room at the station. All the adrenaline from her meeting with Zachary Sutton and the potential lead on Ivan had leeched away during the drive back. Three separate texts and one phone call to Noah to see how he was feeling went unanswered. She prayed that Chief Chitwood's door was closed or that he was otherwise engaged, but she wasn't that lucky; the moment her rear end hit her desk chair, Chitwood's voice boomed across the room. "Quinn!"

She swiveled in her chair and looked at him standing in his office doorway, his trademark wispy white hair floating wildly around his balding head. "Sir?" she said.

Josie was prepared for a tirade about the attention the Colette Fraley-Beth Pratt case was drawing with the latest fire but all he said was, "How's Fraley feeling? You talk to him this morning?"

Josie swiped a hand over her face. "Yeah," she said. "I did. He was still a little dazed, had some pain, but he was okay."

Chitwood nodded. "I stopped in during the night after he was out of surgery, but you were both asleep."

It was exactly what Josie would have done when she was chief and two of her officers had narrowly escaped a fire, but didn't seem in keeping with Chitwood's abrasive personality. She wondered if perhaps he was warming up a little? He said, "You, Mettner and Palmer, in my office at four sharp to brief me on this catastrophe—and I expect some progress."

"Maybe not," Josie muttered under her breath as Chitwood's office door slammed.

She had just found a current address for Brody Wolicki when Gretchen appeared beside her, depositing a paper coffee cup and a bag from Komorrah's Koffee onto her desk.

Josie snatched up the bag and tore it open to find two cheese Danishes inside. She looked up at Gretchen who sat at her own desk, sipping from her coffee. With mock seriousness, Josie said, "I think we should get married."

Gretchen laughed, drops of coffee spilling down her chin. She wiped them away with the sleeve of her jacket. "Noah might have something to say about that."

Josie bit into a Danish and shook her head. "No, I don't think so."

She filled Gretchen in on the morning's awkwardness with Noah and his sister.

"Well," Gretchen said. "It is better if he's not in the area. Safer. If he wants time, give him time. He does love you, you know."

Josie sighed. She wasn't sure that was going to be enough, but there were more serious issues to attend to than her own hurt feelings. "Well I've got some exciting developments—I think. Let's get Mett up here." She called him on his cell phone and five minutes later, he was sitting at Noah's empty desk so Josie could fill them in on the Wolicki article and on her meeting with Sutton. Mettner tapped away excitedly on his phone as Josie spoke.

"How long do you think it will take to get the personnel records?" he asked.

Josie shrugged. "If they go back that far? Possibly a week. I asked Sutton before I left. How'd it go with the Catholic church?"

Mettner nodded to Gretchen who picked up a sheaf of papers from her desk and handed it to Josie. "Here is a list of students enrolled in St. Agatha's elementary school between 1958 and 1966. Colette's name is on here. No one named Ivan."

"What?" Josie said, skimming the names on the pages. "Are you kidding me?"

"I wish I was," Gretchen said. "Especially if those personnel records don't pan out. Anyway, that's the bad news. The good news is that I've got another lead. Look at the faculty names."

Josie found the names of the nuns and lay teachers who had taught at St. Agatha's when Colette was a student there. "I see them."

"There was a nun there, Sister Mary Elsa. Her real name is Tracy Schmidt. She left the church in 1967."

"Left the church?"

"Yes, left it. Apparently, it was quite the scandal."

Josie raised a brow. "How do you know that?"

Gretchen smiled. "The church secretary is in her late seventies. She's been working in the school office since she was twenty five years old."

"But she's never heard of an Ivan?"

"No, but she said she was never great with student names," Mettner said.

Josie laughed. "Well, that's a good school secretary."

"That's a lot of students to remember," Mettner replied. "All those decades of working at the school. Faculty and staff last a lot longer. What she does remember is the gossip, and Sister Mary Elsa, otherwise known as Tracy Schmidt's departure from the church was quite a scandal."

"What happened?" Josie asked, setting the list aside and taking a sip of her coffee.

Gretchen said, "She's not sure why she left, just that she left. That was the scandal. Nuns take their vows for a lifetime. Back then it was quite a big deal for a nun to break her vows and leave the church."

"So," Josie said. "The school secretary thinks that this nun might know something?"

"Apparently she and Colette were quite close," Mettner said.

"And then, at some point in high school, Colette switched to Episcopalian and never looked back," Josie said.

"Yes. They both left the Catholic church," Gretchen pointed out. "So there's definitely something there."

"Something that's going to lead us to this Ivan person?" Josie asked hopefully.

Gretchen shrugged. "Hard to say. Won't know unless we ask."

Mettner stood up. "Let's go talk to Tracy Schmidt."

"Hopefully she's still alive," Josie said.

CHAPTER FORTY

While Mettner and Josie looked into finding Tracy Schmidt, Gretchen did a search for Brody Wolicki and texted Josie and Mettner her results. He was still alive but he had moved to Sullivan County, a remote area in northern Pennsylvania and about three hours from Denton. Josie's ex-fiancé, Luke Creighton's sister had a farm up in Sullivan County, so Josie had been there before. She called the number listed for Wolicki twice, but he didn't answer. After a brief discussion with Mettner, they decided she would drive up there first thing in the morning to follow up on the belt buckle lead.

The ex-nun, Tracy Schmidt, was still alive and in her eighties and living in a run-down part of Denton. Her apartment was in a five-story crumbling brick building on a block where weeds grew from the cracks in the pavement and broken glass and litter gathered in every concrete crevice within sight. The building next to Schmidt's was condemned, its top floors burned out from a fire several years earlier. The windows of the lower floors had been smashed out, boarded up, and then someone had broken through some of those boards. Josie knew from the patrol officers that there were a few homeless people who routinely stayed on the lower floor. The building on the other side had a Chinese restaurant and a small laundromat on the ground floor, and the top floors looked to be apartments. Directly across the street were several stout two-story rowhouses crammed together. The corner house had a mini-market on the first floor. A couple of men in hoodies stood outside smoking cigarettes.

Josie and Mettner parked outside Schmidt's building and made their way inside two unlocked wooden doors with smoked glass. There were some metal mailboxes affixed to a wall to the left and a set of stairs to the right. "She's in number four," Josie said, pointing to the mailbox with the name "Schmidt" written on it in thick black marker.

They climbed the creaky steps to the second floor. A musty smell filled the air and threadbare burgundy carpet lined the hallway, softly illuminated by two hanging lights, giving off a vague yellow glow. The doors to the units were wooden and looked as though they'd been painted many times over the years, so that now they all looked some kind of indeterminate dark brown color. At the door marked "4", they stopped and Mettner knocked. A few moments passed, and he knocked again.

For a second, Josie wondered if Tracy Schmidt was dead inside, smothered, her body sprawled across the floor. But then they heard movement and a woman's voice call out, "Just a minute."

Footsteps could be heard padding across the floor before the door finally squeaked open. An elderly woman with stooped shoulders, short gray hair and a thin frame stared back at them. She wore navy blue sweatpants and a matching sweatshirt. A pair of pink slippers added a splash of color to her ensemble. Wrinkles bunched and sagged on every inch of exposed skin, from her long face to her arthritic hands. Thick glasses rested on her narrow nose and yet she squinted at them. "Who're you?" she asked.

Josie let Mettner make the introductions. Before they had even pulled out their credentials, she waved them inside, moving slowly and carefully. It was a studio apartment, Josie soon realized, no bigger than Josie's own living room. There were only two places to sit—her twin bed or the saggy mauve recliner right next to it. A tray table sat next to the recliner, holding a remote control, a cup of coffee, some tissues and several pill bottles. At the foot of the bed was a small table with a television on it, and a dresser. Opposite the bed and recliner was a small countertop, sink and stove. A wooden door painted black was cracked open next to the kitchen area. Josie could make out the bone white of a porcelain toilet.

"Sit," Tracy Schmidt said. She lowered herself into the recliner.

Josie and Mettner sat on the edge of the twin bed on top of an ancient floral comforter. Mettner pulled out his phone and opened his note-taking app. "Thank you for speaking with us, Ms. Schmidt."

The woman waved her hand in the air again. "Don't get many visitors. Not anymore. You're here to talk about St. Agatha's, are you?"

Josie said, "We know it was a long time ago, but we were hoping you could help us. Do you remember a student named Colette Riggs? She would have been in St. Agatha's between 1958 and 1966."

Tracy nodded. "Lettie. That's what she was called back then. That's what I knew her as—she just died. I saw it in the paper. Couldn't get to the funeral, though. I don't get around too well anymore. I guess she was killed, then. Is that what it means when an obituary says the person 'died suddenly'?"

Mettner said, "Sometimes, I think it does."

"What does St. Agatha's have to do with it?"

Josie said, "We're not entirely sure yet. But we're trying to track down someone she went to school with at St. Agatha's—a man. We didn't see his name on the list of students although Colette's was on it. She told her husband that his name was Ivan. Evidently, her mother knew him as well."

Two spots of pink rose in Tracy's cheeks. She blinked several times. "I know the one."

Josie's heart did a quick double tap; the thought that they might actually get some answers to one of their lines of inquiry sent adrenaline surging through her veins.

"Was he a student there?" Mettner asked.

"Yes. He was. Same grade as Lettie. They were close, those two. You see, both their mothers worked in the rectory. They were charity cases. They only went to St. Agatha's because their mothers were employees. They got discounted tuition."

"If he was a student there, then why isn't his name on the list?" Josie asked. "Colette's name is there."

Tracy blinked rapidly again. One trembling hand reached over to the tray table and plucked a tissue from the box. She used it to dab beneath her rheumy eyes. "It's cause of what happened. Those bastards took his name out of the records so there would be no evidence."

Josie felt a prickle along the nape of her neck. "What happened?"

"What do you think happened?" Tracy snapped. "One of the priests got hold of poor Ivan and started messing with him. Doing… things to him."

Mettner said, "Ivan told?"

"No, of course not. Back then you didn't tell about things like that. Especially not boys. It was Lettie who told. She saw them one time. Ivan was an altar boy and one day, Lettie's mother sent her into the sacristy to dust, and she saw the priest interfering with Ivan."

"Who did she tell?" Josie asked. She knew that even now, sex abuse scandals in the Catholic Church were extremely touchy subjects, and many victims did not get the justice that was their due even when they did alert their parents and the authorities about what was happening.

"Me," Tracy said. "She came to me, crying, upset. We were close, me and Lettie. She was such a sweet thing. A fiery, sweet thing. Ivan didn't want her to tell anyone at all. They were in the eighth grade, and they'd be going off to high school. He was convinced once the year was over, he would have to see the priest a lot less. I think he just didn't want anyone to know. He was ashamed."

"That's terrible," Josie said as Mettner tapped away on his phone. "What did you do?"

"I went to my mother superior. She said we should pray for the Father's soul."

"That's *it*?" Mettner said.

Tracy shook her head. "It wasn't enough. Not for me. Not for Lettie. I told Lettie I needed some time to figure out what to do, but she decided that wasn't right. None of us adults were moving fast enough for her. Or maybe she knew that nothing would change—that no one of any importance would believe a couple of kids and a nun. Or even if they did, they wouldn't care."

Josie said, "What did she do?"

"Her mother was in charge of cooking for the priests. In charge of all their meals. Lettie used to deliver them to their rooms. Breakfast and dinner at any rate—when she wasn't in school. That particular priest started getting pretty sick. Couldn't stay out of the restroom for very long. Certainly not long enough to perform his duties or interfere with any of the altar boys. He started losing weight. Then Lettie wrote to the bishop all on her own, and the bishop and some of his auxiliaries—they were like his assistants—they swarmed on St. Agatha's like hellfire, trying to shut those children up. They didn't chastise the priest, just Lettie and Ivan. It so was sad. Colette's mother nearly lost her job, and Ivan and his mother had to leave town."

"What was Colette giving the priest?" Josie asked. "Did you ever find out?"

Tracy smiled for the first time since they'd been there. "Castor oil. Lots and lots of it. Not sure how he never figured it out. I know I should have been angry with her, and I did pray for her, but I understood… I understood her helplessness. I was never that brave."

"But you left the church," Mettner said softly. "That was brave, especially back then. Not many options for an excommunicated nun, I'm guessing."

"That's very true, my dear," Tracy agreed with a sigh. "Sometimes I wonder if it was worth it. I worked odd jobs my whole life till I couldn't work anymore. I barely get by here, but I've got enough for this place. I couldn't stay in the church knowing what that man was doing and knowing that no one was going to stop him."

"I'm sorry," Mettner said. "I can't imagine how difficult it must have been."

Josie said, "Did you ever hear from Ivan again?"

Tracy shook her head.

"Do you remember his last name, by any chance?"

"Hmmm," she said. "I'm not sure. It was a German name. Began with a U. I'd have to think on that."

Mettner handed her a business card. "If you remember, can you give us a call right away? It's important."

CHAPTER FORTY-ONE

"Brave," Josie said for the fifth time in the car on the way back to the station. "Colette was brave."

"She was extremely brave. She must have been what? Thirteen?" Mettner said.

"I think she was incredibly brave," Josie said. "It's consistent with the woman Noah knew his mother to be and the woman I knew. A good person. Not a serial killer. Not someone who kept terrible secrets."

"That's true," Mettner said.

"Do you think someone who would do something like that for a friend—even a childhood friend—would have multiple extra-marital affairs?" Josie asked.

"Hard to say," Mettner responded. "People change."

"Not that much," Josie said. "I think we're missing something. She refused to keep the secret when Ivan was being hurt by a priest—even at her own peril, and her mother's. Her mother could have lost her job from the way it sounded."

"She was a whistleblower."

"Right. So why was she keeping secrets about the Pratt brothers?" Josie asked. "She somehow came into possession of something that Samuel Pratt would have had on his person the day he was killed, and the flash drive—well, it's possible Drew had that on him when he went missing."

"So you think she definitely knew what happened to them," Mettner said.

"I don't know. I'm guessing. My point is that she was keeping secrets. Big secrets. Why keep those secrets when she was so willing before to call out a Catholic priest during a time when that was simply not done?"

"She grew up," Mettner said. "You're not so brave after you grow up."

Josie gave a humorless laugh. "True. But she did get Ivan a job. She cared enough about him to go to her boss and outright ask him to hire the guy."

Mettner said, "So she had a strong connection to this Ivan person. With the Pratts—you think she was blowing the whistle on something? Or she just knew what really happened to them?"

"I don't know," Josie muttered, feeling more frustrated than ever. Exhaustion was catching up with her. She pressed her fingers into her eyelids. "I keep thinking about what Mason Pratt said about Beth—how she believed the simplest and most obvious explanation was the right one."

"So we're back to the extra-marital affairs," Mettner said. "Samuel Pratt, possibly this Ivan."

Josie slapped both hands on her thighs. "And that doesn't seem right. I can't see Colette repeatedly cheating on her husband. But I also can't see her as some kind of serial killer—or accomplice to one."

"Maybe Ivan can shed some light on the situation."

"If we can find him."

Mettner pulled into the municipal lot behind the police station. "How many German surnames can there be in the state that begin with a U? We'll find him. Don't worry about that."

As soon as they sat down at their desks to brief Gretchen, Chitwood's door flew open and his voice rolled loudly across the room. "Mettner! Palmer! Quinn! Briefing in my office, now!"

Josie and Gretchen sighed heavily in unison and trudged into Chitwood's office with Mettner in tow. The Chief sat behind his desk and waited for them to take their seats. Josie and Gretchen sat while Mettner remained standing between their chairs. Then Chitwood pointed at Mettner and said, "Go."

He scrolled through the notes on his phone as he filled him in on everything they had discovered in the last couple of days as well as the leads they had yet to follow. Chitwood listened intently, chewing the inside of his cheek as Mettner spoke. When he was finished, he said, "So Palmer and I are gonna look for this Ivan guy, and Quinn's gonna run up to Sullivan County to see this Wolicki guy."

They nodded. Chitwood leaned forward, elbows on his desk. "So far we've managed to keep the press out of this, although I had a couple of people from the TV station calling about the Pratt fire. I'm gonna have to tell them something soon, so get your asses in gear and get me some real answers. Also, we got some stuff back from the Pratt scene."

"Beth or Mason?" Josie asked.

"Mason."

"What is it?" Mettner asked.

"A shoe print. Size eleven. It was in the dirt in Mason's backyard. Scuff marks and mud on the fence. We think the attacker jumped the fence there. Hummel casted it, measured it. Treads didn't match Mason or any of our staff. The tread looks like it came from a boot manufactured by a company called Coyote Run. They make different kinds of boots. They distribute all over the country, though mostly at hunting and sporting goods retailers."

Mettner started scrolling through his notes, but Josie was ahead of him. "Are you sure? The shoe size found at Colette's murder scene was a size ten."

Mettner stopped scrolling and pointed to his phone screen. "Right. Size ten."

Chitwood stared at Josie with a raised brow. "It's your team that processed the scene. You think they got one of these shoe print measurements wrong?"

Josie bristled. She knew damn well her Evidence Response Team wouldn't screw something like that up. She had thought perhaps Chitwood had misunderstood either the ERT officer or their report, but she didn't say that. "So we may be talking about two suspects."

"Shit," Gretchen said. "This changes everything."

"No," Josie said firmly. "Not really. We still work the leads. This started with Colette Fraley so we stay on her—find this Ivan person, try to find the owner of the belt buckle. We work the same leads. Just now we know we're looking for two different people. What each one of them did specifically is something we can figure out once we've caught them. We should have someone visit hunting and sporting goods retailers in the county and see if they can get a list of customers who bought this type of boot in the last year or so and work from there. Most of those places have rewards cards that get scanned every time the customer makes a purchase, so even if our guy paid cash, the retailers might be able to track the purchase by his reward card."

Mettner said, "I'll write up a warrant."

Gretchen added, "And I'll try to find Ivan."

CHAPTER FORTY-TWO

After work, Josie went to visit Noah. He was asleep and Laura sat guard by his bed. She didn't acknowledge Josie even though Josie sat on the other side of Noah's bed for three hours, until the staff kicked them both out, citing the end of visiting hours. Josie drove around aimlessly for an hour, passing the liquor store near her house twice, wanting desperately to go in and get a bottle of Wild Turkey. Instead, she turned back to the hospital and used her police credentials to get back onto the floor where Noah's room was located. The lights were off in his room, but the television played on low. She felt a wave of relief to finally be alone with him. She walked over to the bed and stroked his thick hair. His eyes fluttered open. "Hey," he said. "What time is it?"

"It's late," Josie said. "I was here earlier, but you were sleeping. How do you feel?"

"Lots of pain," he answered. He looked past her. "Is Laura still here?"

Josie tried not to show the hurt on her face. "No, she had to leave. Noah, I—"

"I'm going home with her tomorrow."

"I know. I just wanted to… I just… things between us have been…"

"Josie, I meant what I said this morning. With everything that's going on, I can't even think straight. I really do need a break."

"Stay here," Josie said suddenly. "I'll take a leave of absence. You can stay with me. I won't work. Chitwood let Gretchen off the desk on a limited basis. Between her and Mettner, they're both perfectly capable of handling the case. I'll take care of you."

He shook his head. "No, I need to get out of here. Away from here. I need to be with my family right now."

A stab of pain pierced her chest. Maybe it shouldn't have, but it felt like rejection.

"Laura and Grady will take good care of me," he said.

Josie swallowed over the lump in her throat. "I have no doubt."

He closed his eyes. Josie waited but he didn't open them again. Instead, he started to snore. She was dismissed.

On her way home, she stopped at the liquor store and bought the Wild Turkey. She curled up with it on her living room couch but before she could even open it, she was fast asleep.

*

Brody Wolicki was someone who still had a landline instead of a cell phone. Although from what Josie knew about Sullivan County, the cell service wasn't great so a landline was your best bet if you ever needed to reach the outside world. Josie tried Wolicki's number a half dozen times before she drove to Sullivan County. There was no answer, which made her stomach turn almost the entire drive though she tried to reason with the panicked voice in the back of her mind: he could be on vacation or in the hospital, or he could have been out to breakfast when she called. Still, she couldn't shake the feeling of dread building in her stomach as she got off Route 80 at the Buckhorn exit and took Route 42 into the mountains. As she passed the county line, the roads got narrower and more winding. She tried punching Wolicki's rural address into her GPS, but it didn't recognize it. She stopped at a general store in Laporte to see if she could secure an actual map, but they didn't have any. The cashier knew the Wolicki place, though, and gave her some vague directions.

She went north past the fringes of World's End State Park, then into Dushore and through the only traffic light in the entire county.

She took the unmarked road the general store clerk had told her to turn onto, following it up into the mountains where the homes were spread several miles apart. Taking three turns that failed to bring her to the Wolicki property, she found herself back out on one of the main routes. After an hour of aimless driving, reluctantly, Josie turned toward Carrieann Creighton's farm. It was the only place she really knew how to find in Sullivan County. Things with Luke hadn't worked out, but there had never been any hard feelings between Josie and his sister. Carrieann had put herself in jeopardy to help Josie during the missing girls case. Josie was sure she would help her now, especially since all she needed was directions. She hoped Carrieann could help her find Brody Wolicki's home.

The two-story stone house hadn't changed much since Josie had been there last, several years earlier. As she drove up the bumpy gravel driveway that stretched over a quarter mile from the road to the front porch, she saw the shutters had been recently painted. They gleamed white in the sunlight. A bloodhound with a droopy face and long ears lay on the front porch, its head resting on its paws. It didn't even look up when Josie parked and got out of her car, but its tail wagged slightly as she climbed the steps. "Hey, boy," Josie whispered. She squatted down and offered the dog her knuckles which he sniffed disinterestedly.

A male voice from the front door said, "That's Blue. As you can see, he's quite the guard dog."

The storm door creaked open and Luke stepped out. Josie's heart caught in her throat. He was over six foot tall and had always dwarfed her. In the years since she had last seen him, he had gained weight, but in muscle, not fat. Gone was the high and tight haircut he had been required to keep while with the state police. Now his dark brown hair was long and a thick beard covered his face. He was dressed in torn, dirty jeans and a thermal undershirt, white turned gray with wear. Heavy boots covered his feet. He smiled at her. "Never thought I'd see you again."

Josie licked her dry lips and stood. "I was looking for Carrieann."

He took a step toward her. "She had to do some deliveries. She'll be back tonight or tomorrow."

A long moment stretched out between them. Finally, Josie could stand the silence no longer. "Do you... do you live here now?"

"Yeah. It's not so bad. I did six months in prison. I'm on probation. I had a really good lawyer. I help Carrieann out with the farm, and I get to live here rent-free."

"That's great," Josie said. "I mean that you've..."

She broke off. What could she say? It was great that he hadn't gone to prison for many years? It was great that he wasn't homeless? It was great that he could no longer pursue the career he had loved so much?

"Josie," Luke said, his voice firm. "I'm fine. Really. Things have worked out."

"I'm glad," she said.

He took another step so they were only two feet apart. "They worked out for you, too, huh? I saw the *Dateline* about you and Trinity."

Josie couldn't suppress her smile. "Instant family, yes. It's... good."

"What did you need Carrieann for? Maybe I can help."

She felt her heartbeat settle into a normal rhythm. Work was solid ground. She told him she needed to talk to Brody Wolicki about a case she was working on.

Luke scratched his head and for the first time, Josie noticed the scarring on his hand. During the case that had destroyed his career, ended their relationship and sent him to prison, he'd been tortured. Both hands had been crushed, and it had required multiple surgeries to repair them. Silvered scars ran along the back of his hand and the lengths of his fingers. His index and middle fingers still looked flattened and deformed. Josie swallowed, trying to focus on his words.

" ... think that's on the other side of Dushore. He's got that outdoor shooting range on his property. If you want, I can drive you out there."

"Yes," Josie said. "Please."

CHAPTER FORTY-THREE

The conversation came easier during the twenty-minute drive out to Brody Wolicki's property. Mostly, Luke asked her questions about her family and all that had happened since they'd last seen one another. As they talked, Josie fired off a text to Noah asking him how he felt and if he'd been discharged yet. No response.

"So, you and Noah, huh?" Luke said.

"How do you know that?"

He laughed and turned the steering wheel of his truck. Josie noticed the little finger on his other hand was also permanently deformed, its tip twisting out slightly. But he didn't seem to have any difficulty with either hand. "I just figured. You two always had your heads together. Plus, it was pretty obvious he had it bad for you."

Josie humphed and looked out the window, watching the forest roll past. Not so much anymore, she thought.

Luke said, "I'm happy for you. Noah's a good guy." Then, "Here we go."

Brody Wolicki's driveway was barely noticeable in the brush at the side of the road, but Luke pulled in like he did it every day. He must have seen her staring at him because he said, "Like I said, he's got an outdoor range. Lots of guys around here come over to use it."

The truck bumped along the dirt driveway through the thick foliage all around. A small cabin came into view. It was a drab brown and its roof looked as though it had been patched many times with various materials. One wall of the structure was covered in moss. Off to the side, Josie could see another path which she assumed led to the shooting range that Luke had talked about. They got out and Luke followed her onto the small porch. She rapped on the door and waited. They stayed silent, listening for any movement inside. Another rap on the door went unanswered. With a sigh, Josie turned to step off the porch, hoping maybe Wolicki was out at the shooting range. Luke said, "No one up here locks their doors. Brody! Hey, Brody!" He twisted the doorknob and the door opened. The moment Josie turned back, the smell hit her, provoking an instant gob of vomit that shot from her stomach into her esophagus. Her hand went to her weapon even though the logical part of her brain told her whatever violence had been visited on Brody Wolicki had happened long before she and Luke arrived.

Carefully, she stepped inside, covering her mouth with the back of her forearm. Still, her eyes watered from the rancid smell. The cabin was not big. A single room encompassed both the living room and kitchen. She saw two doors in a small hallway to the right and guessed they were likely the bedroom and bathroom. It was sparsely furnished with mismatched furniture that looked like it had been bought at Good Will. An ugly teal shag carpet formed an oval in the center of the living area, between a saggy brown two-seat couch and a wood-burning stove that was now cold.

On the carpet lay what Josie guessed was Brody Wolicki's body. It was hard to tell, though. She had only seen his driver's license photo in the police database, and the body before her was a greasy, black, bloated facsimile of a man. Her mind was already working. Josie knew that in the first twenty-four to seventy-two hours after death, aerobic bacteria in the body used up all the oxygen inside, paving the way for the increase in anaerobic bacteria. Once the anaerobic bacteria started to proliferate in the intestinal tract, they produced foul-smelling gases which led to bloating. The bacterial bloat, as Dr. Feist sometimes called it, happened between four and ten days after death.

Brody Wolicki had been dead for some time.

Josie turned to speak to Luke but he wasn't there. She walked back outside and found him leaning against his truck, his face pale.

In his trembling hands was his phone. As she got closer, she could hear him mumbling. "Have to get out of here… have to call… have to get out… can't stay."

Josie reached out and touched Luke's arm. He startled and his phone fell into the dirt at his feet. He dropped to the ground and picked it up. "Have to call," he said. "911. Have to call 911."

His index finger trembled as he tried to punch in his passcode. Josie felt a wave of sympathy and sadness. She knelt down next to him and put an arm across his broad shoulders. "Luke," she said softly. "It's okay. I'm going to call."

Without looking at her, he said, "I can't be here."

She took his phone out of his hands and tucked it into his jacket pocket. She leaned in and used her fingers to turn his face so he would look at her. "Luke, it's okay. You don't need to do anything but wait in the truck, okay? I'm going to call 911."

As he stumbled to his feet, Josie took out her cell phone. She dialed 911 as Luke climbed unsteadily into the driver's seat and rested his forehead against the steering wheel.

"911, where's your emergency?" the dispatcher answered.

Josie gave the address.

"What type of emergency are you having, ma'am?"

"There's a dead body here. I need the police."

CHAPTER FORTY-FOUR

Within the hour, Brody Wolicki's tiny cabin was swarmed with sheriff's deputies and state police as well as a coroner's van. Josie and Luke sat on Luke's tailgate and waited while the scene was processed, answering questions whenever necessary about why they had come to Wolicki's property. They watched men and women go in and out of the cabin, some racing out and vomiting outside the scene perimeter. Every so often the horrific smell wafted over to where they sat, and Luke would get up and pace for several minutes while Josie checked her phone and texted Noah again—still getting no response. For the fourth time, Luke sat beside her again on the tailgate, one hand scratching at his beard. It had taken time, but the color had come back into his face and he seemed more composed, for which Josie was glad. A few years back, during the case that ultimately ruined his career and sent him to prison, he had walked in on a crime scene involving his best friend. Josie hadn't realized how deeply the experience had affected him until she saw his reaction to finding Wolicki's body.

From behind the cabin, dressed in a white Tyvek suit, State Police Detective Heather Loughlin emerged. She pulled off her skull cap as she approached them, shaking her long, blonde hair loose. Josie had already briefed her when she arrived. They'd worked together before, most recently on a case involving Gretchen. Heather said, "Looks like this guy was burning documents out back."

Josie groaned. "You've got to be kidding me."

Heather shook her head. "Come on," she said. "I'll get you a suit and you can come around back and look."

Once Josie was suited up, she and Heather logged into the crime scene with the sheriff's deputy guarding the perimeter, and Heather took her to the back of the cabin where two large, rusty metal barrels stood about thirty feet away from the cabin's back door. Empty cardboard boxes were piled up next to the barrels. Beyond that, about fifty feet away was a small shed, its brown siding also covered in moss, and its door standing open.

Heather said, "Apparently Wolicki was a bit of a hoarder. The cabin's filled with things—some photo albums, old cassette tapes, a gun safe, and a bunch of taxidermy animals in his bedroom." She pointed to the shed. "He had a lot of stuff in the shed, which appears to have been burnt in these barrels. He lived alone out here, as I'm sure you can guess. Most of the local folks knew him—like Luke out there—and he let a lot of people use his shooting range. He doesn't have any relatives. No one nearby who would check on him regularly. I think eventually someone coming to use the range would have found him."

As they stepped up to the two barrels, Heather motioned inside of one which was filled with blackened ash and slips of paper. "It's not hot," she said. "Looks like it's been there a while."

"By the looks of his body, it's possible he's been dead as long as ten days," Josie said. "Has it rained in the last ten days?"

"Last rain here was nine days ago."

"So whoever did this must have done it within the last eight days."

Heather cocked her head to the side. "You think someone else could have burned all this stuff?"

Josie sighed. "Yes." With gloved fingers she probed some of the paper inside the barrel. Most of what remained appeared to be handwritten notes. One scrap had a couple of shooting club names which Josie recognized from her library research, along with a list of guns. The more scraps she turned up, the heavier her heart felt. The killer—or killers—had been way ahead of her. They obviously knew the significance of the belt buckle and had known it long before Josie discovered it—before she had even sent Mettner to Rockview to ask the residents about it. They had come here and murdered Wolicki and destroyed all documentation he had of his former shooting league and any evidence of who the belt buckle had belonged to. For just a moment she wondered if they had some kind of leak at the Denton Police Department, or even if Noah's sister and brother-in-law were somehow involved. But that didn't make sense since Laura and Grady hadn't known they were going to talk to Beth and Mason Pratt, and both of them had been attacked before Josie and Mettner could get to them. Wolicki had been murdered long before Denton PD even knew about him. Plus, the only people in the department who knew Josie was coming to see him were Chitwood, Mettner and Gretchen.

She picked her way over to the shed and peeked inside. All the walls were lined with wooden shelves. One whole wall was completely empty. That would have been the one that held all of Wolicki's old records. The other walls were filled with tools, weed-killer, potting soil, rakes, shovels, pruners, extension cords and an air compressor. Josie turned back to Heather. "Any idea of the cause of death?"

"Hard to say, especially given the shape the body is in, but there's no obvious trauma we can see. We can't even say this is a murder at this point."

Together they walked back to the front of the house. "Oh, it's a murder all right. When you get that coroner's report it will say he was asphyxiated. Just you wait."

CHAPTER FORTY-FIVE

Josie drove Luke's truck back to the farm. He was still largely silent and only seemed to perk up once there inside the farmhouse. She followed him into the kitchen where he immediately started poking around in the fridge and the cabinets and pulling out pans. "You hungry?" he asked.

It was after dinnertime, and she hadn't eaten all day. Just watching him pull things out of the fridge made her stomach growl. She sat at the table and pulled out her cell phone—still nothing from Noah so she fired off another text pleading with him not to shut her out—and set it on the counter. She'd have to call Gretchen, but she didn't have the heart to do it just then. "I'm starving," she told Luke.

He worked quickly and deftly, even with his scarred and mangled hands, to whip up something that smelled positively delicious, while outside the sunlight disappeared behind the horizon. She heard the storm door creak and a moment later, Blue the bloodhound came loping into the kitchen. With a sigh, he plopped down in front of his food and water bowls.

Luke said, "He knows how to open the door."

"Really?" Josie said. "Well, that's the first time I've ever seen something like that."

Luke smiled and patted Blue's head as he moved from the stove to the fridge and back. After he made his final touches to the meal he was making, he took Blue's bowl and dumped some of the concoction into it. The dog waited patiently for his bowl to be returned while Luke let it cool on the counter. "I hope you like steak stir-fry," Luke said, presenting her with a plate.

Her mouth filled up with saliva as she took the fork he offered. "I always loved your cooking," she said. "Thank you."

He got his own plate and sat across from her. They ate in silence for several minutes. Josie tried to focus on the wonderful flavor of the meal, but her mind kept returning to the scene at Wolicki's and the fact that one of their last remaining leads had been blown. She just hoped that Gretchen had been able to find Ivan. She checked her email, but there was nothing from anyone at Sutton Stone Enterprises. Not that she expected that lead to pan out. Who kept personnel records for almost forty years?

"You okay?" Luke asked.

"Oh, yes. Fine," Josie answered.

"Need to call Noah? I can step out."

"Oh no, we're not—things aren't really going that well right now. I do need to call Gretchen though about the case."

"Got it," Luke said. "I have to get something. Be right back."

With a heavy feeling in the pit of her stomach, Josie called Gretchen's cell phone. She picked up on the third ring and said, "You wouldn't believe how many Ivans there are in this state whose last names begin with U. Underwood, Ulrich, Ulster, Umstead… I'm still looking, though. I can definitely narrow by age range. What's going on there? Good news, I hope? You still in Sullivan County?"

Josie told her.

"Well, that raises a lot of questions," Gretchen said.

"Exactly."

They spoke for a few more minutes, Gretchen having the same thought as Josie about leaks, but they both ultimately agreed that didn't exactly fit. The killer had been looking for the items Colette was hiding and obviously hadn't found them on the day of her murder, so he was trying to eliminate whatever it was the items would lead police to discover. The problem for Josie, Mettner and Gretchen was that whoever they were dealing with knew the significance of all three items. No closer to answers than the day before, they agreed to go at it again the next day. Gretchen promised to update Mettner and hung up. Josie finished her meal and took her plate to the sink. Luke appeared in the doorway with a bottle of red wine in one hand and a half-filled bottle of Wild Turkey in the other.

He grinned.

Josie smiled awkwardly. "Oh, yeah. I don't really… I haven't had a drink in a long time."

Luke said, "So you're not drinking anymore? Not even a glass of wine?"

Josie shifted uncomfortably. She could think of nothing she'd like more in that moment than to drown her frustration in a tall glass of wine followed by numerous shots of Wild Turkey, but since the case that had shattered her world and given her a new family, she'd stopped drinking. "I don't make good decisions when I drink," she told him.

He set the bottles on the counter. "I'm not asking you to make a decision. Well, that's not entirely true. Carrieann won't be back until tomorrow which normally wouldn't be a problem, except today really got to me."

His eyes drifted away from hers, and one of his hands clasped the neck of the wine bottle.

"Luke, I really shouldn't."

He looked back up at her. "You're going to drive three hours home and then what? Go to your empty house?"

Josie almost shot back that her house was pretty full these days, but the truth was that tonight there would be no one there to greet her.

"Josie," Luke said. "I'm not making a pass at you if that's what you're worried about. It's just really good to see you."

She nodded. "I appreciate the invitation," she said. "But I really should get home."

They said their goodbyes, and she was halfway down the driveway when her cell phone finally dinged. It was a text message from Noah.

Except it wasn't from Noah. The message read: *This is Laura. Please stop texting Noah. He'll contact you when he's ready to talk.*

Josie braked and sucked in several deep breaths, blinking hard against the hurt and the sudden sting in her eyes. Punching the steering wheel, she spun the car around and drove back up to Luke's house. This time, Blue greeted her at the door, tail wagging. She let herself inside where Luke was sitting alone at the kitchen table with a shot of Wild Turkey in front of him. He looked startled when he saw her. She sat across from him, picked up his shot and slugged it down, the liquid burning all the way down to her stomach.

"Change of plans," she said.

CHAPTER FORTY-SIX

The pounding in Josie's head was like a jackhammer. She opened one eye, but the sunlight streaming into the room was like a thousand spikes in her cornea. She threw an arm across her face. The room. What room was she in? She peeked over her arm, looking around at unfamiliar surroundings. Her mind worked to orient itself. From beside her came the sound of a sigh. She turned her head to see a man's bare back. She knew instantly it was Luke, although she didn't remember going to bed with him.

She tossed the covers off her, swung her legs over the edge of the bed and sat up, one of her hands pressed against her left temple. The room tipped to the side, and the throbbing in her head was so intense she could barely breathe. She tried to remember how long it had been since she was well and truly hungover. A long time, she realized. She looked down at herself. She still wore her underwear and the tank top she'd had on under her clothes.

Groaning softly, she stood, dizziness assailing her. Holding on to the bed to steady herself, she fished her jeans and polo shirt off the floor and pulled them on. For a moment, she stared at Luke's sleeping form, trying desperately to remember the night before. She remembered leaving, coming back, and doing shots. She vaguely remembered opening the bottle of wine while they watched television in the living room. She remembered laughing. That was it. Dropping to her knees, she swiped a hand beneath the bed, hoping to find her sneakers. Had she kicked them off downstairs?

The sound of tires over gravel outside caused nausea to roil in her stomach. She opened the bedroom door and nearly fell on her face. Blue lay across the threshold on the other side. The dog's mournful eyes glanced up at her, but he didn't move. Josie looked from the dog back into the room. A large tan dog bed lay at the foot of the bed. Why had Luke shut Blue out in the hallway? Josie didn't want to think about it. She stepped over the dog and raced down the stairs just as she heard footsteps creaking on the porch. Her shoes were in the living room. She pushed her feet into them, snatched her keys and cell phone from the kitchen table and flung the front door open, expecting Carrieann but instead finding her twin sister, Trinity Payne.

"Wh-what are you doing here?" Josie said. She raised a hand over her eyes to shield them from the sunlight and the spears it poked all the way into the back of her head.

Trinity stood with her hands on her hips, looking stylish in a pair of tight jeans, knee-high brown leather boots and a clingy cashmere sweater cinched with a belt around her waist. But her face was pinched and angry. "Nice hair," Trinity remarked.

Josie reached up and patted down one side of her brown hair, feeling the tangles catch against her fingertips. "Why are you here?" Josie said. "And how the hell did you find me?"

Trinity waved a hand in front of her face, her nose wrinkling. "My God, your breath." She leaned in and sniffed at Josie. "Wild Turkey again, huh?"

Josie put a hand on her own hip and eyed Trinity head-on. "I asked you a question."

Trinity spun on her heel and started walking back out to the driveway. "Get in the car, Josie."

Josie stood and watched as a young woman emerged from the Lexus Trinity had arrived in. Trinity said something to her, and she looked over at Josie.

"Now, Josie," Trinity said.

Josie trudged down the porch steps and into the driveway. Trinity took her keys from her hand and gave them to the young woman.

"This is my assistant. She'll drive your car back to Denton. You're coming with me."

Josie felt too sick to argue. The bumpy ride out to the road gave her the dry heaves. Trinity pulled open a small door on the top of the center console and took out a pack of gum which she tossed into Josie's lap. Then she pointed to the glove compartment and said, "There's some ibuprofen in there. Take it."

It took three tries to get the childproof cap off. Josie swallowed three pills dry and popped a piece of gum in her mouth. She closed her eyes and waited for Trinity to explain herself. It didn't take long.

"What is wrong with you?" Trinity began. "You barely escape a fire, and I have to find out from one of my local press contacts? Josie, this is not how you treat family."

Without opening her eyes, Josie muttered, "I didn't 'barely escape'."

"Oh really? How did you get out of the house?"

Sheepishly, Josie admitted, "I jumped out the window."

Trinity made a sound of exasperation.

"Don't you have to be in New York City for work?" Josie said.

"I took a personal day. My contact at WYEP called me late last night. She told me there was a lot of suspicious stuff happening in Denton; Beth Pratt dying; her house burning to the ground. Then she said, 'Oh yeah, some police detective's mom's house burned down.' So I looked into it and found out it was Noah's mom's house. I called you but you didn't answer. Then I called the station. Talked to Sergeant Lamay who told me the whole story. I called you again. No answer. I called Noah and guess what he told me? That you two were taking time apart and that he didn't know where you were. Then guess what I did?"

"You called me again," Josie said with a sigh. "How did you find out I was here?"

"Gretchen. She said you were supposed to come home last night, but you didn't. She sent a unit to your house. You weren't there."

Josie felt the sting of a punch on her shoulder. "Ow," she said, opening her eyes finally. Guilt assailed her when she saw the tears glistening in Trinity's eyes. "I didn't wait thirty years to find my sister to have you die on me in the middle of the damn woods."

"I wasn't in any danger," Josie said.

"But I didn't know that. I would ask why you didn't answer your phone, but it's pretty obvious."

Josie was going to defend herself but then realized there was no defense. Shame already burned her cheeks. She had acted irresponsibly—so irresponsibly she didn't even know what happened the night before. She took out her phone and looked at the time. It was nine a.m. so there was still time to salvage the day. Maybe Chitwood wouldn't have her ass in a sling after all. At least he wasn't one of the two dozen missed calls and texts. Her heart stopped momentarily when she saw a call from Noah received late the night before. Probably after Trinity called him.

She put her phone back into her pocket and put her head in her hands. After a moment, she heard Trinity sigh and felt a manicured hand squeeze her shoulder. "It'll be okay," she said softly.

"Will it?" Josie croaked. Her mouth felt like it was filled with cotton.

Trinity squeezed her shoulder again and then without looking away from the road, she reached behind Josie's seat and grabbed her purse. She put it in Josie's lap. "I've got something that will cheer you up."

Josie raised a brow. "A Coach purse? Not really my style."

Trinity rolled her eyes. "Just look in there. There's an envelope. Open it."

Josie riffled through the contents of Trinity's purse until she found an unmarked white envelope. She slipped her index finger under the sealed edge and opened it. Inside were several small photos, no more than three by five inches. They were all yellowed and faded, but Josie recognized the faces in the first one immediately—their parents, Christian and Shannon Payne. They were over thirty years younger, thinner, and much less gray, and they beamed at the camera. Each of them held a baby swaddled in a blanket. The other photos were of the babies, their little pink faces peeking out from their bundles. Tears stung Josie's eyes as her breath caught in her throat.

"It's us," she said. "Where did you get these? I thought everything was destroyed in the fire."

"It was," Trinity said. "But Mom had a roll of film that she had taken to the Photomat to be developed when our house burned down and we were separated. She remembered a few weeks after the fire. She's kept them in a safe deposit box ever since because these were the only photos she ever had of you."

"Of the two of us together," Josie said.

"Yes. She gave them to me when she was in New York last weekend. I had them scanned so now there are digital copies, but I wanted you to see the originals. You can keep them."

Josie clutched them to her chest. "Thank you."

Her heart felt full. As quickly as she had spiraled out of control, Trinity was reeling her back in and grounding her. This was what it felt like to have a real family. Maybe Trinity was right. It would be okay. There might even be a way to solve this awful case before anyone else was killed. Her mind turned to practical matters. She'd have to call Gretchen when her headache subsided a bit and see if she had managed to narrow down her list of Ivans. She'd also have to check in with Mettner to see if he'd had any luck with the hunting and sports retailers and getting a list of customers who had bought size eleven Coyote Run boots. Her fingers stroked the brittle edges of the photographs as she tried to tamp down her disappointment over losing the belt buckle lead. Poor Brody Wolicki. He was just living his life peacefully in his small wooded cabin with no idea at all that he had something a killer wanted to keep secret.

She pulled the photos away from her chest and stared at them again. Her mother had missed her for thirty long years with nothing but these few photographs to sustain her.

"Oh my God," Josie said suddenly.

Quickly, she tucked the photos back into the envelope. She touched Trinity's forearm. "Turn around," she said. "Turn around right now."

"What are you talking about?" Trinity said.

Josie took out her cell phone and dialed Heather Loughlin. As the phone rang, she said, "Just go back the way we came and I'll tell you how to get there. I need to get back to the Wolicki scene."

CHAPTER FORTY-SEVEN

Josie stood outside of Wolicki's cabin, waiting for Detective Heather Loughlin. The crime scene tape fluttered from tree to tree, cordoning off the cabin, even though the scene had been processed. Trinity wandered around outside the perimeter, talking on her cell phone to various work contacts. Josie's cell phone rang. Gretchen's name blinked on the screen.

"What've you got?" Josie said when she answered.

"Ivan Ulrich," Gretchen replied. "I think he's our guy. His age fits and his mother, who died in 1999, lived in Denton around the time he would have been at St. Agatha's. I found her obituary, and it actually says she worked at St. Agatha's, so I'm pretty sure he's our guy. He lives in Bellewood. I'm contacting Bellewood PD now to let them know Mettner will be coming down that way to interview him. I'll go with him."

"Does he have a criminal record?" Josie asked.

"Clean as a whistle," Gretchen said. "I'm trying to track down some more information on him now—like whether he ever worked for Sutton Stone Enterprises. You hear from their records department?"

"No," Josie said. "But I'll give Sutton a call and see if he can expedite their search, and I'll give him Ivan Ulrich's name and date of birth. I'll give him your email address. I think I might have another lead up here on the belt buckle, but it may take me a few hours."

They hung up and Josie dialed Zachary Sutton who answered right away, listened to her request, and promised to get in contact with his records department immediately. She was saying goodbye when Heather Loughlin pulled up in an unmarked state police vehicle. Heather got out of the car, her face paling when she saw Trinity. "What's she doing here?"

Josie laughed. "Relax. She's not here as a reporter. She's here as my sister. She doesn't even know anything about the case. I need to get in there and see the photo albums."

Heather gave Trinity a long look as if trying to decide something and then popped her trunk, reached in and pulled out a Tyvek suit which she handed to Josie. "She stays out here. Suit up and I'll take you inside."

Five minutes later, Josie and Heather were inside Brody Wolicki's bedroom, and Josie was trying not to dry heave at the smell that still lingered in the small cabin. Being hungover at a crime scene was not the best idea Josie had ever had, but she needed to take one last shot at finding out who owned the belt buckle hidden in Colette's sewing machine. Wolicki's twin bed was barely visible amongst the mounds of hunting gear and taxidermy piled into the tiny room.

Josie said, "When you said a 'bit' of a hoarder, I think you were being conservative."

Heather laughed and picked up a taxidermy deer head from the floor and carried it into the hallway to make room for them to work. Josie followed suit until they had removed a stuffed rabbit, a family of stuffed squirrels and an elk head which required two of them to get it out of the room.

"Why didn't he hang any of these?" Josie groused as they struggled to get the elk head through the doorway.

"Maybe he didn't want them over his bed staring at him at night," Heather joked.

When they had cleared out the animals and a few boxes of cassette tapes, they reached the photo albums, piled high from floor to shoulder height. "Tell me again what we're looking for?" Heather asked as Josie handed her an album.

As they worked, sweat poured down Josie's back in rivulets. She was certain Heather could smell last night's booze oozing from her pores but she didn't say anything. "We're looking for a photo of the 1973 Tri-County Shooting League champion." She took out her cell phone and showed Heather a photo of the belt buckle.

Two hours later, Josie was beginning to wonder if she had been crazy to think Brody Wolicki had kept photos of his years with the shooting league. Most of the albums were of local wildlife and hunting expeditions. There were many filled with people Brody had clearly been close to—Christmas pictures of people gathered around a tree; people celebrating what looked like a retirement party at a bar; people at a local football game together. Finally, near the bottom of the pile, they hit pay dirt; an old album, its cover nearly disintegrating in Josie's hands, but filled with what were obviously photographs of the shooting league. A thrill of excitement flooded her body when she found the 1972 champion, proudly holding his rifle while he stood next to a bullet-ridden target. A man next to him—Josie assumed this was Brody—held out a belt buckle much like the one Colette had hidden. Gingerly, Josie pulled the photo from beneath the plastic casing and turned it over. There was a name next to the words: League Champion, 1972.

She frantically flipped through the rest of the pages until she found the next photo of a man—short, burly, wearing jeans, a western-style shirt and a cowboy hat—holding a rifle beside a shredded target. Beneath a bushy moustache, his smile was wide and toothy. Next to him was Brody Wolicki with the mystery belt buckle in his hand. On the back of the photo, it said: Craig Bridges, League Champion, 1973.

"I've got it!" Josie said. "I found it!"

CHAPTER FORTY-EIGHT

Josie took a shower before she went to the station house, washing off the booze, sweat and shame of the night before. She had to keep her focus on the task at hand. She had a new lead in the Fraley/Pratt case, and she needed to get on it. She left Trinity at her house. As promised, Trinity's assistant had brought Josie's vehicle back to Denton and parked it in her driveway. On the way to the station house she called Noah, but he didn't answer. She didn't leave a message.

Gretchen was at her desk, tapping away at her computer.

Josie sat down across from her. "Did you guys interview Ivan Ulrich?"

"He wasn't home. Bellewood put a unit on his apartment for us. As soon as he shows up, they'll call."

"Did you look up Craig Bridges?"

Gretchen nodded. "Yeah. He's been missing since 1990."

"What do you mean? What happened?"

Gretchen looked down at her desk where her notepad sat. "I searched every database I could and then the internet. Through the databases I found out that he had been living in Hagerstown, Maryland although he used to live in Pennsylvania—near Bellewood actually. He seemed to drop off the face of the earth in 1990, but I couldn't find any evidence that he was deceased, so I checked NamUs."

NamUs was the National Missing and Unidentified Persons System. "What did you get?"

Gretchen handed her a printout. "I also called the Hagerstown PD to get some of the details. They had to pull the file cause it's so old."

As Josie studied the sparse details in the NamUs report, her body went cold. "This can't be right."

"Creepy, right?" Gretchen agreed. "But I talked to Hagerstown PD. Craig Bridges drove to the bank of the Potomac River, left his personal possessions in his locked car and disappeared. He hasn't been seen since."

"Friends? Family?" Josie asked.

"Hagerstown PD said that he had a roommate and that was it, but apparently he and Bridges were very close. They said every couple of years the roommate calls to see if any work has been done on the file."

"No signs of foul play?"

"None. Plus, Bridges was an alcoholic with a history of depression. So that doesn't help. If his body had ever been found, there's a good chance it would have been ruled a suicide."

"Basically the same circumstances as Samuel Pratt," Josie said. "What's the roommate's name? Is he still alive? Did you try to get in touch with him?"

Gretchen nodded. "He is still alive. His name is Earl Butler. He moved to Fairfield in Lenore County after Bridges disappeared."

"That's only an hour south of here," Josie said.

"Yeah, I tried calling the number I could find for him twice, but there was no answer so I called the local PD and had them do a welfare check. Door's locked, no answer, no signs that anything is wrong."

Josie felt a sick stirring in her stomach. "I'm going to drive down there."

"And do what?" Gretchen said.

"So far this guy—or these guys—have killed Colette, Beth Pratt, Brody Wolicki and tried to kill Mason Pratt. They've burned down two houses. They know who we're going to talk to before we ever even get there. I'm not wasting one more second before making sure that Earl Butler is alive and well. You stay here—Mettner will need you once Ivan Ulrich shows up. Did Sutton's people send you over any records?"

"No, not yet."

Josie pulled a scrap of paper out of her jeans. "This is the name and number of the woman who works at the off-site storage facility. Sutton gave it to me in case we didn't hear from his people before the end of the day."

Gretchen took it. "I'll give her a call. Maybe Mettner and I will even take a ride down there while I'm waiting to hear back from Bellewood PD about our friend Ivan."

"Let me know if anything breaks."

CHAPTER FORTY-NINE

Josie drove as fast as she legally could to Fairfield. It was in Lenore County which was south of Denton. It mostly consisted of farm and gameland with gentle rolling hills and lots of wooded areas. The narrow roads were like black ribbons snaking through the largely deserted area. Earl Butler's home was along a rural route where the houses were several acres apart and set back from the road. It was a one-story modular home with tan siding and a brown roof. Three wooden steps led to the front door. There were no flower beds or garden, but the lawn was neatly kept. An old Ford sedan sat in the short gravel driveway. Josie parked behind it and got out, momentarily resting a hand on its hood. It was cold.

She walked up to the door and knocked, ears strained for any noise inside. There was nothing. Her eyes tracked the door frame. No doorbell. She knocked again. She waited several minutes before circling the house and peeking in the windows. Most were covered by heavy curtains or miniblinds. She could see into the kitchen but it was empty. A small table with two chairs sat to one side. On the table was a plate with half a sandwich on it. From where she stood, she thought it looked like someone had taken a bite out of it. The back door was only one step up from a small concrete patio. Josie knocked on that as well and listened. She thought she heard a faint voice, but she couldn't be sure.

She walked around the house again, and this time called out Earl Butler's name. "Mr. Butler? You in there? You okay, sir?" Every few steps she would stop and listen. Only once more did she think she heard a faint sound, but she couldn't make out exactly what it was. A feeling of dread, heavy and cloying, had settled over her shoulders. Her gut churned, signaling to her that something wasn't right. But her head reasoned that she was just being paranoid because of everything that had happened in the last two weeks. She circled the house once more, trying both the front and back doors but they were locked. The windows were locked as well though she could probably easily break in if she smashed the glass in one of them. But then what? What if the house was empty and Earl Butler came home to find that a strange woman had broken into his home? Josie knew that even her status as a police officer couldn't protect her from having charges pressed against her. She'd need a warrant to get in without a key, and she was in a county that was not her own. That could take a day or more to get and that was if a judge would even allow it. She could try to track down people who knew Earl Butler to find out when he'd last been seen and if anyone had a spare key.

A spare key.

Josie looked around but didn't see anywhere that Earl might have hidden a key. There were no plants or porch furniture outside. She walked again around the house, checking the perimeter for stones. She then checked the wheel wells of his car to see if he had a magnetic case where he might hide a key, but there was nothing. She was about to give up, was in fact walking to her car, when she spotted a sprinkler head in the middle of the front yard. It was green and blended in with the grass which was why she hadn't noticed it before. She zigzagged across the lawn, looking for additional sprinkler heads but there was only that one. It was a long shot, but on the job, she'd seen secret key compartments in just about every design she could think of—including sprinkler heads. Dropping to her knees, she used both hands to gently probe the sprinkler. If it was attached to an underground system, it wasn't going to come out of the ground—certainly not without her breaking it. But it pulled right out. It wasn't attached to anything. The bottom part of it was a hollow compartment shaped like a spike. A minute later she managed to twist the thing open, and a key fell into her palm.

She put the sprinkler head back where she'd gotten it and sprinted toward the door, using the key to unlock it. The house was dim and it took a moment for her eyes to adjust. Her heart raced as she took in the scene before her. Immediately to the right was what Josie assumed was a living room although now it looked like a tornado had blown through. Furniture was upended; lamps broken and tossed to the floor; magazines and mail torn and discarded; a television with a cracked screen lay on the living room carpet. Beyond that was a dining room, judging by the table and chairs, although the table was askew, two of the chairs had been overturned and what looked like a large china cabinet had fallen on its face.

The faint sound Josie thought she had heard outside came again, making her jump. Her service weapon was in her hand, her eyes searching everywhere. "Mr. Butler," she called.

This time, she registered it as a man's raspy voice, trying to call out. Her feet carried her deeper into the dining room and that was when she saw a pair of feet covered in tan moccasin slippers protruding from beneath the china cabinet. "Mr. Butler!" she cried.

Holstering her gun she bent at the knees and cupped her palms beneath the edge of one side. It was heavy, far heavier than she had anticipated. Josie was sure she wouldn't be able to lift it by herself. But then came the sound of that pitiful gasping voice, begging her for help. Adrenaline shot through her, and a cry tore from her throat as she lifted the china cabinet from the ground. The sound of glass breaking shattered the silence of the house as Earl's dinnerware scattered across the floor. Once Josie righted the large piece of furniture, she looked down to see him on his back, wearing a pair of khaki pants and a flannel shirt. His hair was gray and thinning and white stubble dotted his ashen face. His lips were almost blue. Josie knelt beside him and felt his pulse while she took out her phone and dialed 911.

"Mr. Butler," she said. "My name is Josie Quinn. I'm a detective from Denton. I'm going to get you help. Just hang in there."

CHAPTER FIFTY

An hour later, Josie sat by Earl Butler's bed in the Emergency department of a nearby hospital. On the other side sat a sheriff's deputy from Lenore County. Since the attack on Butler had taken place there, it was out of her jurisdiction, but because she was trying to solve a string of murders and she had saved Butler, she was allowed to sit in on the interview. An oxygen tank whirred in the corner of the room, and Earl strained to talk over it. Some color had come back into his face. A lifetime of wrinkles jostled when he spoke, and the nasal cannula bobbed on his upper lip.

"This man came yesterday. Said he wanted to talk about my old friend, Craig Bridges. We were in Vietnam together, me and Craig. Real close. We used to be roommates, but then Craig disappeared. Police thought maybe he killed himself but I knew better. So this guy shows up. It's been almost thirty years. I thought… I thought this is it, I'll find out what happened to Craig. So I let him in."

He sucked in several breaths before continuing, "He was stocky and muscular and bald. Shaved head, not bald from genetics. He was probably in his sixties but real fit. He just attacked me. Knocked me down, got on top of me, put his hands over my mouth and nose. I knew he was trying to kill me so eventually I stopped fighting. I went real still. I was betting he wouldn't check my pulse and he didn't."

"But he knocked over the cabinet," Josie said.

Earl nodded. "Pinned my legs. I couldn't get out. I heard him going through the house like he was looking for something. I didn't dare try to move in case he wanted to finish the job. Then he left.

I heard the police come this morning and tried to call out, but I couldn't. Thank God you came. I'm not as young as I used to be. Have a lot of trouble getting around."

Josie smiled at him. She glanced at the sheriff's deputy and he nodded at her, giving her permission to ask her questions. "Mr. Butler, I want to show you a photo." She took out her phone and found the photo of the belt buckle to show him. "Do you recognize this?"

He fidgeted with the nasal cannula, pressing his lips together and puckering them, pressing and puckering. Finally, he spoke, his voice husky. "That was Craig's. Where did you get that? He loved that thing. You know, he struggled when he came back from 'Nam. We all did. But he told me joining the shooting league helped him. He was good at it, and he said it was nice to shoot targets and not the enemy."

"Did he wear it all the time?" Josie asked.

Earl nodded.

"Was he wearing it the day he disappeared?"

"Yes."

"Mr. Butler, I've read the police file in connection with his disappearance. Can you tell me what you think happened?"

Earl nodded again. He looked away from her, straight ahead, as though he was staring into the past. "I think they got him. He always said they would."

Josie's spine straightened. "They who?"

"When we came home from the war, I went back to Maryland, and Craig went home to Pennsylvania. He was real depressed, didn't do much with himself at first. Then he started at the shooting league, met some friends there. One of 'em got him a job at a quarry. Good money."

"Wait," Josie said. "A quarry? The Sutton quarry?"

"Yeah, that's the one. He liked working there. Was just a laborer but it was work. He was getting his life together. Then something happened. I asked him, cause it was in all the papers back then, if he was there when they had the big accident."

Josie could have kicked herself for not looking more closely at Sutton Stone Enterprises, but why would she? None of the clues they'd found had implicated the company except perhaps the elusive Ivan. She had found out about Ivan before she knew what the belt buckle meant, and Bridges had worked for Sutton before Colette became employed there. "What accident?" she asked.

"One of the cranes failed and fell on a trailer. Killed four people. Craig was there. He never set foot in that place again after that. He injured his leg somehow. The company gave him a lot of money. I guess so he wouldn't get lawyers involved. Anyway, he took the money and came down to Maryland. Showed up on my doorstep. He was real messed up after that. More messed up than when we came home from the war."

Josie kinked a brow. "But surely what you two saw in Vietnam was worse than anything he saw as a civilian."

Earl shrugged. "I thought so but it was the quarry accident that gave him nightmares. He never got over it. I thought there was more to the story. I tried to get him to tell me—many times—but he wouldn't. Finally one night we were real drunk, and I brought it up again and he told me he couldn't tell me what really happened. That it would put me in danger. He said even though he took the money, he wasn't really safe, that one day they would come for him because he knew too much. He was always looking over his shoulder."

Josie calculated the dates in her head. She could look up the accident in the library in Denton, if it had been covered in the papers, but it would have had to have taken place in the mid-to-late seventies. Before Colette came to work for the Suttons and even before Zachary Sutton took over for his father. Which meant that whatever happened had been handled by Zachary Sutton's father, who was deceased and had been for many years. What could possibly be so damning that even now, Sutton Stone Enterprises would kill to cover it up? Was Sutton Stone behind it? Josie was betting that Ivan Ulrich was the man who had set Colette's house on fire and tried to kill Earl Butler. But according to Zachary Sutton, he hadn't worked for them that long. Why was Ivan targeting people? He wouldn't even have been working for the quarry when the accident happened or when Bridges went missing. Unless Sutton had lied.

Josie said, "Will you excuse me for a minute?"

Earl nodded. As Josie stepped out of the room, the deputy started asking him more questions. She called both Mettner and Gretchen to fill them in. Then she asked Gretchen to call Sutton's records department and ask them to check for Ivan Ulrich as an employee for the last thirty-five years, not just for the time period that Josie and Sutton had discussed. She promised to be back in an hour and hung up. Once she was assured that Earl Butler was going to be just fine, she left her contact information with the deputy and headed back to Denton, her head spinning.

The pieces didn't fit. There weren't enough connections between all the victims. What did Colette Fraley have to do with any of them? By all accounts, she hadn't even known the Pratt brothers or Craig Bridges. She worked at the same quarry as Bridges a couple of years later, but that was it. Where did Ivan fit in? The affair theory no longer seemed viable once Bridges was figured into the equation. Still, she wondered, was Ivan working alone? No, she thought, clearly he wasn't because they'd found two different shoe prints at two different scenes. Was there a connection to Sutton? There had to be. But if Sutton was somehow involved, what did any of it have to do with Drew and Samuel Pratt? Were the Pratt brothers' cases not connected to the Bridges case? But why did Colette have personal items from both the Pratt brothers, who had no connection to the quarry, and Bridges?

When the Denton station house came back into view, it was a welcome relief. Except for the press vans parked out front. "Oh no," she muttered. She parked in the municipal lot and called Trinity, trying to keep the note of accusation out of her voice. "There's an awful lot of press down here at the police station," she said to her sister. "Do you know anything about this?"

"No," Trinity snapped. "I don't. You could have given me a heads-up that there was some kind of development with the Drew Pratt case. Instead I had to find out from someone at WYEP."

"And what did your WYEP contact say?" Josie asked.

"That Drew Pratt's daughter was murdered and a few days later, someone torched her house."

"That has nothing to do with Drew Pratt," Josie argued.

"Maybe not but given the fact that her father went missing under such suspicious circumstances, you know that his case is going to be in the limelight again. Reporters will try to make connections between the two."

Before Josie could stop it, a laugh erupted from her lips. "Good luck with that."

"What's so funny?" Trinity asked, an edge of annoyance to her voice.

"I have to go," Josie said. "We'll talk later, I promise."

She fought her way through the onslaught of reporters shouting questions at her and thrusting their microphones and cameras her way, keeping her eyes on the door and saying nothing. Chitwood could be heard hollering all the way in the first-floor lobby. Josie took the stairs and poked her head into the great room, where he paced like a caged lion, yelling about "the damn press" and "this unholy circus" he now had to deal with because someone on the staff "obviously couldn't keep your damn mouth shut" and that when he found out who leaked about the Beth Pratt case, he was going to "have their ass." Never mind that all any enterprising reporter had to do was ask around Beth Pratt's neighbors or co-workers to find out she'd been murdered. It had never been a matter of keeping her death and the arson of her home a secret, it had simply been a matter of making sure as little attention was drawn to it as possible.

Gretchen and Mettner stood in the corner of the room with cups of coffee in hand, watching Chitwood pace. When Josie caught Gretchen's eye, she sauntered past her desk where she casually picked up a piece of paper, then walked over to the door and entered the stairwell. They closed the door, muffling the sounds of Chitwood's rage.

Gretchen handed Josie the printout of an article from the *Bellewood Record* from May of 1974. Quickly, Josie scanned it. It confirmed what Earl Butler had told her about there being an accident at the quarry that killed four people. Except it hadn't happened on any work site. There had been an encampment, the article said, where Sutton Stone Enterprises had set up temporary living quarters for their workers. It was basically a number of trailers. It was still under construction when one of the cranes had fallen onto a trailer and crushed it, killing all four workers inside. The company had taken full responsibility and compensated the families generously. End of story.

As Josie finished the article, she said, "So why did they pay off Craig Bridges? This obviously wasn't a secret, and the company handled it."

Gretchen said, "Exactly what Mett and I were thinking."

"There's more to this," Josie said. "There has to be."

"I agree," Gretchen said. "We can look into it, but right now, Ivan Ulrich is home. I just got a call from Bellewood PD. Maybe you and Mettner should go talk to him?"

"No," Josie said. "Not yet. I think we need more information."

"Like what?"

"I don't know. I still think we're missing something. Did you hear back from Sutton's records department?"

"We went down there. Talked to the girl." Gretchen handed Josie her coffee mug and took a pair of reading glasses out of one pocket and her phone out of the other. She positioned the glasses on her nose and started scrolling on her phone. "I might already have an email. Yes, here it is." Josie waited a long moment while Gretchen read over an email. Then Gretchen gave a low whistle. "Well, this is interesting. Ivan Ulrich has been an independent contractor for Sutton Stone Enterprises since 1983."

"An independent contractor? What do you mean?"

"He was hired as a full-time laborer back in 1981," Gretchen said.

"Which is what Zachary Sutton told me."

"Then in 1983, he was taken off the payroll but retained as a 'security consultant.' He was paid per job after that, it looks like."

"A security consultant?"

They looked at one another. They both knew exactly what that meant. Gretchen said, "He's Sutton's muscle."

CHAPTER FIFTY-ONE

Bob Chitwood stood behind his desk, arms crossed over his thin chest, regarding Josie, Mettner and Gretchen with guarded optimism. Finally, his voice had lowered to a normal volume. He lifted one hand and pointed an index finger at them. "You're telling me that this Ivan Ulrich person worked as Zachary Sutton's 'security consultant' for over thirty years, and Sutton lied about it."

"Yes," Josie said. "I mean, he said his memory wasn't that great anymore, but I don't buy that. Also, Ivan would have been acting as his muscle when Craig Bridges disappeared, when Samuel Pratt died, and when Drew Pratt went missing."

"Which means that Ivan—who was close to Colette—could have been responsible for whatever happened to Bridges and the Pratt brothers," Mettner added.

"So, what? You think he collected these items and gave them to Colette?" Chitwood asked. "And doesn't Laura Fraley-Hall work for Sutton? Isn't she a big shot there? You said she'd never heard of this Ivan."

"She's the vice president and heads up the quarry in Bethlehem. It's possible she's never met Ivan or had reason to meet him. He's an independent contractor," Josie said. "Which means he doesn't report to the quarry or any of the offices. He only works when Sutton tells him to—at least based on the personnel records we got."

"We should still bring her in," Chitwood said.

Josie could imagine how well that was going to go over. She had been wondering herself just how much Laura knew and didn't know and how much of her divisive behavior toward Josie and Noah had to do with her hiding something. Josie couldn't see Laura murdering her own mother, much less while eight months pregnant. Besides that, she had a solid alibi. But it wouldn't surprise Josie if Laura knew something critical and was hiding it to protect herself.

"Yes, we'll need to bring her in," Josie said. "I think it's possible that Ivan got the belt buckle, arrowhead, and flash drive and gave them to Colette, although we believe that Colette may have been with both Pratt brothers on the last days they were seen by anyone so she could have gotten the arrowhead and the flash drive herself."

"You think Colette Fraley killed the Pratt brothers?" Chitwood asked.

"Possibly," Gretchen said.

"No," Josie said.

Chitwood looked from one of them to the other, his eyes alight with interest. Then he turned to Mettner. "You want to weigh in?"

Mettner shook his head. "I'd like to hear what these two fine detectives have to say first."

Chitwood raised a brow. "You're a smart man, Mett."

Josie said, "I just don't think that physically Colette Fraley would have been able to overcome either one of the Pratt brothers. I think it's more likely that Ivan Ulrich knew she had met with them, and he killed them and then, as a warning he gave her a personal effect from each one. He wanted her to understand what would happen if she kept trying to expose Sutton's secret—people would die. Innocent people. He gave her those things so she would never forget."

"You think she was having affairs with these men?" Chitwood asked, looking to Gretchen.

"It makes the most sense," Gretchen said. "Except for Bridges who wasn't living around here when he disappeared. But Detective Quinn disagrees."

Chitwood raised a brow in Josie's direction. "Quinn. Just because Colette was Noah's mother doesn't make her a saint."

Josie shifted in her seat. "Yeah, I know that. That's not why I think Colette was innocent in all of this. Colette kind of *was* a saint, sir. The way she lived her life flies completely against the notion that she would have had multiple extra-marital affairs. Or that morally she would have been capable of something like what we're talking about—which is allowing Ivan to kill these men and never saying a word about it."

"People have secrets, Quinn. Big, disgusting, appalling secrets."

"With all due respect, sir, I know that better than anyone," Josie said dryly.

She waited for his retaliation, for some mean-spirited comment delivered in a shout or for him to threaten her job, but all he did was laugh. It was, Josie realized, possibly the first time she'd ever heard the sound come from him. He laughed for a good thirty seconds as he pulled his desk chair out and plopped into it. Finally, he said, "Yeah, both of you know that better than any criminal I've ever met, huh?"

"Sir," Josie said, sitting up straight, ready to defend herself and Gretchen, but Chitwood waved her off.

"Forget it, Quinn," he said. "I'm just saying you're right. What do you think is going on here?"

"Colette was the assistant to the owner and head of the company—first for Sutton, senior and then for Sutton, junior. She would have seen things almost no one else in the company would have seen."

"Like what?" Chitwood asked.

Josie shrugged. "I'm not sure. Everything. She would have been privy to the content of phone calls, meetings, internal memos, records. I think she found something—the same something that Craig Bridges knew about that got him killed."

"But what?" Chitwood asked.

"That's what we don't know yet, sir," Gretchen said.

"So you don't think she was having an affair with either of the Pratt brothers?" Chitwood said.

"No, I don't."

"All right, let's say you're right. Colette is the head secretary. She comes across something the company doesn't want the public to know about. She talks to Bridges because he was there."

Josie nodded. "So Sutton has Ivan make Bridges disappear."

"I can see her going to Drew Pratt because he was a prosecutor," Chitwood said. "But why Samuel Pratt? He was a college professor."

Mettner chimed in, "Maybe because he was Drew Pratt's brother?"

Josie said, "But Drew Pratt never even figured out who C.F. was so that doesn't make sense. Unless Ivan killed Samuel Pratt before he could put Colette in touch with his brother."

"Why not just approach Drew Pratt directly?" Chitwood argued. "I knew Drew. He was approachable."

"We're still missing something," Josie insisted.

"Well, if there's something in the internal Sutton records, no way is Sutton going to just give that up. I mean, we can get a warrant, but if you had something so damning you'd be willing to kill over it in your records, why would you keep it around?" Gretchen said.

"And why didn't Sutton ever have Colette killed if he knew she knew something big that could jeopardize the company?" Chitwood said.

Josie said, "I don't know. I don't have it all put together yet, but I think we should pick up Ivan. We can hold him until Lenore County expedites him. Earl Butler will be able to make a positive ID. We bring in Laura Fraley-Hall and Zachary Sutton. We get a warrant for the Sutton Stone Enterprise records in connection with the crane accident. While we've got Sutton and Laura here, we execute it."

"Who's the second person?" Chitwood asked. "The second shoe print?"

"We don't know yet," Josie said.

Mettner added, "I served warrants on all the hunting and sporting retailers in the county, but that information will take a day or two for them to produce."

Josie said, "This is what we've got to work with. I say we run with it. We'll turn the second person up eventually, either through the list we get from the retailers or through the course of the investigation."

Chitwood clapped his hands together. "Get some people together then and get on it. We've got the press breathing down our necks. I want this shit solved yesterday."

CHAPTER FIFTY-TWO

It was late in the day so they wrote up their warrant and had it signed by a judge. They resolved to round up all the players the next morning and have Mettner and Hummel serve the warrant while Josie and Gretchen questioned Ivan Ulrich, Laura, and Zachary Sutton. Mettner deferred to them since they were the more experienced interviewers. Josie drove home feeling both jittery and exhausted. Her body thirsted for another drink even as the headache from the morning's hangover still lingered at the periphery of her brain. She felt relieved when she saw Trinity's rented Lexus in her driveway. Trinity met her at the door, bouncing up and down on her toes. Josie could tell by the excited twinkle in her eyes and the breathy way she said, "Hey" that something was up.

Trinity said, "Someone's here to see you!" in a low and eager voice.

Josie froze like a deer in headlights in the foyer. For some reason, she thought it was Luke. She'd left without saying goodbye. She had no memory of whatever had happened between them, but he probably recalled every second. What would she say to him? Had he really driven all the way to Denton to see her? Surely he didn't believe they would be getting back together in any way, even if they *had* slept together, and she was sure she would never do that, no matter how drunk, because she loved Noah. She hadn't seen his vehicle, or any other vehicles, in the driveway. Besides, it was extremely unlikely that Trinity would be this excited to see Luke.

Josie leaned to the left and peeked over Trinity's shoulder to see Noah sitting on her couch, his casted leg up on her coffee table and a pair of crutches propped up against the couch beside him. Relief and trepidation flooded through her at once. Trinity winked at her and said, "I'll be upstairs. Gonna grab a shower before I head back to New York."

"Hey," Noah said, smiling at her. He patted the couch. "Have a seat."

Josie perched on the edge of her sofa. "How did you get here?"

"Grady brought me. Laura will probably kill him, but I had to come back."

"How are you feeling?" she asked.

"I've been better. You okay? You had Trinity worried. Me too."

"Uh yeah. I'm fine. Sorry. I was following a lead, was all. What are you—what are you doing here?"

He reached over and took her hand, and Josie felt at once warmed and guilty. "I needed to apologize to you. Laura got ahold of my phone, and well... I did need to get out of Denton, but I was wrong to shut you out the way I did. I'm sorry. I'm really struggling with all of this."

"I know," Josie said.

"I'm still not thrilled that you spoke with my dad."

Josie sighed. "Well, you're not going to be thrilled about what happens next then. We need to bring Laura in for a formal interview. Chitwood's going to call her himself tomorrow."

Noah's posture tensed. "Laura? Why?"

"Not for anything we think she did wrong, but we think there are things that went on at Sutton Stone Enterprises that your mother found out about and that Sutton was trying to cover up. We need to know how much Laura knew about it, if anything."

Noah said, "She didn't know anything. She can't have. If it was something really bad, she wouldn't hide it. I know she wouldn't."

"Then it shouldn't be an issue to bring her in and ask her," Josie said.

Noah raked a hand over his face. Josie could see his internal struggle; he'd come here to reconcile with her—for which she was grateful—but there was still the issue of his mother's murder case and everything that came after, and whether or not his family was somehow involved in something nefarious. "Noah, I'm not your enemy. If you were on the other side of this, you would realize that. I'm trying to solve a case. Your mother's murder. I can't turn the other way just because there are things that would be unpleasant for you or Laura or Theo."

A moment passed between them. Finally, Noah said, "I know. You're right. I was on the other side once, remember?"

A knock on the door startled them before Josie could answer him. It was Gretchen with a file in one hand and a pizza in the other. Mettner stood awkwardly behind her. "I thought we could go over the case," she said as she bustled into the foyer. Then she saw Noah on the couch. Her face reddened. "I'm sorry. I didn't realize… hey, Fraley. How're you feeling?"

He waved. "I've been better."

Mettner gave Noah a mock salute which he returned. Gretchen turned back toward the door, pushing Mettner back onto the front stoop. "We'll go," she said.

Noah called, "Don't leave on my account. I'm pretty tired. I was going to go upstairs and get some sleep. The painkillers make me drowsy."

Gretchen looked to Josie, who nodded, and then headed toward the kitchen, waving a clearly uncomfortable Mettner along with her. Josie helped Noah upstairs to her bedroom where he was out within seconds of hitting her mattress. She said goodbye to Trinity and settled at the kitchen table with pizza and the Fraley and Pratt files.

"Do you think it's in here?" Mettner asked.

"What's that?" Josie said, pulling over a stack of reports from the scene at Colette's house after her murder.

"The thing we're missing?"

"Don't know, but this is a good place to start."

They sifted through pages and notes for an hour, speaking little, each of them making their own notes on individual notepads and Mettner using his phone app.

"You know what I don't get?" Josie said finally. "All Colette had were three random items that would mean nothing to almost anyone who found them. So why is Ivan or his accomplice or whoever working so hard to silence so many people—Colette, Beth and Mason Pratt, Wolicki, Earl Butler— and burning down Colette's house?"

"Maybe he thought someone would start asking questions once they found the flash drive?" Gretchen suggested. "I mean that's what set us on this path."

As Josie paged through the report from the murder scene at Colette's once more, she came to the photos of the various rooms in the house, the backyard and Colette's body. "No," Josie said. "I don't think that's it. I mean, earlier we talked about the possibility of Ivan having brought her the items. Only he and Colette would have understood the significance of them."

Mettner put down the slice of pizza he'd been chomping on and leaned forward. "And what was the significance?"

"He was showing her what would happen if she didn't keep quiet," Josie answered. "They were warnings, not proof. We're looking at this all wrong. We need to know what Colette found— what she still had—that this guy has been looking for. She had to have had something. Something incriminating."

"And Ivan didn't know what she did with it," Gretchen said, following Josie's train of thought.

"Right. For all he knew, she might have sent something to one of the Pratt children. Maybe that's why he had to kill her. She was about to blow the whistle," Josie said.

"Why now, though?" Mettner asked. "If she knew about something incriminating as early as 1990 when Craig Bridges went missing, why would she suddenly decide to blow the whistle now?"

Josie paged through more photos, coming to a picture of the empty dining room where she and Noah were supposed to sit down with Colette for dinner that evening, then one of the kitchen where the drawers had been riffled through but no attempts to cook anything had been made. Josie felt a piece of the giant, confusing puzzle click into place. "Maybe because she knew she had dementia," she said. "I mean, she was in the early stages of it. She didn't know how long she would be lucid."

"So she decided she'd come clean with whatever she knew. Except she didn't get the chance," Mettner said. "Neither Beth Pratt nor Mason Pratt had received anything from Colette or ever even heard of her before we came asking questions."

"Which means she was still in possession of whatever it was that she was murdered for," Josie said.

The next photo Josie came to was of Officer Chan holding up a dirt-encrusted rosary. Then photos of the small shovel Colette had been using to dig up the garden. "Oh my God," Josie said. She stood up abruptly, her chair scraping the tile.

"What are you doing?" Gretchen asked.

"I'm going to wake Noah up. I need to know the address of the house he grew up in."

CHAPTER FIFTY-THREE

By seven the next morning, Josie, Noah, Gretchen, Chitwood, Mettner and Hummel were all assembled outside of Noah's child-hood home. It was only a few blocks away from Denton's city park—a two-story Cape Cod with gray siding and bright blue trim. It was larger than the home Colette had been living in at the time of her death, but Noah had told Josie that after her husband left, she had had to downsize.

While the rest of them stood on the sidewalk, Noah sat in the passenger's seat of Josie's vehicle, his cast dangling out the open door. "You sure about this?" he asked Josie.

She wasn't, but it was worth a shot. They could bring in Ivan and Zachary Sutton and question them relentlessly, but without some actual evidence or knowledge of what it was that Colette was hiding, they were likely to get nowhere. Both men could ask for attorneys and without being able to tie them to any crimes, they'd be out of reach permanently. While they had a little bit of leverage on Ivan Ulrich since Earl Butler could identify him, Josie didn't think it was enough for Ivan to give them a full confession accounting of all his crimes.

"Yes," Josie said. "I'm sure."

Chitwood squinted against the morning sun as he turned to look at her. "You sure it's not at the other house? She was digging at the other house."

"No," Josie said firmly. "It's here. Laura said she'd been burying rosaries since they were kids. Whatever Colette found, she found when her children were young. This is where they were living. What better way to keep it out of the wrong person's hands than to leave it buried here when she moved?"

"Then why was she digging when she died?" Noah asked.

Josie grimaced. "I think she may have been confused, because of the dementia."

Chitwood sighed. "You better be right about this, Quinn. I'm about to knock on this family's door and ask to dig up their backyard, and we don't even know what the hell we're looking for. By the way, I'm going to call on Laura Fraley-Hall, you and Gretchen are picking up Ivan Ulrich, and Mettner and Hummel are going to round up Zachary Sutton before they serve the warrant. I don't really have the manpower for this nonsense."

As if on cue, an old Toyota Camry rolled down the street, stopping behind Josie's vehicle. "Don't worry," Josie said as Sergeant Dan Lamay stepped out. To Lamay she called, "Did you bring it?"

"Sure did, boss." Lamay limped along on his bad knee to the trunk which he popped open. Reaching inside, he pulled out a metal detector.

Gretchen gave Josie a smile of admiration. Chitwood said, "What if she didn't hide this thing—whatever the hell it is—in something metal? You ever think of that, Quinn?"

"Sir," Josie answered. "If she didn't then we'll have to dig up the whole yard, but if she *did* bury it in something metal, and Lamay can locate it, then we only have to dig up one spot."

Chitwood shook his head but ambled up the walkway. "Let's hope they let us do this," he mumbled. "'Cause I don't think I can get a warrant for something this goddamn vague."

In the fifteen minutes that Bob Chitwood was inside the house, Josie had a barrage of second thoughts about sending him in to ask the homeowner to let them dig in their yard. Chitwood was the least personable of them all. He even chafed easygoing Noah. But he emerged with a grin on his face, waving to Lamay and telling him to "hurry the hell up." To the rest of them, he said, "Get your asses moving. We've got a lot of work to do today."

CHAPTER FIFTY-FOUR

Two and a half hours later, they had Ivan Ulrich in one interrogation room and Zachary Sutton in another. Neither of them knew the other man was being questioned. In a strange twist, Sutton had given the team the most trouble about coming in and demanded they call his lawyer before he would even leave his office, while Ivan Ulrich agreed to drive to the Denton police station with Josie and Gretchen with no questions asked. In fact, the only thing he had asked them was, "Can I get my wallet?" Now, he sat peacefully at the table, sipping at the coffee Josie had offered him. He was definitely burly and well-muscled as both Colette's neighbor and Earl Butler had described. His bald head gleamed beneath the fluorescent lights. Beneath fathomless dark eyes, his nose looked permanently smashed in. Black and gray whiskers stubbled his chin. He had a hard face and a flat affect. Josie could see why Sutton would want to use him as muscle. Although he had been pleasant and cooperative with Josie and Gretchen, she could easily see him turning intimidating and frightening.

A woman's voice carried down the hallway. Josie recognized it at once as Laura Fraley-Hall's before she turned the corner with Chitwood at her back. "This is some kind of joke, right?" she said indignantly. "I mean, this has to be a joke. I know you're not suggesting that you want to question me in relation to my own mother's murder case. What the hell kind of department are you running here?"

Chitwood shook his head. "Relax. My detective here, Palmer, just needs to ask you some questions."

Laura rested her hands on her enormous belly. "You can't treat me like this," she went on. "I'm about to give birth."

"Hey," Chitwood snapped. "I can do whatever the h—"

Gretchen cut him off. "Hi Laura. Thanks for coming. This isn't an interrogation. In fact, why don't we go back downstairs? There's a conference room down there that's pretty comfortable. Right down the hall we've got some snacks. I can get you something to eat or drink or send the Chief out to get you whatever you want. Are you hungry?"

Laura bristled but seemed to calm down a bit, her posture loosening. Chitwood glared at Gretchen but kept quiet. To Gretchen, Laura said, "Thank you. Maybe some decaf tea and crackers."

Gretchen glanced pointedly at Chitwood whose face turned beet red. Still, he spun on his heel and walked off to fulfill Laura's request.

Laura said, "I don't understand what's going on here."

Josie said, "I'm so sorry, Laura. It's just that there have been some developments in your mom's case. We really need your help is all."

"Yeah," Gretchen added. "Sorry about the Chief. He can be really abrasive sometimes."

Laura laughed. "Oh, well, that's the nicest word for dickhead I've ever heard."

Josie couldn't stop the bark of laughter that escaped her mouth. She sincerely hoped that when this was over, Laura would be exonerated and they could form some type of real relationship. One where Laura wasn't trying to keep Josie from her brother. But for now they had to play Chitwood's foils. He was bad cop; they were good cop.

In the conference room, they waited until Laura was settled in one of the comfy leather spin chairs with her tea and crackers in front of her before they started asking questions.

Gretchen began with, "You told Detective Quinn that you'd never heard of a man named Ivan, is that right?"

"Correct. Why do you ask?"

"So the name Ivan Ulrich doesn't mean anything to you?"

Laura's eyes were wide and blank. "No, should it? Is that the name of my mother's childhood friend?"

Josie said, "Yes, and the name of a security consultant who has been retained by Sutton Stone Enterprises since 1983."

Confusion crinkled Laura's brow. "A security consultant? What do you mean? We have an outfit we contract with for site security. I can give you their information."

"So Sutton Stone Enterprises doesn't contract with security consultants?" Gretchen asked.

"Not that I'm aware of. I mean, it's certainly not a practice that I know anything about. Maybe Mr. Sutton consulted with him when he was choosing the site security outfit?"

"Not that kind of consultant," Gretchen said.

"We believe that Mr. Sutton was contracting with Mr. Ulrich for... muscle."

Laura laughed. "Muscle? What does that mean? What, like a bodyguard? Mr. Sutton hardly needs a bodyguard. We run a number of quarries. Not dangerous stuff."

Josie said, "Not a bodyguard. More like... an enforcer. A fixer, if you will."

"What?" Laura said, looking from Josie to Gretchen and back as though waiting for a punchline. "What on God's green earth would Mr. Sutton need a 'fixer' for?"

Ignoring her question, Gretchen asked, "So you've never heard of or come into contact with Ivan Ulrich in the context of your work?"

"What? No. I never heard of him until the other day when Josie said my father mentioned him."

Gretchen asked, "Did your mother ever mention work issues to you?"

"No," Laura said. "But she worked in Mr. Sutton's office. I was usually traveling—at least until I took over the Bethlehem site."

"So she never mentioned anything she might have found or stumbled onto while she worked for Sutton that would have been cause for concern?" Josie asked.

Something flickered in Laura's eyes. She looked down at her tea. "She said something weird once, but it was during one of her… episodes. You know, when she was showing early signs of dementia. I didn't take it seriously. It didn't even really make sense."

"How long ago was this? What did she say?" Gretchen asked.

Laura put her hands on the top of her belly. "It was last year. She said, 'I know what they did. It was a big cover-up.' So I asked her what who did and she said the Suttons. I asked if she meant Mr. Sutton, her old boss, and she said, 'It wasn't just him.' Then I asked her what she was talking about and she said, 'If I talk, they'll kill me, and maybe you, too.' I pressed her on it, but she was off on some other tangent. The thing is that she said a lot of strange and paranoid-sounding things when she wasn't lucid. I really didn't take it seriously."

"Did you ask her about it when she was lucid?" Josie asked.

"Of course," Laura said. "She laughed and said she'd been watching too many crime dramas on television, probably."

"Was that the only time she ever said anything like that?" Gretchen asked.

Laura's hands stroked her belly. Her face crumpled a little. "Well, I mean, she said something strange after that, but I honestly didn't even bother asking her about it because I just thought it was the dementia talking."

"What did she say?" Josie asked.

"She said, 'I know where the bodies are, all the bodies.'"

CHAPTER FIFTY-FIVE

Josie and Gretchen left Laura in the conference room and headed upstairs to where the interrogation rooms were. They checked the closed-circuit video feed to see that Ivan hadn't moved very much while he was waiting. His coffee cup was empty but other than that, he seemed content to sit very still until someone joined him. He was someone who was very used to being obedient, Josie thought.

"You believe her?" Gretchen asked.

Josie sighed. "I don't know. It's hard to believe she didn't know that Sutton had someone in the wings to do dirty work. But I do believe that she has no idea what Colette was hiding. Your mom's getting dementia, saying all kinds of odd things… knowing the person Colette was, her saying she knew where the bodies were would seem completely outlandish if I were her daughter. I would have believed her when she said she'd been watching too many crime dramas."

"But Colette was telling the truth," Gretchen said. "She did know something. She definitely knew what happened to Bridges and the Pratt brothers."

"Yeah," Josie agreed. She took out her cell phone and called Lamay, but he hadn't found anything besides an old wrench buried in the yard. "Keep going," Josie urged him. "It's important." She hung up and pocketed her phone. "Let's take a crack at Ivan Ulrich."

"Wait," Gretchen said as her phone chirped. "It's Mettner. He got an email from the legal department at Landon's Sporting Goods outside of Bellewood. Ivan Ulrich's name is on the list of customers who purchased size eleven Coyote Run boots from their store in the last six months. They tracked it through his customer rewards card."

"Perfect," Josie said. "Let's go."

They read Ivan his rights and Josie waited for him to ask for an attorney, but he didn't. Maybe he didn't realize how much trouble he was in, Josie thought.

Gretchen started by asking where he was on dates and times of the recent spate of crimes: Colette's murder, Beth Pratt's murder, the fire at Beth Pratt's house, the attack on Mason Pratt, the fire at Colette's home, Wolicki's murder, and the attack on Earl Butler. He had the same alibi for each date: a lady friend who could confirm that he'd been with her during each of those times. He wrote her name, address and phone number down for them, but Josie set it aside. This woman was obviously someone he had convinced to lie for him. Josie wasn't buying any of it.

They asked him if he had known Colette, and he confirmed that they'd gone to Catholic school together and that both their mothers had worked in the rectory. He confirmed that one of the priests had been 'doing bad things' to him and that Colette blew the whistle, eventually leading his mother to pack up and move them away.

"When did you see Colette again?" Josie asked him.

"It was many years," Ivan said. "We were both out of high school. My mother had just died. I was going to be evicted from our apartment. I came to Denton looking for her. I asked her for help. She got me the job at the quarry."

"What kind of work did you do?" Gretchen asked.

He laughed. "I moved rocks from one place to another. After the rock splitters did their jobs, a bunch of us would come in to move the slabs and any debris, haul it elsewhere."

"How long did you do that?" Josie asked.

"Maybe a year."

"Then what happened?" Gretchen asked.

"Mr. Sutton—junior—said he had easier work for me. Security stuff."

"What kind of security stuff?" Josie asked.

"He had an outside business come in and provide security for the sites, but he didn't trust them. So he asked me to periodically check on things without the outside business knowing. Like a checks and balances system."

"That's it?" Gretchen said.

"Well, sometimes the workers would get into disputes, and I'd go down to the sites and mediate. Try and get things worked out before anything got violent."

Josie didn't believe this for a second, but she was certain that both Ivan and Sutton had long ago realized that one day they might be asked questions like these so they had ready answers. Innocuous answers.

"Did you ever provide any services for Mr. Sutton that required you to carry out a violent act?" Josie asked pointedly.

A smile froze on Ivan's face. "Violent? What do you mean?"

Gretchen said, "Did Mr. Sutton ever ask you to intimidate anyone? Assault them?"

"That would be illegal," Ivan said.

Josie noted he didn't say no. She took out her phone and swiped to a photo of Drew Pratt. "Have you ever seen this man?"

He stared at the picture for a long moment and then said, "No, I haven't."

She got the same answer when she showed him photos of Samuel Pratt and Craig Bridges. Josie decided to move on for the moment. "After you became a security consultant for Mr. Sutton, how often did you see Colette?"

"Not often. I'd run into her from time to time, but I never had much reason to be up in the big office."

"Mr. Ulrich," Josie said. "Did you ever have a romantic or sexual relationship with Colette Fraley?"

He looked somewhat stunned but quickly gathered himself. "No," he said.

"Did you want to?" Gretchen asked.

He looked into his empty coffee cup. "Yes. I loved Colette very much. But she was never interested in me in that way. Plus, she was married. She had a family."

"That doesn't necessarily stop people," Josie pointed out.

He met her eyes, his dark irises flashing with anger. "Colette would never do something like that. She was loyal. A good person. A good wife and mother."

"Did she ever have an affair with Zachary Sutton?" Josie pressed.

He shook his head. "No, never. It was a very professional relationship."

"How about other lovers? Do you know if Colette had other lovers?"

"I don't know," Ivan admitted. "But I doubt it. I told you, she wasn't like that. She wasn't that kind of person."

"Lots of people aren't that kind of person," Gretchen said. "Until they are."

He slapped a palm onto the table suddenly. Both Josie and Gretchen managed to keep completely still instead of startling. "*Not* Colette," he hissed.

"Okay, fair enough," Gretchen relented. She turned her chair around and grabbed a paper evidence bag from the table along the wall. After snapping on a pair of gloves pulled from her pocket, she dumped the contents of the bag onto the table and spread them out before Ivan. The flash drive. The arrowhead. The belt buckle.

"Do you recognize these things?" Gretchen asked.

Again Josie saw the slightest flicker in his façade. "No," he said. "I've never seen them."

"What's your shoe size?" Josie asked.

Bewildered, he met Josie's eyes. "I'm sorry. What?"

"Your shoe size. What size shoe do you wear?"

"A size eleven. What does that have to do with anything?"

Josie asked, "Do you own a pair of Coyote Run boots?"

"I don't know what kind. I have lots of boots," he said.

"Did you buy a pair of boots at Landon's Sporting Goods in the last few months?"

"What?" For the first time, his expression showed signs of frustration. "I don't know. I guess so."

Gretchen asked, "What if I told you I had a receipt for a pair you bought there four months ago? Size eleven Coyote Run boots in tan. Would you dispute that?"

"No," he said. "I wouldn't dispute it. I've bought many boots from there."

He had already given his lady friend as an alibi for the night that Mason Pratt was attacked. If they wanted to prove beyond a doubt that it was his boot print, there was more work to be done. They'd have to get a warrant for his apartment so they could take his boots into evidence and then perhaps they could take soil samples from the treads. Or they could hire an expert in footprint analysis to take a footprint from Ivan and then compare it to the one found at Mason Pratt's house, for which they'd need his consent. In the meantime, Josie didn't want their line of questioning to send up enough red flags for him to ask for an attorney.

"Do you have a partner?" Josie asked. "Someone else you work with when you're doing these security consultant duties for Sutton Stone Enterprises?"

"No," Ivan answered. "I work alone."

"Are you aware whether or not Mr. Sutton has any additional security consultants on his payroll?"

"I don't know," Ivan said. "You have to ask him."

Gretchen smiled. "We will. Tell me, where were you yesterday afternoon?"

He stared at Gretchen. "I was with my lady friend. We went for a drive."

Josie said, "I think we're done here, but there's one more person who would like a word. Do you mind hanging around for just a little longer?"

A muscle ticked in his jaw, but he said, "Sure."

CHAPTER FIFTY-SIX

Outside of Ivan's interrogation room, Josie told Gretchen, "We need a warrant for those boots so we can make a comparison. That could take a while, and we may be not be able to hold him that long. Call someone from the Lenore County sheriff's office and have them come up here to talk to him. We'll need a picture of him. Maybe they can give Earl Butler a photo lineup."

"He lies as easily as he breathes," Gretchen remarked, taking out her phone to make the call.

Josie walked over to the closed circuit viewing room to peek in on Zachary Sutton. His lawyer had arrived and was meeting with him so the feed had been turned off.

"He's not gonna say a damn word," Chitwood said, walking up behind her. "I cut Laura loose. She said she and her husband would be at Noah's house for the night."

Josie had dropped Noah off at his own house before coming to the station house with assurances from him that he would be fine on crutches for the day. At least now both Laura and Grady would be there with him should he need anything.

They walked back to the great room. Josie sat at her desk and called Lamay again, but he hadn't found anything yet. She was beginning to feel like a real idiot. Then again, it had only been a guess that Colette might bury whatever she had found in something metal. "Keep looking," Josie said. "Also, how big is the yard? I didn't think any of the yards on that block were very big."

"They're not, but if it's just me with a shovel it will take a while. I'm double and triple checking, boss," Lamay assured her.

She hung up just as Gretchen sat down at her own desk. "Lenore County deputy is on his way. About forty-five minutes, but you know we can't hold him even that long if he demands to leave."

"I know. We need more."

"We could go at him," Gretchen suggested. "Lay everything out for him. Tell him we know what he did."

"I don't want to play our cards too soon," Josie said. "He's not just going to give us what we want. Neither is Sutton. As soon as he realizes we don't have enough to charge him with anything, he'll be gone. I don't think we have enough yet to bluff our way into getting him to confess. Have you heard from Mettner and Hummel about the warrant for the Sutton Stone records pertaining to the accident?"

Gretchen looked at her phone. "As of fifteen minutes ago they were still searching through documents. What do you really expect them to find?"

Josie opened one of the case document boxes on her desk and sifted through its contents. It was the collection of personal effects that Drew Pratt had taken from his brother's office after his death. She paged through Drew Pratt's notebook and his notes on the mysterious C.F. With a sigh, she set that aside and picked up the document beneath it, which was Samuel Pratt's curriculum vitae. It was an impressive array of accomplishments.

"I don't know," Josie answered. "I don't know that Zachary Sutton would keep records of criminal activity in his company files anyway. I just know we need something else before we go at these two full tilt."

Josie paged through it again, reading over the decades of publications he'd made in his field.

Rural Archaeological Pottery in Medieval Italy.
Archaeological Recovery and Forensic Analysis of Twentieth-Century Mass Graves.

Stone Tools in Ancient Rome: Classification, Function and Behavior.
Recent Archaeological Developments in Research Methods in the
Balkan Region 6500 to 4200 BC.
Radiocarbon dating and forensic considerations of Mass Graves in
Northern Macedonia. Reassessing the Emergence of Village Life in
the Jiroft Culture of Iran.

She heard Laura's voice in her head: *She said, 'I know where the*
bodies are. All the bodies.'

"Oh my God," Josie said.

"What is it?" Gretchen said.

"I think I know what happened," Josie said, darting out of her
seat. "Let's go back in."

CHAPTER FIFTY-SEVEN

Ivan looked up when Josie and Gretchen came back in. Josie remained standing and leaned over the table, locking eyes with him. "Let's cut the bullshit, now, Ivan. I know about the mass grave."

His face went very still as the color drained from it. His mouth worked, but no words came out. Josie, encouraged, pressed on. "In 1974 there was an accident at an employee encampment at the quarry. The newspapers reported that four people died. Their families were compensated. But it wasn't just four people, was it? It was more than four. Many more. Craig Bridges knew how many people died that night. He witnessed it. That's why he had nightmares about it for the rest of his life. Nightmares that were worse than what he saw in Vietnam."

Ivan looked at his lap.

Josie spoke louder. "Colette Fraley found evidence of what really happened the night of the crane accident. She found internal documentation of the cover-up. She knew where the bodies were—all of them—and Colette couldn't let it go. She had to do something because that's the kind of person she was. Am I wrong?"

Ivan said nothing.

Josie slapped the table and he jumped. "Colette Fraley saved you from a pedophile priest. She risked both your mothers' jobs, risked being excommunicated from her beloved church. So when she found out that there was a mass grave on Sutton Stone Enterprises' property that the Suttons had covered up, she had to act. Am. I. Wrong?"

The air around her seemed charged, and the temperature in the room had gone up at least ten degrees since Josie stormed in.

A fine sheen of sweat covered Ivan's shiny skull. Slowly, his head turned from side to side.

"Say it," Josie told him.

His words were barely audible. "You're not wrong."

"She contacted Craig Bridges. He was the only survivor of that night. I don't know why he was allowed to live, but the Suttons paid him off, and he went on his way. Until Colette found the documents. Someone found out. Sutton found out. He ordered you to take care of it, so you did. Am I wrong?"

He shook his head again, more quickly this time.

"What did you do?"

He didn't speak.

"Ivan," Josie said. "If you ever cared about Colette in your life—if you ever really and truly loved her—you'll tell the truth. You know that's what she would want. It was the only thing she wanted. For the truth to be told. You know the truth. I need you to say it. What did you do?"

"I did love her," he mumbled.

"Then tell the truth. As things stand, Colette looks like some kind of serial killer. She had personal effects of three men who are either missing or dead hidden in her home. We know that she met with Samuel Pratt at least twice, and we know she met with Drew Pratt on the day he went missing. Is this what you want? For Colette to be remembered as a killer? Do you want her memory tarnished like this?"

"No," Ivan said firmly.

"Then tell me," Josie urged him. "How did Sutton find out that Colette was in touch with Bridges, and what did he order you to do?"

"She was careless," Ivan said quietly. "She had Bridges' name and phone number written on a scrap of paper in her purse. She was looking for something in her purse one day at work and it fell out. Sutton found it. When he asked her about it, she lied to him and said it was someone from her church she was supposed to deliver meals to, but Sutton wasn't buying it. He had me check out the number. Then he told me I needed to make Bridges disappear."

"He told you to kill him?" Josie asked.

Ivan said, "He never said the word kill. But it was clear. He said that Bridges knew something that could endanger the whole company, and I needed to make him go away permanently."

"So you did?"

"No, I didn't want to. I didn't—that wasn't the arrangement we had. He had me intimidate people sometimes, but nothing more than that. Most of the stuff he asked me to do was spying on competitors or people he was trying to make deals with. I was there to find dirt on people. So I said I wouldn't make Bridges disappear. I didn't see why I needed to—Bridges obviously hadn't talked."

"But Colette knew. That changed everything."

"He wanted me to make Colette disappear, too. He said he could find someone else to do the job if I refused."

Gretchen stepped up to the table, staring hard at Ivan. "You made a deal with Sutton."

He looked over at her, as if realizing for the first time she was in the room. "Yes," he said. "I promised him that I could make sure Colette was no longer a threat. I convinced him it would be too suspicious to have a former employee and a current employee go missing or turn up dead so close together, even though Bridges no longer lived in Pennsylvania. I told him Colette was a young mother and a dedicated employee. She was active in her church and well-known in her community. Her disappearance would bring a lot of scrutiny to the company. Scrutiny he might not want. So he said if I made Bridges go away, he'd let me keep my job and he wouldn't harm Colette."

"So you went to Maryland," Josie said.

"I waited in the backseat of Bridges' car one morning. When he got in, I held a gun to his head and told him to drive to a nearby riverbank. Then I made him get out and walk partway into the river. I—I held him under it until he died and let his body go."

"But you kept his belt buckle," Josie said. "And you brought it back to Pennsylvania and gave it to Colette. What did you tell her?"

"I told her it belonged to Bridges and whatever she was doing, she needed to stop. I told her that Sutton had had Bridges killed, and she would be next if she didn't let it go. That's when she told me what she had found—the massacre at the encampment, she called it. I had no idea until she told me."

"But you convinced her to keep quiet," Josie said. "How?"

His chin dropped to his chest. "Her children were young. She was terrified for them. I promised to do what I could to protect her, but I told her that Sutton would have me killed and replaced in a heartbeat if he thought I had failed to shut her up. I convinced her that the best thing for her family was to keep quiet."

"And just like that, she did?"

He nodded. "She had young children. She couldn't put them in danger. It was difficult for her, but she had to protect her family."

"Except that in 1999 she tried to expose Sutton again," Josie said. "She met with Samuel Pratt, an archaeology professor at Denton University. He had studied mass graves all over the world. She wanted to see if he would do a dig near the quarry. Exposing the grave without exposing her. It would have been an incidental finding. How did Sutton find out?"

"He didn't," Ivan said quietly. "He didn't know about Samuel Pratt—or about his brother."

Josie looked over at Gretchen who gave a barely perceptible shrug. Josie turned back to Ivan. "But you knew about him. How?"

His eyes glistened with tears. "I was in love with her. I—I watched her."

"You stalked her."

"No, I kept an eye on her."

Josie decided not to debate the point. "You saw her meeting with Samuel Pratt. She met with him once before he died."

"I researched him. There was only one reason that I could figure why she would be meeting with him. The second time they met, I overheard them talking and there was no doubt. So I waited until Colette left. I approached Dr. Pratt near his car, convinced him to get in and drive to Bellewood. I knew a stretch of riverbank there that was secluded."

"Then what?" Josie asked.

"He begged me to let him go. He said he'd never tell and never speak to Colette again. But it was too late. I already learned that people couldn't let something like that go. I knew what would happen if he exposed Sutton. I'd be killed. Colette and maybe even her family would be killed. So I took him into the river, and I held him under the water until he was gone."

The cold and matter-of-fact way that Ivan described his crimes sent a shiver up Josie's spine. The only time he ever seemed to show emotion was when he spoke of Colette. Was he even capable of the love he said he felt for her or was it just some twisted form of obsession? How could someone who could kill so easily be equally as committed to protecting a woman who didn't love him back? Was Ivan Ulrich a sociopath or just very deeply damaged? Maybe a bit of both, Josie thought. It didn't matter. What mattered was getting the rest of Ivan's confession so they could get him off the street and solve the case.

"You took something from him," Josie said. "To give to Colette as a warning."

"He had this arrowhead with him. I gave it to her and told her she had to stop. She was—she was very angry. Very upset. She told me to leave her alone, that she—" he broke off, swallowed, and tried again, "she never wanted to see me again."

"But you kept 'looking after her', didn't you?" Josie said.

He nodded.

"In spite of your warnings, she made one last effort at exposing Sutton Stone's big secret," Josie said.

"Yes. With Drew Pratt. He was a prosecutor. This could not stand. If Mr. Sutton found out she was talking to a prosecutor, all of us would have been in jeopardy."

"Did Mr. Sutton find out?" Gretchen asked.

"No. I… took care of it."

Josie said, "What did you do?"

"I followed her the day they met at the craft fair. I knew she was up to something because she'd put on this short-haired wig. I saw her in the parking lot, walking back and forth, chain-smoking. Then Drew Pratt drove up. She leaned into the passenger's side window for a minute. Then he got out and they went inside. I trailed them as best I could without her spotting me. I overheard her tell him that she had documents. A file, she said. I didn't know if it was paper or a computer file. So after she left, I made him walk down to the river, with his laptop, too. He had a flash drive. I took it. Then I walked him into the current and drowned him."

Again, Josie felt a wave of sadness. These men had been taken away from their families and loved ones for no other reason than someone else had told them a terrible secret. They were innocent. They had no part in the original crimes. Their families had suffered. Mason Pratt— the last Pratt standing—would suffer for the rest of his life because of this man.

"Did you know what was on the flash drive?" Josie asked him.

"No. I thought perhaps it was what she had given him. I wanted her to know that I was the last person he saw. So I gave the drive back to her. She told me it wasn't hers. I told her I knew she gave it to Pratt. She said that she hadn't given anything to him, but she admitted to having files. Internal company documents, she said. She found them in Sutton senior's office after his death, hidden in a secret panel in his desk. She said no one would ever know where she hid them, and it didn't matter because she was done with trying to expose Sutton."

"You weren't afraid she would try again?" Gretchen said. "She'd already tried three times."

"I knew she wouldn't try again," Ivan said, voice now tinged with sadness. "She didn't want more deaths on her conscience."

Josie wanted to tell him those deaths were on his conscience, not Colette's, but she kept silent.

Ivan continued, "I begged her not to make me kill again. I begged her to pray for my soul. Then Laura was hired by Sutton. Colette promised again to stop, to take it to her grave."

"So what happened?" Gretchen asked. "Why did you kill her?"

Shock whitened his face. "I didn't kill her. I would *never* harm Colette. No one would hurt her. She was a good person."

"Ivan," Josie said. "You've just confessed to three murders. Why are you lying about Colette's?"

He put a hand on the table and thrust his neck toward Josie, eyes earnest. "I didn't kill her."

"But you killed Beth Pratt, burned her house down, attacked Mason Pratt, killed Brody Wolicki and tried to kill Earl Butler," Josie pointed out. "And you burned Colette's house down while me and Noah were still in it."

His head hung again. "I didn't want to."

"Then why did you do it?" Josie said.

For the first time, Ivan looked behind them at the viewing mirror. "I don't want to talk anymore. I want a deal."

"What kind of a deal?" Josie asked.

"The kind where I tell you the rest and help you put away Mr. Sutton. You don't understand. He is still a danger to Laura and all of Colette's children."

Josie raised a brow at him. "You're the one who does his dirty work. Why should we believe that he is a danger to anyone? He's an elderly man now."

"Any man with a gun can be dangerous. I'm telling you. He is unpredictable. Cold. I did the things I did because I had to do them. He is not like that. He… enjoys it."

Josie exchanged a glance with Gretchen. "Give us some time."

Outside the interrogation room, Gretchen said, "What do you think?"

Josie sighed. "It's not up to us. I have to call the DA's office. Although if they know we got information from this guy about Drew Pratt, they'll probably be willing to work with him."

"But he already gave up the Drew Pratt murder. That was his bargaining chip," Gretchen said.

"No. He knows a lot more. If there's really a mass grave out there, and this guy can give it to us then the DA will work with him. Plus, Sutton's a big fish with big lawyers. A witness against him might be the only way to get to him. Also, there was a second person, remember? The size ten shoe print at Colette's house. We need to know if he can name that person."

"I'll call the DA's office," Gretchen said. "You check in with Lamay."

CHAPTER FIFTY-EIGHT

"I got nothing, boss," Lamay said when Josie reached him on his cell phone. "I'm gonna have to dig up the whole yard. You got someone set up for that?"

"Shit, no. I'll have to talk to Chitwood." They hadn't had a plan B.

Lamay was still talking. "I'm thinking if we start at the end of the yard where this grotto is—"

"What did you say?" Josie asked. "About a grotto?"

"There's a small garden grotto here in the backyard. Has a statute of the Virgin Mary in it. Homeowners say it was left there by the Fraleys when they sold the house. It's pretty nice. They never took it down even though they're not religious. They said it felt wrong."

Josie squeezed the bridge of her nose. "Dan," she said. "It's under the grotto."

"You sure?"

"Yes," she said. "I'm sure. Can you move it? Is it small enough for you to move on your own so you can get under it?"

There was a long moment of silence followed by some panting breaths. "I think I need help, boss."

Josie looked over to hers and Gretchen's desks in the great room where Gretchen was now talking with Mettner and Hummel. By the looks on all their faces, the search warrant they'd served that morning hadn't turned up anything useful. "I'm sending Mett and Hummel," she said. "Sit tight."

She dispatched Mettner and Hummel to go help Lamay. They hadn't turned up anything at Sutton Stone's records storage facility other than what Gretchen had already found in the newspapers.

The DA himself showed up a half hour later with one of his assistant DAs in tow. After meeting with Josie, Gretchen and Chitwood and hearing everything they'd already discovered, the prosecutor offered to keep the death penalty off the table if Ivan was willing to testify against Sutton for any part he had in the murders of Beth Pratt and Brody Wolicki; the attacks on Mason Pratt and Earl Butler and the arsons at Beth Pratt and Colette's houses. It took another hour of negotiating with Ivan and convincing him that, given all he'd confessed to already, avoiding the death penalty was the best he could hope for.

"Ivan," Josie told him. "Mr. Sutton is only a few rooms away with his lawyer—don't worry, he doesn't know you're here—this is our chance to make him pay. We're so close. We just need more from you. Tell us what happened after Colette died."

With a long and tortured sigh, Ivan began speaking. "Laura was in contact with Mr. Sutton after Colette's murder. She told him that the police had found certain items hidden in Colette's home."

Josie said, "The flash drive, arrowhead and belt buckle."

"Yes. He asked me why she had such things, and I told him. I didn't think it mattered since Colette was dead. No one would really know what any of those things meant. Maybe the flash drive was a problem because someone might figure out it belonged to Drew Pratt, but she told me it wasn't hers to begin with. The other two items were so random, I didn't think anyone would question them. Then he said that I needed to be sure."

"Sure of what?" Gretchen asked.

"Sure that there was nothing in her possession and nothing she had given to anyone else—one of the Pratts or anyone connected to Craig Bridges—that could implicate him. I told him there wasn't. Even if someone could make the connection between the three of them, no one would ever suspect why they were connected. No one alive knew what Colette knew."

"Except you."

He shrugged. "Even I don't know exactly what happened. I never saw the documents. I don't know where they are. I was afraid maybe the person who killed her had taken them. Laura told Mr. Sutton about her murder. How whoever killed her was looking for something and had ransacked her house. How she was digging in her garden. He was convinced that he was going to be found out. There were too many variables. He wanted whatever Colette had—whatever she took from his father's office. I told him I didn't know where she hid it. He said to torch her house although I didn't at first. I hoped to get over there and search so burning it wouldn't be necessary, but Colette's son was there every day. Finally, I had no choice. I never wanted to hurt her children."

"But you almost killed Noah," Josie said. "And me."

"I'm so sorry. I had no choice."

"You couldn't tell Sutton no?" Gretchen said. "What did he still have over you?"

Mournful eyes turned in Gretchen's direction. "Laura. He told me he'd kill her, and he'd do it himself. He said he'd covered up bigger crimes, and he would make sure he didn't get caught. I didn't care for my own life, but as I said, I didn't want Colette's children to be harmed. And Laura was having a baby."

"So you did whatever Sutton told you to do," Josie said. "And he paid you to do it."

"Yes."

Josie said, "When you couldn't find the documents that Colette had, what happened then?"

"He said he wanted the two remaining Pratt children eliminated."

"Killed?" Josie asked.

He nodded. "Yes, killed. I tried to tell him that this would only draw more attention, which it did. So he told me to burn Beth Pratt's house down. He told me to find anyone who could connect Craig Bridges to the belt buckle found in Colette's home and eliminate them."

"Kill them."

"Yes. He wanted me to burn Brody Wolicki's cabin down, but it would have caused a forest fire. More attention. So I burned all his documents."

"Earl Butler?" Josie asked.

"I was supposed to burn his house to the ground, but he didn't have anything that could come back to Mr. Sutton. So, I—I suffocated him."

Ivan still didn't know that Earl Butler had survived. Josie decided she'd let him find out later.

"Have you ever met Laura Fraley-Hall?" Josie asked.

"No. I've seen her from afar. Colette talked about her. I have never met her."

"Do you believe she knows about any of this?"

"No."

"You know that Mr. Sutton was grooming her to take over the company?"

"Yes. That was why it was even more important to put all of this to rest. The records that Colette had were the only evidence of the bodies near the encampment where the crane fell. Once those were destroyed no one would ever know."

A knock sounded on the door. Josie excused herself to find Hummel standing before her, his uniform covered in dirt but a grin on his face from ear to ear. In his hands was a small plastic insulated cooler.

"A cooler?" Josie said. "Really?"

Hummel slid the top off. "It was duct-taped. Don't worry, we photographed everything before we sliced the tape off. It held up," he said. "Look."

Inside was a folder that had been wrapped in what had to be two dozen plastic freezer bags. "Did you look at it?" Josie asked.

"No, figured you'd want first crack, boss."

"Take it down to the conference room. Get Chitwood and the DA—they're in the Chief's office—I need gloves, and I want photos and video. I'll get Gretchen. Write up a warrant before we open this and have a judge sign it."

"You got it."

It took an hour to get everything and everyone in place. Ivan had been placed under arrest and moved to the holding area. The next day he would be picked up by the county sheriff and taken to their county-wide processing facility in Bellewood. Zachary Sutton and his lawyer waited impatiently in one of the interrogation rooms. Chitwood had handled some initial questioning mostly to keep the lawyer from taking his client and storming out. Those questions had to do with why Sutton had lied about Ivan and his employment status. Sutton had cited his age and poor memory which was all his attorney would allow him to say.

"Sutton's gonna walk if we don't get in there soon," Chitwood told her as they gathered in the conference room.

"The DA's office is working on charges right now based on what Ivan Ulrich told us," Josie said. "This is the final piece. After I see what's in this file, I'll take a crack at Sutton. Even if his lawyer instructs him to say nothing, we can still place him under arrest."

"Here we go," Gretchen said as they all circled the table and she began to peel away the plastic layers with gloved fingers.

As she laid the pages of the document out on the table, they all leaned over and tried to read it. "This is an internal memo," Josie said.

Chitwood said, "I didn't bring my glasses. Who wrote it?"

Josie moved to the end of the table as Gretchen laid out the last typed page. "Sutton Stone Enterprises' head of security in 1974. It's addressed to Zachary Sutton, senior." She returned to the first page which was marked CONFIDENTIAL in large, faded red letters. Scanning it, she read off the pertinent parts to the rest of the crew. "'On May 14, 1974, an accident was reported at the employee encampment on the north side of the quarry…' there are some coordinates here and a hand-drawn map. 'I was asked by

Mr. Sutton, Senior to inspect the encampment. One trailer had been completely crushed by a construction vehicle. Its occupants appeared to be deceased from injuries sustained when the crane struck the trailer. There were sixteen employees onsite. Three employees were inside the trailer which was struck…'" Her heart seized in her chest, and her voice faltered as she summarized the next part. "Eleven employees were found in the remaining trailers, each with gunshot wounds to the head, neck, face and back. One female was found approximately one mile from the encampment with a gunshot wound to the back of the head. One employee, Craig Bridges, was unharmed as he had gone for a brief walk outside the perimeter of the encampment. Upon his return, Bridges reported seeing Zachary Sutton, Jr. exit the driver seat of the crane and then walk from trailer to trailer carrying a rifle. Bridges also reported hearing shouts, screams and gunshots. He then observed Mr. Sutton walk into the woods where he heard a final gunshot. Of the fifteen deceased individuals listed in the appendix to this report, eleven were undocumented workers. This writer was instructed by Mr. Sutton, Jr. to assist him in using heavy equipment to dig a hole…" Josie pointed to the third page. "There are dimensions here and a map with coordinates. Then he says they 'deposited' the bodies of the eleven undocumented deceased into that hole and filled it up. The deaths of the female and the three documented workers in the encampment were publicly reported to have died in a crane accident. Their families were compensated as was Craig Bridges who signed a non-disclosure contract. Jesus."

A heavy silence filled the room as each one of them took in this information. The deaths weren't the result of some accident involving construction equipment. Zachary Sutton had purposefully and coldly murdered fifteen people and then made a calculated effort to cover it up.

"Why would this be documented?" Chitwood said out loud. "Was Sutton's dad some kind of idiot?"

"I don't know," Josie said. "But at the end of the report there is a notation that the land where the grave is located should not be used or sold for development. They wanted to make sure it was never found."

CHAPTER FIFTY-NINE

They photographed the list of names of the murdered so the District Attorney could use them to charge Sutton for murder. Josie took the sheets into the interrogation room where Sutton and his attorney waited. Chitwood, Mettner and Gretchen stood behind her while she placed him under arrest for the murder of fifteen people in 1974 and conspiracy to commit murder and arson for the more recent crimes that Ivan had committed at his behest. With each charge she read off, Josie felt like a small weight lifted from her shoulders even as Sutton's attorney became more and more enraged. But as he reviewed the Affidavits of Probable Cause accompanying the arrest charges, his face grew pale and pinched.

"I'll need a few minutes alone with my client," said the attorney.

Sutton raised a hand in the air, as if to silence the attorney. A strange little smile played on his lips. His eyes found Josie. "Clever girl," he said. "Did you unearth all of this yourself?"

"No," Josie said. "My team did. Also, I'm a grown woman and a detective, and you'll address me as such."

She expected pushback but Sutton merely nodded. His attorney said, "Mr. Sutton, I cannot recommend that you say another word in front of these officers."

"Quiet now, please," Sutton told his lawyer. He looked again at Josie, the smile still in place. "Detective, I knew a girl once. She looked a lot like you." He used his thumb and index finger to lift one of the lapels of his suit jacket. "May I?" He mimed reaching inside the lapel.

Josie nodded.

He took out his wallet and riffled through it, finally peeling an old, square color photograph from the back of one of its compartments. He turned it so they could see the face of a young woman. She did bear a bit of a resemblance to Josie with her dark hair and pale skin, rosy lips and bright blue eyes. "No one would mistake you for sisters," Sutton said, pulling the photo back and staring at it. "It was more of a quality she had that you have as well... a sort of indomitable spirit. I know that sounds corny. She was quick as a whip, too. So smart. So clever."

"What was her name?" Josie asked, going along with him even though she could sense the confusion among her colleagues and Sutton's own lawyer.

"Ellie Grace," Sutton said.

Sadness pricked at her. "The woman in the woods with the gunshot to the back of her head. She wasn't an employee. What was she doing there?"

Sutton's attorney piped up again. "Zachary, really. Please don't say another word."

But Sutton didn't listen. "She was whoring around with the laborers," he answered, his demeanor turning bitter and mean so quickly it nearly gave Josie whiplash. Now she saw what Ivan must have seen. Perhaps the only side of the man that Ivan had ever seen.

"I proposed to Ellie twice, you know," Sutton said. "Twice she turned me down. I thought it was some kind of game that she was playing. Teasing me. Maybe waiting for a bigger ring. Making me work for her affection. But then I saw her in town with one of the workers and again on a Friday night at a bar with him. I started following her. She would go to the encampment in the evenings, disappear into one of the trailers. Then I saw her with another worker having a picnic by the river together. She was so brazen. It was disgusting."

"Did you ask her whether she was dating any of your workers?"

As he spoke, his face flushed. "She said they were better men than me—all of them—and that she'd rather have... have *relations* with every single one of them than settle down with me for a lifetime. She would rather live in squalor, opening her legs for any worthless man who looked her way than become my wife and live a life of luxury."

His eyes were vacant and glassy, staring right through Josie as if he were watching a movie on the wall behind her. "I hated her," he said. "I tried to bring her to her senses, but she was so defiant. I was only going to teach her a lesson. That's all I meant to do. I dragged her out of the trailer, and I—I hit her. One of those bastards came out and stopped me. I was so angry. I wanted them to pay for how they'd disrespected me."

"Disrespected you?" Josie echoed.

"Those workers knew that Ellie was my girlfriend. They should have kept their grubby hands off her."

"Was she your girlfriend?" Josie asked. "Hadn't she turned down your proposal of marriage twice?"

His eyes snapped back into focus. He pointed at his own chest with his index finger. "She was mine, and they defiled her."

"You started with the crane," Josie said, wanting to keep his confession moving along.

"It was close. We hadn't finished installing all of the trailers on that ridge. There was a lot of equipment around. It was positioned perfectly so all I'd have to do is move it around and lower it onto the trailer. Of course, then I had to worry about the rest of the camp and if anyone had seen anything. Ellie begged me to stop. The fear in her eyes—finally, she respected me—it was everything. I felt alive like I never had before. She got on her knees and begged me to stop. I told her that all of it was her fault. That she should have considered her words and actions more carefully."

"Where did you get the rifle?" Josie asked softly.

Sutton's attorney hung his head in his hands.

Sutton answered, "It was in the cab of my truck. I always kept it in there with extra ammunition in case I came across a coyote or a bear on the quarry property."

"You let Bridges live. Did you know he had seen you?"

"Of course not. Not until after. My dad's security man found him. He was the one who insisted we pay him off. He hadn't actually seen any of the shots or the crane come down. He'd only seen me getting out of the crane and walking around with a rifle. I wasn't thrilled about it, but back then whatever my father and his head of security decided was gospel. I couldn't wait to get my hands on the company and get rid of that bastard—hire my own security person who would do whatever I said. It was a shame my father's head of security fell into the quarry one day. Went splat all over the stone at the bottom. Took weeks to get him off the rock so we could use it."

Behind her, Josie could feel her colleagues shrinking back, but she kept her face and posture neutral. She'd been up against worse than this monster before. He was powerless now. Her officers would cuff him and put him in a holding cell, and he'd never breathe free air again. She only had a couple of questions left for him.

"Did you kill Colette Fraley?"

"No."

"Did you order someone to kill Colette Fraley?"

"No."

"Do you know who killed her?"

He met her eyes one last time. "No, my dear—Detective, I do not. But as I said, you're a clever gir—woman. I'm sure you'll figure it out."

CHAPTER SIXTY

Josie felt like she'd run a marathon. She stood at her desk, in the middle of the buzz of low, excited conversation among her team, staring sightlessly at the internal memo Colette had unearthed. She knew she had to do something, had to take the next step in wrapping up the investigation, but exhaustion rooted her to the spot. A gentle hand touched her shoulder. She glanced over to see Mettner smiling at her. "Boss?" he said.

She opened her mouth to correct him for what seemed like the thousandth time. But instead, she smiled back at him. "Mett," she said. "You did an incredible job on this investigation."

He shrugged. "It's not over yet."

Josie nodded. "I know, and we'll find the person who killed Colette, but you should be proud of what you've done."

His gaze swept to the floor but she could see his smile widening and his shoulders loosening with relief. "Thanks, boss." He cleared his throat. "Hey, why don't you take a break? Get some air. I can wrap up the paperwork."

Josie laughed. "You sure? You'll be here all night."

Another shrug. "Part of the job, right?"

She patted his back as she turned to walk away. "You're all right, Mett."

While Mettner and everyone went about writing their reports, and Chitwood and the DA locked themselves in Chitwood's office to plan a press conference, Josie walked out through the back of the station house, near the dumpster and away from the prying eyes of the press camped out front. She called Noah. She wanted to be the first to tell him that his mother wasn't a killer. That Colette had been trapped in an impossible situation, trying to keep her job and protect her family while making attempts to expose a mass murderer. Josie would always wonder why she didn't just go to the press. She had had the internal documents. She had been a whistleblower as young as thirteen years old. What had happened?

Noah's own words came back to her from one of their previous cases. *Sometimes people just get it wrong.* It was true. It was so easy in hindsight to know what someone should have done. But Colette had been a young mother with explosive information on her hands that she could share with no one. Even Ivan, her childhood friend, was not trustworthy. He had been willing to kill to stop her from exposing her boss. They would never know what had been in Colette's heart or mind, but she had tried to do the right thing until she couldn't anymore without risking her own children.

Noah didn't answer. Josie sent him a text asking him to call her. She thought about calling Laura, but there would be too many questions and Josie wanted Noah to hear the information first. Besides that, they still didn't know who had killed Colette. He should hear that from her, with assurances that she wasn't going to quit until she found the killer.

She heard the back door slam closed and looked over to see Gretchen walking toward her. Gretchen pointed to the parking lot exit. "Let's go get some coffee. We've earned it."

They took the long way, walking around an extra city block to avoid the press. Gretchen ordered coffees and their favorite pastries while Josie chose a table in the back of the small café. Her mind swirled with questions and different elements of the case, working from the beginning to where they now sat, trying to see what she had missed.

"Colette's murder was not random," Josie said as soon as Gretchen sat down.

"I know," Gretchen replied. She turned the tray between them so that the cheese Danishes faced Josie and the pecan-crusted croissants faced her. "So let's run it down."

"We can't trust Ivan's alibi," Josie said. "Whoever this lady friend is that he claims to have, she's going to lie for him. So if we ask her if they were together on the night Colette was killed, she's going to say yes."

"Agreed. But Ivan is a size eleven shoe. The print at Colette's was a size ten. Based on that, I tend to believe Ivan when he says he didn't kill her. Clearly, he loved her."

"But the murders were all so similar," Josie said. "Death by suffocation. Even when he killed Craig Bridges and the Pratt brothers, Ivan drowned them. He's never used a weapon. What are the odds of two different killers in this case killing in exactly the same way?"

Gretchen's mouth was full of croissant so she couldn't speak, but she shook her head vigorously.

"Not the same," Josie said.

Gretchen nodded.

"Because someone stuffed Colette's mouth full of dirt."

Gretchen swallowed. "Yes. Think about that for a moment."

Josie said, "It's unnecessary. Based on the knee prints, the large male shoe size, the imprint of Colette's skull in the dirt—she was being pressed very forcefully into the ground."

"So whoever was on top of her was strong," Gretchen added.

"The dirt was a personal thing," Josie said. She tried to envision it; straddling someone, holding their head in place and stuffing handfuls of dirt into their mouth so deep that it lodged in their throat. "He was angry. He didn't just want to silence her. He wanted to shut her the hell up. He wanted to hurt her."

"Who? Gretchen asked. "Who would be that angry with her? Who would want to shut her up? Who would be that close to her?"

Josie's mind cycled through all the players. Then she said, "Come back to the station with me. I need to look at the alibis again."

CHAPTER SIXTY-ONE

Back at the station house, it only took Josie fifteen minutes of reviewing Colette's file to find what she was looking for. She made a call, and her suspicion was confirmed. She immediately called Noah, but he didn't answer.

"We need to go," she told Gretchen.

Josie tried calling Noah again as she and Gretchen raced toward his house. No answer. She tried Laura's phone but got no answer from her either. As the streets of Denton flew past them, Gretchen said, "Call a backup unit."

"We're just asking him to come in," Josie said. "I don't want to spook him."

"They're not answering their phones," Gretchen pointed out.

Josie called dispatch and asked for a backup unit at Noah's house.

The front door was locked, but Josie had a key. She slid the key into the lock and opened the door tentatively. She could hear the sound of the television in the living room and see the glow of the lamp on the end table next to the couch. No one was in the room. She motioned for Gretchen to follow her down the hall toward the kitchen. As they approached, they heard the sounds of Laura and Grady talking.

"Grady, please," Laura said, a desperation to her voice that Josie hadn't heard before. She quickened her step.

Grady said, "I don't want to talk about this in front of him, Laura. He's a cop for chrissake."

Laura shot back, "You didn't do anything illegal, Grady. Just immoral. You're such an asshole. How could you do this? With the baby coming?"

"I thought I could help—"

His words died as Josie and Gretchen reached the doorway. Noah sat at his table, his casted leg propped on another chair, a cup of coffee in front of him. Grady stood near the fridge, one palm on the door handle. Laura was only a few feet away from him, her enormous belly taking up almost all the space between them. Noah looked relieved to see her, but Laura said, "How did you get in here?"

Josie said, "I have a key."

Laura had no response to this. Josie looked at Noah. "You okay?"

"Yeah," he said but his face was pinched. It was his annoyed look. He was fine, but he couldn't take much more of his sister and her husband.

Gretchen said, "What were you two arguing about?"

Laura's voice went up an octave. "That is none of your business."

Noah said, "Grady racked up some gambling debts."

"Noah!" Laura snapped.

"What?" he said. "Josie's my girlfriend—if she'll still have me after the way I've acted the last couple of weeks—so I'm going to tell her anyway. I mean, I assume you guys are going to want your share of Mom's estate pretty soon given your current situation." It was then that Noah seemed to really register Gretchen's presence; that she and Josie weren't there for a social call. "What's going on?" he said.

Josie said, "We need Grady to come down to the station and answer some questions."

Laura laughed but it was a hollow sound that died quickly in her throat. "This is ridiculous," she said. "I think we need to get a lawyer. I mean, how long are you going to stretch this out? What could Grady possibly have to offer you?"

Noah swung his casted leg off the chair and reached for his crutches. He started to stand on his good leg but Grady said, "Sit down, little brother."

The sound of his voice—cool instead of ingratiating—froze Noah in place, half standing, half sitting. "What did you say?" he asked Grady.

Grady took his palm away from the fridge handle. "I said sit down. I'm not going anywhere." He pointed at Josie and Gretchen. "You want to talk? We talk here."

"Fine," Josie said. "The day Colette was murdered, you were working from home, is that correct?"

"Yes, that's correct. But our housekeeper was there. She saw me, and my truck never left the driveway."

Gretchen said, "But Laura's car did, didn't it?"

"Laura was at a work function," Grady said.

Laura looked from Grady to Josie and back to him. "Grady," she said, her voice shaking. "I was driving a company car that day. You know that. Did you take my Jeep out?"

He didn't answer.

Josie said, "We called your housekeeper before we came over here. She saw you when she arrived for work. You went into your study. She called goodbye to you from the hall before she left. You didn't answer. She was in a hurry to get home to dinner so she left."

"So?" Grady said. "So what?"

Gretchen said, "She didn't see you for about three hours before Colette was murdered or after Colette was murdered. She didn't see you at all that day except in the morning."

"I was in my study working," Grady said.

"Then who took my car out, Grady?" Laura demanded.

Josie changed tactics. "What's your shoe size, Grady?"

His brow furrowed. "What?"

"You're a size ten, right?"

He hesitated for just a moment and then scoffed. "Yeah, who cares?"

Trying to keep him off balance, Josie said, "Laura told me that Colette said some pretty strange things when she was having episodes of dementia."

Grady, Laura, and Noah stared at her. Josie forged on. "She once told Laura about some bodies she knew about. She ever say anything like that to you, Grady?"

Grady was so still, Josie wondered if he was still breathing.

Josie said, "Did Colette ever say anything to you about a mass grave on the Sutton Stone quarry property?"

A sharp intake of breath came from Laura. Her hand flew to her chest.

Josie kept her gaze on Grady. "She ever mention anything about how Laura's boss killed a bunch of people and buried them on the quarry property and covered it up? How Colette had the only evidence?"

"What in God's name are you talking about?" Laura cried.

"Laura," Noah said, shooting her a look that said *be quiet.*

"She didn't tell you what it was, did she? That's why you couldn't find it. She wasn't lucid, so she told you she buried it. That's why you had her out in the yard with a shovel, isn't it? What were you going to do with it when you found it?"

"Shut up," Grady said.

"Is this true, Grady?" Laura whimpered.

Josie said, "I'm thinking you were going to use it to blackmail Mr. Sutton. That would have paid off your gambling debts, wouldn't it?"

"Grady," Laura said, her voice small.

Grady said, "Laura was being groomed to take over the company. I was trying to protect her. If something like that came out, it would ruin Sutton Stone Enterprises."

"Oh my God, Grady." Tears streaked Laura's face.

"Colette was getting worse. She would have popped off about it eventually to the wrong person. I had to stop her."

"You son of a bitch," Noah said.

"Did you go there with the intention of killing her?" Gretchen asked. "Or did you just want the evidence?"

"I never meant to kill her," he said.

But Josie didn't believe it for a second. She also didn't believe he'd been protecting Laura's position at Sutton Stone. "Grady," she said. "You're under arrest for the murder of Colette Fraley."

Before she could finish reading him his rights, he lunged forward and grabbed Laura's upper arm, yanking her to him, his chest pressed tightly against her back, his arm wrapped around her neck. With his free hand he fumbled on the counter behind him until his hand touched the butcher's block. Beside Josie, Gretchen drew her weapon and shouted for him to freeze. But his fingers had already found the handle of the largest knife in the block. The room erupted into shouts as he unsheathed it and pressed the point against Laura's distended belly.

"Grady, stop," Noah yelled. He stood on his good leg, using the back of his chair for support.

Josie said, "Don't do this. Put the knife down."

Laura sobbed in his arms. "Grady, what are you doing? Stop. You're going to hurt the baby. Grady, please. Stop this. Don't hurt the baby."

Gretchen kept her weapon trained on him. "Put the knife down and move away from her."

Josie raised both her hands in the air. She reached over and pressed down on the barrel of Gretchen's gun, easing it downward so it pointed to the floor. It wasn't a clean shot anyway, not even at close range. Too much could go wrong, and Josie wasn't willing to risk killing Laura or the baby—or both. "Noah, sit down," she instructed.

From her periphery she saw his fists clenching and unclenching. "Please," Josie said. "Sit."

He glared at Grady for a long moment before sitting back down on the chair. Still, Josie could feel the tension rolling off him in waves. She took a step toward Grady, but he needled the point of the knife harder into Laura's belly, causing her to cry out. A tiny pinprick of blood bloomed on her shirt.

"Look at me, Grady," Josie said.

"Shut up," he yelled.

"Grady, look at me. I'm not armed. Gretchen's not pointing a gun at you. No one here is a threat to you."

"You came here to arrest me."

"I did," Josie said, keeping her voice calm, reasonable-sounding. "That's my job. You know that. Listen, right now you're in a lot of trouble, but I can help you."

"Oh fuck you," he spat. "That's what all cops say right before they screw you over."

"Well, sure, that's true in a sense," Josie said. "And if you weren't holding a knife to your wife's belly right now, I probably wouldn't be inclined to help you, but it's also my job to make sure innocent people don't get hurt, you understand?"

His wild eyes flitted all over the room, but he nodded.

"I don't want anyone to get hurt," Josie said. "You know what I mean, right? Just like you didn't want anyone to get hurt. That's the truth, isn't it, Grady? You never intended for anyone to get hurt." She pointed to Laura who was sagging in his grip. "Especially not Laura or your baby."

She didn't even know if he realized he was doing it, but his head kept nodding along with her words.

"Everyone in this room knows you never meant to hurt anyone. Especially Colette. She was your mother-in-law. She was good to you, wasn't she? Her sweet potato casserole that we had last year at Christmas dinner, that was your favorite, wasn't it?"

"Stop," he said, as tears glistened in his eyes.

Josie pressed on. "You knew that if Colette had something that incriminated Zachary Sutton—something as bad as what she was babbling on about—none of you would be safe once her dementia took hold. You knew the safest thing for all of you was to find whatever evidence she had for yourself so you could decide what the best thing to do was, didn't you?"

"I wasn't going to hurt her," he said. "I swear. But when she wasn't lucid, she didn't make any damn sense. I only went there to find whatever it was she had. Laura was at an all-day work event. No one was going to know. I was just going to get it. That way even if she started saying all these crazy things, people would just think it was the dementia. I would have turned it over to the authorities, I swear."

Lies, all of it, Josie thought, but right now she just had to convince him that they were on the same team, that she believed him and understood him, so he would put the knife down and release Laura.

"I know that," Josie said. "Everyone in this room knows that, Grady. Laura, Noah, me—we're your family."

"I didn't want to hurt her," he said. "But she was just so damn frustrating." He looked at Noah. "You know how she was when she was having one of her episodes. Making no goddamn sense. Not doing one fucking thing you told her or asked her to do. It was like dealing with a fucking toddler."

Josie could see the muscle in Noah's jaw ticking double-time. He was having difficulty keeping his composure, but he understood what Josie was attempting, so he nodded and through gritted teeth, muttered, "Yeah."

Josie said, "We all know how difficult things were becoming, Grady. We get it. You don't have to do this. You don't have to hurt Laura or your baby. Just put the knife down, and we'll talk."

The pressure of the knife on Laura's stomach lessened slightly. Grady said, "You're still going to arrest me."

Josie pursed her lips and looked to the floor as if considering something. Then she said, "Well, yes. I have to do my job, but we can talk about the best way to do this. Listen, there's a backup unit on the way here. If they roll up and find you with a knife to your wife's pregnant belly, there's not much any of us in this room can do to help you. They're going to take you down. If they come in here, and we're all sitting around talking, and you agree to come down to the station peacefully with me and Gretchen, things are going to be a whole lot better for you in the long run."

Gretchen pulled her phone out and looked at it. "They'll be here any second."

He hesitated for a moment. Then slowly, he put the knife back onto the counter. Laura sagged to the ground, sobbing uncontrollably. The second Josie's body was between Grady and his wife, Gretchen surged forward, taking one of his arms, whipping him around and slamming him into the refrigerator.

"Hey, you said we were going to talk," he cried.

Josie helped Gretchen secure his hands behind his back with zip ties. Noah was on the floor, dragging himself over to Laura. He took her in his arms. "Call an ambulance," he said. "This stress can't be good for the baby."

Josie and Gretchen lowered Grady to the floor, face down, and Gretchen read him his rights while Josie called dispatch for an ambulance. Outside, they heard the long wail of the backup unit's siren.

CHAPTER SIXTY-TWO

A Week Later

Josie and Noah sat on her couch. His casted leg was propped up with a pillow on her coffee table. On the television in front of them, the network morning news show that Trinity co-anchored played. They watched the weather, the latest news in politics and then the words *Scandal in Central Pennsylvania* flashed across the screen. Trinity's face appeared as the camera zeroed in on her. As always, she was heavily made up, and her hair was so shiny you could see the reflection of the studio lights in its thick locks.

"She doesn't look that much like you when she's doing the reporter thing," Noah noted.

"I know. I think that's why the resemblance went unnoticed for so long."

Noah reached between them for the remote and turned the sound up. Trinity's eyes burned with intensity. "Today, we're bringing you an exclusive interview with Laura Fraley-Hall, the vice president of Sutton Stone Enterprises, where authorities in Central Pennsylvania recently unraveled a scandal so massive and so complex that it's still sending shockwaves through not just the region but the entire nation. At the center of this scandal, and now left to pick up the pieces, is Ms. Fraley-Hall whose mother was murdered by her husband—setting off a chain of events that would break this story wide open. Welcome, Ms. Fraley-Hall, and thank you for joining us via satellite from your hospital bed in central Pennsylvania where I understand you've been on bed rest for a week."

The screen split into two frames with Trinity on the left and Laura on the right. Although she was in a hospital gown, confined to a bed, Laura had taken care to have someone do her hair and makeup. She looked lovely, in spite of the circumstances.

"Good morning," Laura said. "Yes, it's true. I'm on bed rest."

"First, before we get into what happened, how are you feeling?" Trinity asked with exaggerated concern.

Laura gave a pinched smile. "I'm feeling grateful that my baby is still healthy. Having some pain and Braxton Hicks contractions but otherwise, I'm doing well."

"I'm so glad to hear that. Now, Ms. Fraley, I understand you're the acting head of Sutton Stone Enterprises now that Zachary Sutton has been charged with a number of things, most notably fifteen counts of first-degree murder."

"That's right," Laura said. "I've taken control of the company. This was all in place before any of this happened. Mr. Sutton took steps to make sure that I could transition into his place should he pass on or become… incapacitated."

"Well," Trinity remarked. "He's certainly in no position to run a company now, is he? Given the public relations nightmare all of this is shaping up to be for Sutton Stone, it's very unusual for the new head of the company to come on live television and discuss such sensitive matters. Why did you think it was important to speak with us today?"

Laura looked earnestly into the camera. "The terrible tragedy that took place at our main quarry back in 1974 was the sole act and responsibility of Mr. Sutton. His father and his father's head of security conspired to cover it up. They both passed on decades ago. No one presently employed at this company was aware of what took place, except for my mother, and she did not make me aware of anything she had found out. We employ hundreds of decent, hard-working people at Sutton Stone, and I do not believe that they should be held accountable for something Mr. Sutton did.

Our employees come to work every day and give us their very best. They're caring people who routinely volunteer for the community outreach programs which I have put into place in the last ten years. I think that by being transparent with the public right now, helping authorities in any way that we can, and making sure that we develop internal policies to ensure that something this heinous and tragic never happens again, Sutton Stone will begin to atone for the sins of its former boss."

They went on to discuss the case—all of which was fair game since Ivan Ulrich, Zachary Sutton and Grady had all agreed to plea deals. Ivan and Sutton would spend their lives in prison—avoiding the death penalty by cooperating. Grady agreed to a lesser charge of third degree murder and took forty years. There would be no trials. The Alcott County District Attorney was working with the sheriff's office to make plans to excavate the workers that Sutton had buried outside the encampment at the original quarry site. Unfortunately, the bodies of Craig Bridges and Drew Pratt would likely never be found since so many years had passed and neither had washed up on the banks of the rivers where they'd drowned. But at least their loved ones knew what happened to them.

"You think she'll turn Sutton Stone around?" Josie asked.

Noah stretched his arms over his head. "Yeah, she's a master at spinning things. If Trinity hadn't asked for this interview, she probably would have been after you to set it up."

"We have to pick up the pieces however we can, I suppose," Josie remarked.

She felt Noah's hand slide into hers. "Yes," he said. "We do."

She turned to him. "You're going to be messed up for a long time, you know that, right? Grief is a funny thing."

He smiled. "I know. You have any tips?"

She laughed. "I'm good at being messed up, but not that good."

He squeezed her hand. "Are we okay? You and me?"

Immediately she thought of her night with Luke, the exact details forever out of reach. Had she and Noah even been together at that moment? Was it worth telling him? What would she even say? Did she want to get into all of that again? She thought of something her mother, Shannon, had said to her when she was first reunited with her family, when they were all so overwhelmed with the task of filling the gap of the past thirty years. She had said, "Sometimes, you have to start from where you are." So they did.

Josie squeezed back. "We'll try, okay?"

He raised her hand to his lips and kissed her knuckles. "We'll try," he repeated.

A LETTER FROM LISA

Thank you so much for choosing to read *The Bones She Buried*. If you enjoyed it, and want to keep up-to-date with all my latest releases, just sign up at the following link. Your email address will never be shared, and you can unsubscribe at any time.

www.bookouture.com/lisa-regan

Thank you so much for reading more of Josie's adventures! It means so much to me that you keep returning to Denton again and again to follow her on her latest case.

I love hearing from readers. You can get in touch with me through any of the social media outlets below, including my website and Goodreads page. Also, if you are up for it, I'd really appreciate it if you'd leave a review and perhaps recommend *The Bones She Buried* to other readers. Reviews and word-of-mouth recommendations go a long way in helping readers discover my books for the first time. As always, thank you so much for your support. It means the world to me. I can't wait to hear from you, and I hope to see you next time!

Thanks,
Lisa Regan

Lisa-Regan

@LisalRegan

www.lisaregan.com

ACKNOWLEDGEMENTS

As always, first and foremost, I must thank my amazing readers and loyal fans! Thank you so much for your excitement and passion for this series, and for always spreading the word. I never get tired of hearing from you lovely readers, and sincerely appreciate all the ways you reach out to me to let me know how much you're enjoying Josie's adventures! Thank you to my husband, Fred, and daughter, Morgan, for your love, patience, and encouragement. Thank you to my first readers: Nancy S. Thompson, Dana Mason, Katie Mettner and Torese Hummel. Thank you to my Entrada readers. Thank you to my parents—William Regan, Donna House, Rusty House, Joyce Regan, and Julie House—for your constant support and for never getting tired of hearing good news. Thank you to the following "usual suspects"—people in my life who support and encourage me, spread the word about my books, and generally keep me going: Carrie Butler, Ava McKittrick, Melissia McKittrick, Andrew Brock, Christine & Kevin Brock, Laura Aiello, Helen Conlen, Jean & Dennis Regan, Sean & Cassie House, Marilyn House, Tracy Dauphin, Michael Infinito Jr., Jeff O'Handley, Susan Sole, the Funk family, the Tralies family, the Conlen family, the Regan family, the House family, the McDowells, and the Kays. Thank you to the lovely people at Table 25 for your wisdom, support, and good humor. I'd also like to thank all the lovely bloggers and reviewers who read the first four Josie Quinn books for continuing to read the series and to enthusiastically recommend it to your readers!

Thank you so very much to Sgt. Jason Jay for answering all my law-enforcement questions so quickly and in such great detail that

I can get things as close to authentic as fiction will allow. You are truly wonderful!

Thank you to Oliver Rhodes, Noelle Holten, Kim Nash and the entire team at Bookouture for making this amazing journey both possible and the most fun I've ever had in my life. Last but certainly not least, thank you to the incomparable Jessie Botterill for making every one of my dreams come true, for believing in me and my work, for "getting" my work in ways no one else ever has, and for just being completely and utterly awesome.

Made in the USA
San Bernardino, CA
22 June 2019